American Wasteland

AMERICAN WASTELAND

Stories by Alexander Shalom Joseph

Owl Canyon Press

© 2021 by Alexander Shalom Joseph

First Edition, 2021
All Rights Reserved
Library of Congress Cataloging-in-Publication Data

Joseph, Alexander Shalom
American Wasteland: Stories —1st ed.
p. cm.

ISBN: 978-1-952085-13-0
Library of Congress Control Number: 2021941070

Owl Canyon Press
Boulder, Colorado

Disclaimer

TABLE OF CONTENTS

TABLE OF CONTENTS (CONT.)

PREFACE

One of my favorite stories in Jewish Folklore and Literature is that of the Lamed Vavniks: thirty six Jews from each generation tasked with justifying the existence of humanity to God. Perhaps the best known modern surfacing of the idea of the Lamed Vavniks, specifically a family line which were included in this group of righteous or just men, came in the form of a novel titled The Last of the Just by Andre Schwartz-Bart, a winner of the Jerusalem Prize. After reading this work, I started to want to live like a Lamed Vavnik myself: I wanted to try to use my writing to justify the existence of the humanity I saw to a God I was trying to learn to believe in, in my own way. Instead of having a whole history of a people, from the shtetl to the concentration camps as my setting, as Schwartz-Bart did, I had a working class suburb in Boulder, Colorado and a full time job working as a chimney sweep. It was over the year and a half that I worked this grueling job, my hands and cheeks soot blackened and my fingers always bleeding from sharp wire or splintered wood, climbing rooves in two feet of snow or in 100 degree blue sky sweltering days, that I wrote the short stories herein. In my work truck on lunch break, for eight hours each weekend day at a local café where I could only afford to buy one cup of coffee per sitting, and at a cheap desk in the corner of my rented room: this is where I began to try to make meaning of the lives which surrounded me, to try to justify all the humanity I saw to whatever was above or if not that, to myself.

These stories take place in a contemporary America, a place I like to frame as at the "3 pm stage," a time at which it is too late to start anything but too early to end it either. This in between place, this american wasteland, this often hopeless and grey place is the stage for the following works of fiction. In these stories there are grocery stores, car washes, dive bars, dinner parties, long drives and traffic. In these stories we encounter the country as it sits today, smogged and slow and full of so many lives, so much love and loss and endless hours of work. These are not fantastical stories, they are as real as I could make them. These stories are the truth as I could find it and with them I hoped to find some sense and meaning in the modern madness, between my hours spent climbing dangerously high for $17 an hour. I hope you can find meaning in this mess too.

—Alexander Shalom Joseph

"there is a loneliness in this world so great
you can see it in the slow movement of the hands of a clock
people so tired
mutilated
either by love or no love"
—From "the crunch" by Charles Bukowski

sonder
n. the realization that each random passerby is living a life as
vivid and complex as your own—populated with their own
ambitions, friends, routines, worries and inherited craziness—
an epic story that continues invisibly around you like an ant-
hill sprawling deep underground, with elaborate passageways
to thousands of other lives that you'll never know existed, in
which you might appear only once, as an extra sipping coffee in
the background, as a blur of traffic passing on the highway, as a
lighted window at dusk
— *The Dictionary of Obscure Sorrows*

"....to be lords of our own skull sized kingdoms, to be alone at
the center of all creation"
—"This is Water" By David Foster Wallace

A DAY THAT SHOULD HAVE BEEN GOOD

Today is a holiday.

The clouds that cover about an eighth of the sky look like the smudgy palm prints of a giant hand pressed greasily against the blue window that sits throbbingly above the earth.

She will have a good time today.

She thinks to herself that she will have a good time today if it kills her, although she doesn't say this aloud (to herself) because for one it was a joke (she is not willing to try anywhere near hard enough to have a good time today to merit herself being put at any sort of risk) and for two she tries (even when alone and thinking to herself) to be sensitive about death (specifically suicide) jokes (or about any offensive subjects) because she has had friends who have tried (and one who succeeded) to kill themselves and she, herself, isn't the happiest person and thus and therefore she tries (even when thinking aloud to herself) to not bring up or joke about death (specifically suicide) as to not offend anybody and more importantly as to not give anybody (specifically herself) any bad ideas.

Right now, it is 7:28 am and she is in her king size bed, alone, and is still under the covers and the sheet and has sort of come to out of her shallow sleep in the last couple minutes and is now trying to plan her day and figure out how she will have a good time on this holiday, as her body slowly warms up to normal operating speed.

When she was married (which she is freshly no longer so) she would wear a sexy (in both her and her ex-husband's opinion) white, silk slip to bed each night. She wore the slip because she knew that her husband found it attractive and that he enjoyed the feel of it when he would roll over in the night and pull her close (an act that she enjoyed immensely [even when she and her husband were no longer in love] and that made her both internally and externally extremely warm). And but now with her divorce (the first official proceedings and cold, document signing beginning of which happened two days ago) she wears a baggie and faded band t-shirt to bed and sleeps diagonally across the bed and is not held in the night and often wakes up in the night chilled and disappointed that there is nobody there to hold her.

The bedroom in which she sleeps is professionally designed and is extremely fashionable, like fashionable in a way that it (the bedroom) could be featured in an interior design magazine (and in fact the interior designer who designed the bedroom has been featured and interviewed in many magazines like those which the bedroom in question could be featured). The walls of her bedroom are paneled with wood that is painted white in a faded and, to quote the interior designer who designed the room, "distressed", way that resembles (to the woman in the bed) the wood on the side of an abandoned house or on the salt stained siding of a dilapidated fishing boat. But what the walls look like aside, they are most certainly ascetically pleasing (at least to her, because her ex-husband found the walls quote "pretentiously worn" and discussed having them painted over completely and fully white, the way he thought walls should be painted).

The walls were one of countless things that she and her former hubbie disagreed on. If she ends up with the house (which is uncertain as the dividing up of assets between she and her ex has yet to officially begin) she will leave the walls as they currently are, supposed pretentiousness included. Since her ex-husband moved into a hotel (one month ago) she has awakened each morning (alone) and has wondered if she will be in the house the next day or week or month and at this point she doesn't really care whether or not she gets the house or the vacation home in the Hamptons or the TV or whatever. She just wants to have what she is going to have and learn to live with it. She hates the uncertainty that comes with the possibility of her having to leave her house, but for the moment she has to live with the possibility of leaving it while still living in it for now.

All of this drama over her divorce and her maybe having to move out of her house is why today, she really needs to have a good time and plus it's a holiday; a day on which everybody has a good time (at least that is what she hopes is true, well everybody but her ex-husband, she doesn't really hope for him to have a good time. It's not that she wishes he have a bad time but she mentally notes that she doesn't wish him well either).

It is now 9:04 am and she is in the kitchen in her too big, faded t-shirt and is sitting on the cold countertop, swinging her legs as the water for coffee boils in a florescent orange pot beside her on the stove. She has been out of bed for seven minutes and is not quite convinced that she made the right choice in getting out of bed. She can't think of any reason or excuse that would merit her return to bed and thus she has decided that perhaps some coffee and the subsequent energy via caffeine will help her for one not to return to bed and for two her to begin a day that for all intents and purposes should be a pretty good one. As she sits on the counter top, the water in the pot makes vague sloshing sounds as it heats up to what eventually will be a boil with which (the boiling water) she will make her coffee, she can see through a window in the kitchen (which is across from where she sits) that the day is hot, that there are only smudgy clouds in the sky and that (via smells coming in from the half inch of opening that the widow is opened to) people are already starting to fire up their grills for the inevitably meat heavy meals to come for most people later in the day, as almost required by today's holiday.

And while she is literally alone at the moment in her very modern kitchen (that may or may not remain hers) she is not completely alone in her overall life, although as of a couple of days ago she is legally alone (or as some put it, single). She has on her calendar, many parties and BBQ's and other infor-mal social events to which she has been invited by her many friends and to which she is not in the least bit interested in going. It's not that she dislikes the people that will be in attendance at these various parties, the attendees will mainly be her friends and acquaintances from work, her reason for not wishing to attend these parties and BBQ's and other informal social events that litter her calendar is that she just simply doesn't want to go. She thinks that these parties will be boring and today, more than any day, she feels she should, no, she deserves to have a good, non-boring time although she is not quite sure what activities exactly will merit this so called and so deserved good time.

The water in the fluorescent orange kettle on the stove that is being boiled for her coffee which will hopefully wake her up enough to get her started on what should shape up to be something hopefully memorable is taking too long to boil and she moves the kettle to see just what the hell is taking so long. As she moves the kettle to see just what the hell is taking so long, she realizes that the stove on which the fluorescent orange kettle sits, in which (the kettle) the water should have been boiling many minutes ago, is not in fact turned on and the glowing red metal associated with the turned-on-ness of the stove is as black as metal can possibly be and is in fact (upon her touching the metal) cold to the touch. And she wonders how and why the water was making that sloshing sound if it (the stove, the kettle and the water) was not in fact heating up and as she ponders from where that slosh-ing sound could have been coming, she swings her legs that hang over the lip of the countertop on which she sits, and as she swings her legs, her heels bounce off of the cabinet door beside the stove and below the countertop on which she sits and as her heels hit the cabinet door, the vibrations of her heels hitting the wood vibrate out and up to the stove and shake it, the stove, enough that the kettle which sits atop the stove starts to slightly shake producing a sloshing sound like that which she had previously heard and had previously mistaken for the sound of the water heating up. And but now she understands the cause of the sloshing sound and also understands what is not the cause of the sloshing sounds and she realizes that when water is boiling, it doesn't make much of a sound at all until it is literally boiling and bubbling so much that the kettle whistles and even that whistle is not really the water making a sound but is a sound made by the kettle in reaction to the steam which is what some of the water becomes during the boil. She won-ders how the sloshing sound even made her think that the water was boiling and she sort of mentally scolds herself for mistaking the sound of water being vibrated from heel hits on a cabinet with the sound of water actually boiling and she mentally tries to write a reminder to her future-self, detailing the difference in the sounds of sloshing water and boiling water.

But then she stops thinking about the stupid water and she stops making mental notes and she stops kicking the cabinet door with her heels (which makes the water in the fluorescent orange kettle stop sloshing) and she re-minds herself that self-deprecating, time wasting, overthinking patterns like the thoughts which she has just finished thinking, were picked up in re-sponse to and because of her overly critical ex-husband and she reminds herself that she no longer has to think that way and she makes a mental note to not overthink or over-criticize anything anymore and she reminds herself that today is a holiday and that today is a day on which she should have a good time and that she should start having a good time right now, and well but she should probably have some coffee so that she has energy to do those super fun things that she is basically destined to do today.

One of the reasons that she is not very interested in going to any of the parties that she has been invited to is that she is absolutely, 100% positive that while at one of whichever of these parties she ended up going to, that somebody would ask her about her divorce and that the tone of the question about her divorce would be a tone that is presented in a way that is most certainly an attempt to be caring but that has this undertone of a unique kind of pity and an I-am-better-than-you feeling to it that she just cannot and will not deal with anymore. Ever since she and her newly ex-husband announced to the world that they were getting a divorce, she has been having the same demeaning conversation over and over again and even the first time she had this conversation (which was with a friend of her mother's in the bread aisle of a supermarket) she was not at all having it and now that she has had this conversation hundreds of times and is now, actually legally divorced (not just a divorcee-to-be) she wants nothing less than to talk about or think about why she is divorced; what happened to her marriage; how she is feeling about it all nor any of the other pseudo-caring, basically insulting questions that she has been asked way too many times by people who have no business asking her about anything in her personal life.

Basically, what she hates about these conversations is that for one, the people in these conversations presume that and attempt to make her marriage up for public scrutiny, which (apparently unbeknownst to everybody else) it (her failed marriage) certainly is not and is her business alone and is not up for public scrutiny and for two, these conversations make her feel guilty for feeling sort of happy about the divorce from a man with whom she shared very few interests and very many silent dinners.

And as she has been thinking about these stupid conversations, which she is not actually going to have to have today because she is most certainly not going to any of those parties to which she has been invited, she has been swinging her legs and has been (once again) hitting the cabinet door with her heels and from within the deep recesses of her thoughts about the conversations that she is not going to have she has heard the faint sloshing of the water in the fluorescent orange kettle and she suddenly comes to the realization that she has not yet, in fact, turned the burner below the kettle on, so thus and therefore her much needed coffee is no closer to being ready than it was a couple of minutes ago when she realized for the first time that the stove was not, in fact, on. She also realizes that now, in this moment, the stove is still not on and that thinking and reminiscing about all of the times this morning which she has forgotten to turn on the stove will not help her get her much needed coffee any faster. And so now she turns the burner on and gets her French press ready with the correct number of scoops in the bottom and she gets her favorite coffee mug out (a cup that she will most certainly not let her husband [well, ex-husband] and his lawyer take, if she can help it) so that she can (when her water is finally boiled) make her coffee and then head out into what should definitely be a great and relaxing and much needed holiday.

It is now 10:14 am and she has showered and drank her coffee and she has gathered a few things together (although she did not do those things in that order) and she is now in her car in traffic chewing bubble gum and impatiently snapping bubbles as the air conditioning of her car blasts her face with a frigid and slightly chemical smelling air that (the air from the air conditioner) makes her hair (which is shoulder length and jet black) lazily twirl.

The windows in her car are up, even though she would like them to be down. Her windows are up because there are many cars in front of her and in front of those cars, there are even more cars and in front of those cars there are even more cars (etc.) and all of those cars in front of one another are all on and exhausting fumes which she would rather not breathe. There is so much traffic because for one it is a holiday and everybody seems to be out and about attempting to make use of the day off as well as the hot weather and for two there is some sort of accident on the road ahead. What she cannot see but what she has heard (via a traffic report played through the radio and the speakers of her car) is that the accident on the road ahead included an RV (or some sort of tow behind trailer connected to a pickup truck) as well as the three cars behind and next to the trailer and the truck. And basically, according to the nasally and awkwardly enunciating radio traffic report reporter (who is not really the radio traffic report reporter, but more of a fill in for the usual radio traffic report reporter because the usual guy is off presumably enjoying his holiday, while this fill in reporter has decided to work during the holiday in order to try and get some experience being the lead traffic reporter while the usual guy is gone) the tow behind trailer thing somehow became dislodged and disconnected from the hitch on the back of the pick-up truck which had been pulling it and it (the tow behind trailer) spun around and more or less disintegrated and sort of exploded (but in a way without fire) as it spun and collided with the cars on all sides but in front of the truck from which it had become dislodged. And apparently (according to the fill in radio reporter) the trailer, at the moment which it dislodged from the truck, had within it two children and the mother of those two children (the father of the two children had been driving the pickup truck at the time of the accident while the rest of his family relaxed in the trailer/RV/ tow behind thing) and these people had been obviously and terribly thrown about within the trailer as it was itself terribly thrown about and spun and flipped down and around the highway and on top of the cars around the truck. And apparently, the debris and overall chaos of this dislodged trailer and the horrific aftermath is what is causing all of this traffic in which she is stuck and about which she is not thrilled (to say the least).

As she sits in traffic, sweating despite the air conditioning (which her ex always called the 'AC') she pops bubbles with her bubble gum and taps her fingers (which have light pink, bubble gum pink, painted nails) impatiently and rhythmically on the steering wheel on which both of her hands exasperatedly rest.

Her car is a shade of blue that can only be found in the paint of cars and in the middle of the ocean on a hot day when the sky is obscured by dark clouds (that are themselves, the clouds, reflected in the water, which in part creates the color). Her car is one of those cars that some people refer to as 'a bug', although she has never really liked that name for her car (in part because she has never really liked actual bugs that much, and has little to no interest in being reminded of those creepy crawlies every time she thinks of or gets into her car) and thus instead of calling her car by its popular nickname, she refers to it, her car, as her 'little lady', but she is embarrassed by her nickname for her car and thus doesn't really refer to 'her little lady' as 'her little lady' at any time other than in her head (and a couple of times to her now ex-husband, who upon hearing her nickname for her car proceeded to make fun of her relentlessly in a way that at the time seemed playful but now, with the divorce and as she and her 'little lady' are stuck in traffic, seems to have been done with more of a malicious and genuinely mean intent).

Her car is round, and when she is moving quickly down the street it may look, to whomever is able to see the car as it passes by, as if she is steering a dark-blue, half circle of metal and glass down the road (which in some ways, she is).

There is no movement on the road on which she is sitting and basically baking inside of her car (despite the air conditioning) and (based on what the nasally fill in on the radio has heard and subsequently reported to her) it doesn't seem that the traffic will clear up or move for at least another hour. The reason (which the substitute radio reporter gave) is that the EMTs and the fireman and the policeman who responded to the scene of the accident have to (as the radio guy so eloquently put it) 'basically scrape a couple of people off of the road', an act which is apparently made much more difficult and messy than it already sounds like it is on account of the asphalt of the road being hot enough to (as the radio guy once again eloquently put it) 'literally cook an egg on' (sic. As in the literally here is most certainly not a literal literally because there is no real way that the radio man knows how hot the road actually is and if in fact the road is actually, literally, hot enough to cook an egg on and the literally used above [by the high-pitched voice having, fill in radio correspondent] is used in more of a colloquial way than in an actual literal way and said colloquial and subsequently incorrect usage of literally makes her turn off the radio as she is one of those people who believes words should be used for what they are meant to be used for, and she is not one to appreciate malaprops nor the popularized over exaggeration that seems to run rampant today).

And now, in silence and seeping boredom, in her car with her air conditioning on blast and her hair sort of swinging back and forth above her shoulder because of the push of the air conditioner, she starts to look around at those in the car beside her. She is in the leftmost of the two lanes on the highway and the car next to her is almost exactly parallel with her, so as she looks over her passenger seat and through her closed passenger side window and at the people in the car beside her she is looking directly at the person who is driving the car beside hers.

The nearest exit on the highway is about .4 miles away and between she and that exit, in those .4 miles, there are many, many stopped and idling cars filled with impatient and overheated people, who, up until being stuck in this traffic jam, were headed (like she too was) to go do those things, those fun things that are done with the intention of relaxing and having fun on a day, a holiday, like today. And behind her, .6 miles away, there is another exit off of the highway and, like those in front of her, there are a lot of cars filled with hot and angry people between her car and said exit.

The accident up ahead happened right in front of the exit and thus there is now no way to exit in a forward fashion until the accident is clear. And due to a metal guardrail on the right side of the road and a cement barrier on the left, there is no way for people to drive off of the road to go around the accident. Thus there is only one way (besides waiting) to get off of the highway and to not have to wait in this traffic and that way is for everybody to agree to somehow simultaneously back their cars up for .6 miles to the nearest, unblocked exit and somehow organize a turn taking exit strategy for each lane until each and every now stuck car is unstuck and free, but that option is not only extremely complicated and unlikely, it would be such an act of cooperation and selfless working together of so many hot and impatient people that the act would literally (in the true sense of the word) be historical and because of that fact (as in the fact that people are too short sighted, selfish and impatient to work together to help anybody but themselves) the only real option to get out of the traffic is to just sit in one's car and wait and hope that those EMTs can scrape those people off of the road as fast as possible, so that everybody else can get on with the holiday. At least that is what she thinks as she sits in her car staring at the man in the car beside her.

The man in the car beside her is who (she imagines) would be the picture in an encyclopedia beside the term 'Average American Dad' i.e. this man is around forty-five (by her best guess, although she is not the best guess of age), and is about twenty-five-pounds overweight (although she can only see the upper half of his torso and his head, she can see enough fat on those visible places to assume that the rest of his body matches). The man is wearing (based on what she can see) a too-small white t shirt, sun glasses that she is sure he thinks are cool but in her opinion aren't and which (the glasses) were most certainly bought in a gas station (for less than five dollars) and one of those hats that are only worn by middle aged dads or by people going on safaris i.e. the hat goes around the man's head and is extended in the back with extra cloth, (enough so that the man's neck is mainly covered by this extra fabric). The hat has a chin string that hangs down and tucks under the man's chin with the purpose of holding the hat on the man's head and this string is fastened so tightly around the man's double chin that it (the string) is making the man's already double chin fold into yet another chin.

However, she can only see the man's string induced triple chin when he is facing forward, which he is currently not doing because he is currently leaning sidewise and backwards towards the backseat of the car and is yelling at his kids (of which there are three, crammed into the back seat and all of which are sun-block-coated to the point of said sunblock looking like body paint, and all of which are pudgy and round headed). And she can see that the man is yelling at his kids but she cannot hear his yells because her windows are closed (but his windows are open in a way that makes her think that this man is the type of dad to keep the air conditioning of the car off to help "build the character" [as he most certainly says] of his children). Or maybe the car which looks old and almost clichély a family car does not in fact have working AC (as her husband used to call it or more as he most likely still calls it, but what is past is her hearing him call it AC because he is no longer her husband or at least won't be really soon.)

And it seems like the problem with the kids in the car next to hers (which she can see because she can see into both the front and back seats of the car beside her) is that the two children on the far sides of the back seat are pinching the back of the arms of the (most likely youngest) kid who is unluckily seated in the middle, between the two other children. And the pinching (as well as what has to be a terrible feeling of being stuck between two people who are trying to torment you) resulted in the child in the middle seat screaming and crying out and this screaming and crying out subsequently led to the father turning back towards the back seat and telling the kid in the middle seat to basically shut up (or at least what she imagines he would say because she cannot hear what the man is saying to his children).

There is no mother in the car, the passenger seat of the car beside her instead holds a cooler that is strapped in with a seatbelt and most likely contains beer, among other food items such as cheese sticks and maybe sandwiches.

She feels claustrophobic watching the two children pester and bully the one in the middle and therefore looks away from the car beside her. She has always found it interesting how, by looking into someone's car (whether or not this someone is actually in the car matters not) one is able to see into the private life and psyche of the someone to whom said car belongs. A person's car tells an unedited, raw story of what the car's owner is really like through the trash and knick-knacks in said car as well as the smells that emanate from said car, well that is at least what she thinks as she sits in her car among her own personal trash and knick-knacks and smells, in traffic on a holiday that so far has been everything but what it should have been. She thinks about how, if someone was to ask what a person would do if locked in a metal box for an extended period of time, she would answer that the question can be simply answered by watching how people already act whilst in their cars i.e.

singing, farting, eating, yelling at passersby and being so utterly consumed with themselves and where they are going that basically everything and anything else around them is more or less basically just in the way. In her opinion cars and the subsequent things people do in and with their cars are the perfect petri dish of humanity at its most human (and vile).

And through the driver's side window of her car she can see a man on the grassy medium that separates the highway going one way from the one going the other way. Well the person kind of looks like a man, at least that is what she initially thought. She thought this person was a man because of their clothing (which was extremely baggy and dirty and most certainly made for men originally) but now as she really focuses in on this person she is not quite sure about whether or not this person is in fact a man after all. And in reality, this person's gender doesn't really matter in the context of why she is intrigued by this person. And so why she is intrigued by this person is because of what this person is doing and what they are doing is laying on their back on the surprisingly luscious and soft looking grass of the median (on the other side of the concrete barrier) with their head resting in their hands and with their legs laid flat and wide spread on the grass. This person, while obviously dirty and most certainly homeless, seems also to be happy and almost catatonically content. The only reason that she can tell that this person is alive (and not some sort of human road kill) is that she can see this person's stomach sort of rippling up and down with each breath and as she looks closer and tries to tune out everything else going on and rolls down her window, she can see and hear that not only is this person alive and breathing but that they are laughing in a low and wet way as they stare up at the sky (a sky which is now completely void of clouds (even the smudgy clouds from earlier are gone) and it (the sky) is a pulsating and deep blue.

It is now 11:27 am and after tapping her fingers basically raw on the steering wheel of her little blue car (the thing she secretly refers to as her little lady), it seems that the traffic is finally clearing up. The car, her car, her little lady, is moving so very slowly forward (moving at about forty feet per hour) and according to the nasally man on the radio (the radio, which she has turned back on after being driven almost to madness by the bland sounds of her own thoughts) the traffic should be cleared up any minute now and she hopes that this man's use of the 'any minute now' cliché is used in a literal sense, i.e. that she soon could be moving, like actually, finally going somewhere and getting to that destination to which she has been trying hard to get, but to which has never quite arrived.

And to top it all off, to put a cherry on top of this shit sandwich of a day that should have been so relaxing and rejuvenating and good, she has had to pee since about thirty minutes ago. And it hasn't been like an, 'I have to pee but I can hold it until there is a bathroom that I can use' kind of having to pee, it has been an 'oh my god, I genuinely am afraid that I may pee my pants right now' sort of bathroom need. In fact, her need to urinate has become so bad at times, that she has started to plan out how she will deal with the (almost inevitable at this point) situation in which she literally pees herself, and she has spent much of the last thirty minutes contemplating if peeing in her pants in her car is more embarrassing than squatting on the highway.

And her need to pee is just a part to a whole of how bad this day that should have been good has ended up, because while she has been paralyzed from the waist down with the fear that if she moves, she will end up having an accident, her mouth has been drier than it has ever been in her entire life. Her mouth has been so dry at points that she has stuck her fingers in her mouth and felt (to her horror) that her tongue was actually, literally dry to the touch. Her throat has been making crackling and wheezing sounds with each intake of car stale air and her lips have become so chapped that they are bleeding and most likely incurably damaged in a couple of places. Somehow being seemingly completely filled with water and needing it more than anything else in the world has made the last hour pass in a sort of meditative and focus-on-not-pissing-one's-pants type of blur and as her car lurches finally forward she hopes she can hold it together long enough to get to a gas station (which will be off of the exit beside which the accident and the deaths occurred and which are hopefully cleaned up enough for her to pass by).

It is now noon. This day should have been so much better than it actually has been and it is still dragging on like something weak and sick pulling something heavy up a hill. She finally gets moving and her speed turns from a drag to a crawl and eventually to the speed of an old man walking with a walker i.e. very, very slow but technically moving. And moving at this old man speed she reaches the exit and turns quickly off. And she speeds over a curb and into the gas station and parks in the spots in front of the gas station reserved for people who are not purchasing gas but may be buying other things (or who have to use the bathroom). And so, she parks her car between two jaggedly painted yellow lines in front of a spit and who knows what else stained sidewalk that itself is in front of a gas station which is fluorescently lit and is noticeably glowing with a fake looking and migraine inducing chemical white light even in the middle of the day.

She gets out of her car now and is in such a hurry to get into the gas station to use the bathroom that she accidently slams the car door onto her dress, which (her dress) is soft and slightly bumpy to the touch and is a Mediterranean Sea type of bright blue and, because of being caught in the door of her car, is slightly wrinkling and stretching out as she tries to walk forward towards the doors of the gas station before noticing that her dress is caught. And then she does in fact realize that her dress is caught in the door because she has walked a couple of feet forward and her dress felt (all of a sudden) unbelievably and uncharacteristically tight. And so, luckily she sort of backwards-walks back to her car and then unlocks the door and as she embarrassedly looks around to see if anybody saw her do what she did, she sees a man standing about ten feet from her and she realizes that this man is perhaps the person whom she wishes to see the least out of literally anybody in the entire world. Like she would actually prefer to watch something horrific happen, such as a tow behind trailer disconnect from its hitch and spin and send its occupants flying and splattering onto the sun boiled unforgiving asphalt, rather than have to face this man.

She and this man who she sees now were supposed to be something. She and this man were supposed to be a certain type of everything. All her life she wanted to find somebody, find someone, find a one and she always imagined that when she did find that one, how she would feel. She always considered herself a rationalist and had no false pre-conceptions about how, by finding the one (a one, anyone, someone, somebody, some body to lay beside, a body, anybody) that all of her problems would be fixed. That's to say that she knew life would always twist on and that even when she found that person, how potholes and problems and rain and whatever other things that can come up, would still come up. Yeah, she knew all of her problems wouldn't be solved through love or the finding of the one, but she figured that somehow with this person, this anyone; her anyone, those blows dealt by life would somehow be softer.

All throughout her life she pictured; envisioned; prayed for that inevitable day on which she would finally meet this one. And finally, she had met this person and although it wasn't a love at first sight, it grew quickly into something that truly did resemble what she had always so deeply desired. And it was good, for a while. It was all she ever dreamed it would be, and maybe more.

That's not to say it was perfect by any means, but maybe it was real and true, he was real, and they were together for better or worse and sometimes life's blows did feel a bit less harsh with him there for her to fall back on.

And but things, as they so often do, got worse and like a police siren in the distance, the tragedy seemed far away or at least she hoped that the tragedy was not in her doorstep, in her home, but like things that seem far away often do, tragedy got closer and eventually arrived.

And for her tragedies are only real and so deeply horrific when they are happening to her and even during said happening it felt like this tragedy was just a nightmare from which she will soon wake, but she never woke for she was never unconscious to the horror.

But it was real and tragedy struck and with this striking she lost that thing which she had always so deeply wanted and had supposedly, finally, got. And but with that tragedy of her divorce and the end of that dream of dreams, she realized that her marriage to this someone had not in fact been a dream at all. It had been a blank grey screen; he had been a blank grey screen onto which she had projected all of her expectations of what she had always hoped her one would be. And in the divorce, she realized that the man she married had not in fact been the one or a one or anyone at all. He had just been some man she had hoped so hard was the one that she had convinced herself he was, even though he certainly was not. So, with the heartbreak of losing a husband, she was also filled with a white fury and this fury within her, spelled out; yelled out a truth that she eventually realized she had known all along and that truth was basically that there was no such thing as what she had always, so deeply, wanted.

And with this whole deal with the divorce and the breaking of her false reality; her false truth, came the infuriation that she now so often faces. She hates it when people give her that sorrowful look and line about how they hope she is doing ok about her divorce. She hates having to pretend like she is somehow worse off because of the divorce. She hates speaking to people about the divorce because they presume, incorrectly that she is sad because of it, when she is most certainly not. She hates it when people presume that she is somehow still in love with the man who used to be her husband. The divorce is a blessing in her opinion, and could've, should've come much sooner, and the presumption that she is still somehow still in love with her ex could not be more incorrect because as she realized through the process of the separation, she did not, in fact, ever love her husband (her ex) but was merely in love with the idea of being in love with somebody (and that somebody just happened to have been him). And in regards to her supposed and presumed sadness about her divorce she is not in fact sad about the divorce itself but is sad about the truth that sprung from the ashes of the burnt and beat to death thing that her marriage had become. And that truth was simply that in her desperate quest to find that one, a one, she had (through a special type of cognitively dissonant self-illusion) fantasized into reality the idea that she had found what she was looking for when, in truth, she had most certainly not (and probably never will). And all of this goes through her head as she sort of lightly tugs at the edge of her dress that is caught in the door of her royal blue "little lady' and as she looks up and at the man who, through the process of removing him from her heart and her life, showed her that her deepest want had not only not been attained in the first place but that it (her deepest want i.e. a somebody of her own) would be practically impossible and highly improbable for her to ever get with or without him, because the want, in itself, was based on a fantasy and was never anything more than that.

And so now she tugs the dress loose from the car door, luckily without ripping it but unluckily leaving a soot colored smudge on the edge of the dress which was caught in the door. And as she tugs the dress free from the metal's oily grasp, the man (who was standing still up until this point) starts to move and as he gets closer to her and to the glass door of the gas station, she realizes that for one he did not see her nor her dress stuck in the door of the car and for two that the man was not in fact that man who she thought he was and that this man is merely a man who is about her age with a similar haircut to the man to whom she was once married (who is most certainly not the man now walking to the gas station's glass door). She was so obsessed with seeing her ex (or more not seeing him) that she imagined in her panicked, dress stuck in the door state, that the only person who could make her day any worse upon mere sight was right in front of her, when in fact he had not been there at all.

It is now 12:14pm and she is almost to the bathroom of the gas station, well more accurately she is almost back at the bathroom of the gas station because after getting her dress unstuck from the car door and seeing through her imagined sighting of he-who-she-most-certainly-doesn't-want-to-see, she ran into the gas station and to where the bathroom is located only to see a sign hand written on white notebook paper in green marker and taped to the wall beside the doorframe of the bathroom, which informed her that the bathroom key was located at the front counter of the gas station and that use of the bathroom in this particular gas station was/is restricted to paying customers of this gas station only.

After reading the sign (and wondering to herself if the phrase "paying customer" is redundant and what a "non-paying customer" would actually be and if that would be a paradox and if a "non-paying customer" would be allowed in the bathroom) she sort of waddled to the front counter of the store only to find that at the front counter there was a line of three men who, if they were not directly related were most certainly distant cousins because of their shared amount of body (mostly shoulder and back) hair and overall roundness in body shape. And so, she waited for each of the round, hairy, bald spot having men, to respectively buy a pack of cigarettes, a stick of peppered beef jerky and a bag of gummy bears. And when she finally arrived at the counter the mustachioed man behind the counter, in response to her asking for the bathroom key, said that the bathroom was for paying custom-ers only and that if she wanted to get the bathroom key and subsequently use the bathroom that she would have to buy something. In response to the mustachioed man's response to her original question she internally squirmed with the use of the phrase "paying customer" and externally pleaded with the man to just give her the key and that she would buy something when she was finished, but that she just really had to use the bathroom as soon as possible, like it was kind of an emergency, to which the mustachioed man behind the counter said basically no. Then she waddled, now in pain from having to pee so badly, back to her car to get her wallet. From her car with her wallet in hand she waddled back into the store and to a cooler in which there were many plastic bottles one of which (a bottle filled with water) she took from the cooler and with it held in the hand that was not holding her wallet, waddled back to the counter where there (thank god) was not a line and placed the bottle on the countertop and put a bill on the counter and told the mustachioed man to keep the change. From beneath the counter the mustachioed man slowly produced a large wooden spoon through the end of which a hole was drilled and through that hole a pink ribbon was hung and from that pink ribbon hung the key to the bathroom. And while she was watching the man pull the spoon and the ribbon and the key from beneath the counter she saw water droplets of condensation on the side of the water bottle and remembered her super dry mouth and she grabbed the water bottle and twisted the top off and drank about half the bottle in one sip. She then slammed the bottle down onto the counter and so quickly grabbed the spoon and the key from the man's hand that he actually flinched and as she swiped the spoon from his hand she asked him if she could leave her bottle of water on the counter while she was in the bathroom, to which the man shook his head no but she left the bottle of water on the counter anyway and sprint-waddled to the bathroom.

And so now at 12:14pm on a day that should have been so much better than it is, she is finally nearing the door to the bathroom, with the spoon attached key in hand. And after relieving herself, her day; her much deserved holiday; the break she so dearly needs, will hopefully begin to turn into the thing she has so hoped it will be. And as her day hopefully gets better she can hopefully leave her thoughts of her ex, and frankly everything about this day so far, behind as she and her little lady drift into the noonday sun of what she hopes will be something quite enjoyable.

It is a holiday after all, she thinks as she turns the key to the bathroom door, and it is her right to have an enjoyable day and she damn well will (or at least she hopes so).

ANNOTATED LOVE LETTER

Remember that day[1]? We drove down the dirt road[2] and we stopped by the river [3]. Things were simple then [4], things were good, and life was the way I had always hoped it could be.

Well, I know that things aren't that way anymore[5] and I know that the spark and the heat that it once created (between us) has dulled. And I know that today, well this morning, is something special for you (and for me) and for us[6]. And this morning, in the dark, before I go to work, I am leaving you this note[7] and these flowers[8] and this thing in the box[9] and I hope that they are enough[10].

Yours,

Me.

p.s. there is no need to make or get dinner tonight, I've got it covered[11].

[one] a day that was more cold than warm, if I remember correctly, and which was towards the end of November in the middle of a week (maybe a Wednesday) on a year in which November was not a month that had much snow at all but instead had a sort of low hanging (like an unwanted beer belly) fog cover that seemed to constantly and chillingly blow chokingly humid air onto the dirt roads that surrounded our house for not only most of November but also December and the beginning of January as well. And that day was special in some ways, as in I am sure it was somebody's birthday somewhere (or more likely many thousands of people's birthdays) but it was neither of our birthdays, and it was not a holiday (at least not one that we were observing) but it was still special because we were together and even though we were so busy those days, every moment that we had free of work or sleep or whatever, we tried to spend together because those were the times, the minutes, the seconds and dry-lipped kisses that kept us going and doing those things we did so we could continue to survive together. And it was foggy out and it was an evening (or maybe later than that) in the middle of a week in which we were both working more than forty hours. We both had to work at like 6am the next day. Because of our early shifts in the morning, it was maybe a bit irresponsible for us to be out that night (well that day) in the fog and maybe we should've been at home winding down and getting ready to get a solid amount of sleep to be like fully rested and refreshed for the next day, but none of that really mattered. What did matter was the fact that we were together and that we both would've happily stayed up all night together and would've had to slog through work the next day, but it would've been worth it to not sleep if we got to spend that time together, awake and warm, instead.

[two] and that dirt road was the place that we would always go when we were together, when we didn't have enough time or money to actually go any real places or do any real-life things, but those real things we could've done were always too expensive and reality was subjective anyway and we had more fun on that dirt road that at any of those other places anyway. And that day, that evening, that night, we drove in the fog down that dirt road in your old, teal car that squeaked and whistled as it coasted and hopped over potholes and puddles. And in that car, there were empty bags and bottles from snacks and drinks that we or you or me had had in the past and had thrown behind the front seats, and the back seats were folded down and covered with a blanket

that was once black but now was grey with dog hair from your dog, but that day, that evening, that night in the fog, it was just me and you. We left the dog at home because she was asleep under the kitchen table and looked so cozy and warm and sort of innocent beneath that table, that we decided to let her stay asleep and we left in your teal car to go for a drive down our favorite road. That evening the dog was back at home but there was a lot of dog hair and trash in the car and the tank was almost empty (the light was on, telling us we needed to get gas) but we didn't care about any of that, we didn't care about the shambles, because we had each other, because I had your hand in both of mine and on the radio (even though the speakers were blown and the words were garbled almost beyond recognition) one of our favorite songs was playing (it was the one with the minor chords and the two singers).

three and that river was cold then, but wasn't completely frozen over yet. And the water was flowing fast that night and the fog was so low above the river that it looked like the river was kind of coming from the sky and the clouds, and I remember you said that to me as we were parked at a pull off beside the river, that, the river, sort of followed the winding dirt road. And we had the windows up and the defrost in the car was on, but we were breathing too much maybe and the windows were fogged up anyway, so we got out of the car, even though we were not wearing enough clothes to keep us warm we still went outside. And we sat on the hood of the car and looked out at the river and didn't speak, and I put my arm around your shoulders and pulled you in close and you wrapped your arms around my chest and you wrapped one of your legs around mine (that way that I always told you drove me crazy, but in a good way) and you rested your head in the crook of my shoulder. And then you told me, that you were in one of your favorite places, because I was keeping you warm and with one eye you could see my neck and my face and the stubble on both but with the other eye you could see the sky and the trees and with your ears you could hear the river and with your body you could feel my breathing and I could feel yours too. And your breath came out in a small cloud that matched the texture and color of the fog but smelled kind of like strawberries and I always wondered how you always smelled so good those days, even when you had eaten the same things as me. How did you always smell like strawberries, even in the morning when I would lean over and kiss you to wake you up, I could never understand that.

four ever since I was a little kid, I imagined that adults just woke up and got to do whatever they wanted to do. I always imagined that adults everywhere, while I suffered in school, were just having fun. When I became an adult, I obviously realized that my previous outlook on adult life was not correct and in fact that I had wasted my childhood hoping to have fun in adulthood when in reality it was the other way around. When we met (remember that night in the snow?) I was working and everything seemed muted; void of color; grey. Adulthood was a grind that seemed to never end and childhood's hopes were dashed and dead thanks to the grinding of machines and the bright white of office computer screens. But that night in the snow and the new life that has followed, has been what I hoped I could be. No matter what we are doing (whether its waking up late and staying in bed reading and laughing or taking drives down our road or making dinner together or just sitting still and letting the rain soak us so wet that our clothes sag and droop and we have to cuddle to get warm and dry again) with you that dream of somehow doing just what I want has come true. What I am saying is that you are just what I want and what I need and what I have always wanted and what I have always needed, even if I don't say it as often as I should.

five I know that the days seem long and sometimes we are so quiet that the air between us seems cold and hard. I know that sometimes I don't say what I mean, and I know that sometimes you look at me in that way that only you can and I know that look means that you are considering us, as in me and you and if us two are meant to be together. And I know when it's snowing and the sun is hidden behind white and the wind sounds like a train whistle as it whips across the roof and work is still there but it's harder in the dark, I know that you want it to be easy to come home and I want that too and I know that sometimes it's not and it's a different but equally nasty kind of cold inside. And I want you to know I am sorry for that and I am sorry for the times you have smiled even though you were tired and that I didn't smile back. I'm sorry for the times that you touched my back or my kissed my neck and I pulled away, and it's not that I didn't want you to touch me (you know I always do or maybe you don't know, but I do) and I'm sorry for the coldness that I sometimes radiate.

six as in today is that day that we first met, but two years after.

seven and as you can see, this note is written on the paper from that notebook that you got for me so I could try and practice my drawings that you have always said are really promising. And I want you to know that I appreciate your support and your love and everything you have done for me and those days that you have worked longer than normal, as in a double or as in overtime, so that you could get some extra money to pay for these little presents that you always leave for me in the morning. And that is why this morning, before I leave for the day (a day that I wish I could spend with you) I am leaving some little presents around the house, like you have often done for me.

eight and these flowers are the ones you said were pretty that night by the river under the stars. When we were laying on the hood and you looked down and pointed at these light purple flowers by the river and even though that was just the beginning, before we shared a bed every night and before we were an us, I remembered that you pointed out those flowers and last night (before you got home from work) I went back to that riverbank and I picked those flowers that you pointed out. And these flowers are sort of like us, they have had two years to bloom and grow, and even though they are older now and their color has faded a bit and their petals seem a bit rougher and more worn than before, they seem stronger and their roots are thicker. These two flowers that I picked are for you and me and they are also for us.

nine and this thing in the box is a photograph that I had printed of me. It's that photo that you took that day after we had finally dried off after sitting in the rain and in the photo I am sitting with a towel around my neck and my hair is all over the place and I'm smiling this big, wide goofy smile that only you can make me do and I'm sort of looking at the camera (but I'm really looking at you). And I know it's not a necklace and I know it's not some fancy ring, this photo is me at my finest and my finest is when I am with you. And I have only become who I am today because of you and the warmth that comes with the smile that you and only you can make me wear has made me into something softer. Those calluses and those tightly drawn muscles in my chest that you always put your soft hands on; those hard parts of me; those things I have locked away; those tears I never cried because I was told I shouldn't; those muffled screams: you have melted me into something soft and warm like you and I am new because of it. Without those soft touches, without those whispers of love in the night; without those drives to the river and those wide eyes that just cut me down, without all that I would be out in the cold. I would be that thing I thought I would never be. Without those eyes and that way that you listen when I need you to, I would be just some person who had grown up to a life of grey, of work, of blankness; the opposite of what I had always dreamed. And with this photograph in the box that I'm leaving with this note and those flowers that I picked just for you, I hope that you will keep it with you (somewhere safe and secret that only you know) and when you look at it I hope you will remember that I will try to be, always, what you have been to me, there, whenever you need.

ten and I hope that I am enough

eleven I'll be making that dish we had that night after we saw your parents and you were upset and I pulled the car over and stopped at the little place and you were too mad to talk and I kissed your hand and you gave me that look that you give (the scary one) but I knew you weren't mad at me and you eventually came around and you cried during the meal and you said (later) that that night you told me things that you had told nobody else and I know that was a hard night for you but it was one of the best nights for me because I was there for you and I could support you like you have always done so well for me. And I want to make you this meal, that you said you enjoyed because I want you to know, that if you are down and on those days when our spark is dim or fading, that I will be there to kiss your hand and to be there, whenever you need.

A Story About Leaving in the Lifespan of a Cigarette

There is a blankness in leaving; a stale breath held in anticipation of being gone. There is a loss of warmth; a protective numbness that comes when one has decided to go; to move; to flee; to run away.

The chair at the desk in the room is blue. The chair sits atop a pole that connects to three legs at the end of which, each leg, there is a spinning wheel. The wheels of the desk chair rest on a light brown, cheap, wooden floor that often causes splinters in the feet or holes in the socks of those that walk upon it. The back of the chair has a protruding rounded bump that is supposed to help support the lumbar of whomever is seated in it, the chair. As stated the chair is blue, but more specifically the blue color of the chair is that type of throbbing seemingly endless blue of a cloudless July sky in a dry place. Somehow the dryness of the ground beneath said cloudless sky adds to the blueness and therefore the seeming endlessness of said sky, and that dry climate blue sky is what the color of the chair is, although the base with the single pole that leads to the three, wheeled legs is a matte black.

In leaving and during the two weeks before departure from the soon to be left place, there is a social release that takes place for the one whom is about to leave. The day by day people, the friendly but not exactly friends, become suddenly somehow important and time with these people, since time is now finite, somehow becomes a priority for the person who is about to leave. Passersby and those faces recognized but not cherished somehow become exactly what they have never been, because now whatever they could have been will never be and somehow all expectations fade and come true at once. A two-week friendship is a perfect friendship because it ends before or just after things become serious. This fact about the same two-week time period is enhanced even more when imposed on a romantic relationship. A two-week-relationship, especially but not exclusively, when said two weeks are during a time in which one or both of the involved parties are due to leave at the end of said two weeks, feels to both parties somehow perfect yet at the sometime filled with emptiness and incurable angst.

Besides the chair, in the room there is a desk, the same color and type of wood as the floor, a dresser, the same color and type of wood as the desk, and a queen-sized bed with a floral print bedspread and matching floral print pillowcases. Beside the bed on the floor between it, the bed, and the dresser, there is an open, black suitcase half filled with carefully folded clothes that, the clothes, are mainly shades of blue, white and grey. There are two people in this room and it is in this room that they have lived together for some time, although their time together is soon due to end for one of these people is leaving soon, and that soon means the person is leaving in the morning, which is tomorrow, as it is currently nighttime, although it is not late and not yet dark out.

During those both too long and too short two weeks, much time is spent staring at walls that are seemingly, reluctantly becoming emptier and beige-er, always beige-er, or staring at floors filled with cardboard boxes labeled with black markers that, the labels, denote the contents of each box. During this time, whomever is leaving, is present in body, physically, but as each day passes, the soon-to-be-gone-individual disappears piece by emotional piece into the space between where this person is leaving from and where this person is going to.

The room is on the second floor of a three-story apartment building. On the east wall of the room, about six feet apart from each other, there are two, square windows that look out onto another identical in color and shape, also three-story apartment building that, the apartment building across the street like the building in which the room in question is located, is made of a forest-mud colored brick. At the left-most of the windows, stands a woman. She has wavy brown hair that extends to her lower back, brown eyes that are darker than the brown of her hair, and soft skin that is a wet-desert-sand shade of brown that is in between the color of her hair and her eyes. The woman at the window smokes a cigarette, a cigarette which she holds in her left hand and smoke from which she blows through the screen of the open window. Her left elbow rests upon the sill of the window and she is sort of leaning forward towards the screen of the window but not close enough to touch the screen with her ruby lips from which she is blowing smoke from the cigarette that she is holding in a hand that is a connected to a forearm and an elbow which she is leaning on the window sill. Her right hand is balanced on her right hip, fingers pointed down towards the floor, in a sort of impatient and anxious posture as she smokes her cigarette, that, the cigarette, has just been lit. The woman is wearing a light-grey T-shirt that has slowly disappearing creases crisscrossing it from when, moments ago when she put it on, it was carefully folded and resting atop other carefully folded clothing in the half filled, black suitcase on the wooden floor between the bed with the floral print bedspread and the wooden dresser. The light-grey, slightly creased T-shirt does not belong to her, is the only article of clothing that she is wearing and extends to almost exactly halfway down her thigh. The nails on her fingers and on her toes, with the exception of the nail on her right, ring finger which she broke earlier in the day, are painted a hard-boiled-egg-shell-white.

The two-week-friendship or romantic relationship can be wonderfully sweet, if not also almost always extremely bittersweet. During the two weeks, though, the one who is about to leave will, along with the joy of the new relationship, deal with the crushing feelings that accompany the loses of the relationships in the soon-to-be-left-place that have lasted longer than just two weeks and are more emotionally impactful and deeper than whatever the two-week, honeymoon-period, sepia-toned, fantasy could ever be. In the two weeks prior to departure, during which the one set to depart will be head-in-the-clouds-giddy with the honey-golden-warmth that accompanies new love and friendship, the people actually involved and important to the soon to depart individual seem to fade out of existence and are replaced by these newer and much less complex relationships. The people, who up until the t-minus two-weeks departure date, have been a large part of the soon-to-be-gone's life, are themselves floating in a haze of disbelief and experience a minor sort of grief that accompanies the departure of a loved (or maybe even just liked) one. This feeling of low-level-grief and dis-connection is felt by both parties, the leaver and the soon-to-be-left-behind. The pain of this grief often causes both parties to retreat, one into themselves and one into their new two-week-long-relationships, thus causing the tragedy of one spending their finals days with everybody or anybody other than those with whom they should be spending their final days.

The sort of grief described above is what the woman at the window is feeling as she blows her cigarette smoke out through the screen of the window into the hot night and as she absently flicks the ash of the smoldering cigarette onto the sill where it, the ash, falls beside where her elbow, on which she leans, rests.

That sort of grief, described above and felt by the woman at the window, is also felt by the other in the room. The other in the room, is a man, is the one who is leaving and is seated on the dry-sky-blue chair beside the desk, in between the two windows, at the left of which the woman is smoking the cigarette and feeling something like despair.

The man is wearing a long-sleeved, button down shirt made of linen. It is the color of butter left on the counter and is creaseless. The shirt is creaseless because the man picked up the shirt just hours ago from the dry cleaners. The recently pressed and ironed shirt worn by the man in the sky-blue chair is unbuttoned completely, exposing the night-sky-black hair on the man's chest and stomach. The man has eyes that are the sort of electric green seen in a stoplight but often glow with something much more melancholic than electricity. The man's hair is messy and as dark as that on his chest. A strand of hair about an inch wide and three inches long hangs down his forehead, partially covering his left eye. The man in the chair, besides the unbuttoned creaseless, linen shirt is wearing light-grey boxer briefs. He has his back and the chair turned away from the desk, the wall and the windows, at the left of which the woman leans against the sill, almost finished with her cigarette. The man is facing and is less than three feet away from the bed on which the floral-patterned-bedspread lays in disarray in a pile on the lower third of the bed. The general lack of clothing on both of the people in the room is the result of sex that has recently ended and was not very pleasurable for either party and left both people feeling more empty and in more pain than before. The man has hair on his face but not enough hair to be called a beard, but long enough for him not to be called clean shaven. One of his arms rests on his leg and the other supports his head, the elbow of the hand that supports his head rests on his knee and the fingers of the hand that supports his head are stroking the pokey hairs on his neck and cheeks in a slow, semi-conscious movement as he stares blankly at the bed.

The problem with these two-week-relationships is that no matter how much fun is had or emotion is felt, there is an underlying sense of rot that accompanies each and every moment, like the moment is spoiled before it even begins, but neither party wants to comment on or do anything about it. The problem with these two-week-relationships is that they are not real.

More than the fact of what they are not is what they are and that is a mere idea, a fantasy, a briefly indulged mirage. What these two-week-relationships are is a daydream meant to distract from the deep loss and holes made during the process of uprooting. These two-week-relationships are just that ideas and are thus and therefore as fleeting as a passing thought and while one can be momentarily lost in an especially alluring or exceptionally distract-ing-from-reality-passing-thought, reality will always slowly fade back into sight and real life, no matter how much one doesn't want it to, will drag on forward. Now these tangential distractions, these what-could-have-beens al-ways end and they end in a quick way. With the ending, the one who is bound to leave usually crawls (mainly figuratively but sometimes literally) back to those neglected ones that will soon be left. This crawling back mostly hap-pens on the night before departure and what follows, after the return, is the most painful and drawn out and dramatic goodbye that often never involves an actual verbal goodbye because that in itself is too painful for either party to make real by speaking into truth.

It is the night before the man in the room will leave and earlier today, in the morning, unshaven and wide-eyed with heartbreak and guilt, he crawled back from his two-week-failed-distractions. He crawled back to she-who-has been dreading saying goodbye, she who is the one with whom he should have spent his final days, but couldn't out of fear and shame in having to leave this woman he loves.

Besides the clothes on the bodies of the two in the room, folded in the suitcase or messily shoved in the drawers of the wooden dresser, there are, scattered across the floor in a shrapnel-esque pattern; a black necktie, two black men's socks, a black men's sports coat, a sky-blue woman's dress with a zipper on the back and a pair white woman's underwear. A white bra hangs by one of the clasps used to secure the bra on the bottom right corner of the bed, half hanging and resting on the bed and half resting on the hardwood floor, close to the bare feet of the man seated in the chair. Outside there are sounds and they can be heard through the open window through the screen of which the woman is blowing out the last puffs of smoke from the nub that used to be her cigarette. Those sounds are of cars passing, multiple siren clad vehicles responding to hopefully faraway emergencies and the sound of sizzling from the stove of the occupants of the ground floor apartment of the building in view of the windows of the room in which the man and the woman are existing in silence.

Upon hearing of the leaving, the one or ones who are soon to be left will wear an empty smile, like the smile worn by a politician caught in a career ending scandal and trying, desperately, to hold onto things that are so clearly falling apart (or in the case of those soon to be left, disappearing). Now this smile is a mix of anger and of pain; this smile is built from the shards of broken expectations and dashed, long-held hopes. But for the two in the room, on the hot night before the departure, these smiles have long since faded to flat mouthed kisses and stares at nothing much at all. The night before leaving is often spent by both the-soon-to-be-left and the-soon-to-be-gone in the paradoxically tense state of having so much to say, everything to say, but saying nothing at all.

The woman, now standing straight up but still looking out the window, has finished her cigarette and stamps out what is left of it onto the sill on which her elbow previously rested. The man twists the sky-blue chair in her direction. His eyes are on the floor. She breaches the distance between them in two barefoot steps, one of which is over a black men's sock. As she steps towards him, she brushes a strand of hair behind her ear. With both of her hands placed on his shoulders, she pushes him back against the sky-blue, plastic chair. The woman, with the cigarette still on her breath, climbs onto the man's lap, looping her soft but strong legs around his hips. The woman pulls the man's head against her chest. The man wraps his arms around her mid back. They are both warm in each other's embrace, they both know that this type of warmth is not easily found and that it, the warmth of them together, is fleeting.

There is a point, at the latest possible of points, before the departure when the one-who-will-soon-leave is somehow allowed this departure by the one-who-will-be-left, with some type of embrace. There are often tears that accompany this embrace.

The light-grey t-shirt that belongs to the man, which is being worn by the woman seated on his lap, is slowly being darkened at various spots across the woman's chest at which the man's head rests. That is to say the man in the chair is weeping and his tears are soaking into the shirt which the woman is wearing as she holds his head gently and softly strokes his hair with her egg shell white fingernails. The woman does not want to cry tonight, instead, as the man cries into her chest, she looks at the wall behind the desk and notices that it is similar in color to the paint on her nails. She knows that if she starts to cry, she will not stop, she will cry all night and this crying will make it that much harder for him to leave and for her to let him leave. He has to leave, they both know that, but neither of them want him to, but he still has to and he still will and when the morning comes, he will have to go and then he will be gone.

The worst piece of leaving are the lies that are told to one's self as they leave or as they are left. There are promises to keep in touch, vague plans made of a return journey, embraces held for too long, goodbyes never really said. The sad truth about leaving is that one loses touch as soon as they walk away. Most often there is no return journey.

The man in the chair and the woman atop him embrace, as outside, the sun goes down and the city beyond the windows slowly goes dark.

In the morning, the man will get dressed in the grey morning light and constant traffic sounds. As he dresses in his recently dry-cleaned suit on which he will never stop finding strands of her brown hair, the man will watch the woman in the bed, half covered by the floral bedspread, sleep. Although the woman will not be asleep, she will not have slept. Instead, she will have spent the night pulling his arms around her and hoping that somehow he will never let go, but knowing that he will, that he has to, that he has to let go.

He will be dressed; the suitcase will be upright and leaning against the dresser. The man will kiss the woman on her sleep warm, and rich-brown, cheek. And as he kisses her cheek he will leave his lips upon her face long enough for him to have to gasp for air when he finally pulls away.

The woman will pretend to be asleep but she will stir as the man, dragging the suitcase behind him, leaves the room that used to be theirs together but is now only hers, alone.

On the desk or on the chair or on the dresser, the man will have left the light-grey, t-shirt; a keepsake maybe.

In the morning, the man will go.

In the morning, the woman will pretend to be asleep.

In the morning, the light will reluctantly shine on.

A WASH

The car wash is one of those do it yourself kinds of car washes, as in there are no actual employees that work there and if one wants to have their car washed at this particular car wash, one must do it themselves.

To begin the process of washing one's, the person intending to wash their car's car, one must pay with a credit card or change in quarters (no nickels, dimes, pennies, or paper money is accepted) and when the money has been processed by the machine, a timer begins counting down in a way that is similar (but has much less in terms of stakes) to the way timers on bombs count down in action movies.

The timer starts with three minutes and counts down and one would assume that the numbers that move down the screen are seconds, but rumor has it that the timer of the car wash machine has been tampered with by the notoriously shifty absentee owner of the car wash in question and that each second which clicks too quickly by on said timer is actually only one half second, but nobody knows for sure nor has anybody cared enough to bring their own stopwatch to test if there is a discrepancy in the timer on the machine, and even if someone were to do this, it is unclear what they would do in order to fix the problem because for one only the shifty absentee owner of the car wash has access to the programing of the car wash machine and for two the shifty absentee owner of the car wash is never actually at the car wash and there are no other employees to whom the person with the stopwatch could go to, to complain about the allegedly tampered with timer on the car wash machine. So basically the only option this hypothetical time checker would have would be to tape or glue or tack a piece of paper to the machine on which they could write a complaint note and ask for the shifty absentee owner to make the time on the timer actual time, but this option may not do anything either because for one the note could fly away in the wind and for two the note may get wet or covered in soap or in foam (as this note would be hung up in the inside of a car wash after all) and for three (as previously stated) there are no employees to see this note so the only people who would read this note would be customers of the car wash who have no power to fix the issue which the hypothetical time checker would bring up in their note.

And but anyways when the timer starts the person who has just paid has three minutes (well not actually three minutes if the rumors about the tampered timer are true the person has only one and a half minutes) to spray down their car with water, spray their car with a cotton-candy colored foam that has chemical sticky sweet smell (not unlike cotton candy in fact) and then to rinse said foam off of their car with more water, all while watching the timer to make sure they allot enough time to each task as to be able to adequately clean their car. When the timer turns off so does the water and the foam and the music that started when the timer did (music which is most likely classic rock but which plays from speakers that are so garbled and blown that it is practically impossible to tell anything about the music other than the fact that it is in fact music and not just purely radio static), and when the water and the music and the foam all suddenly stop there is an eerie silence broken only by the soft sucking sound of the drain (atop which those wishing to wash their cars are directed to park [by a faded red sign with white lettering, and which [the drain] sits at a decline from the rest of the floor of the car wash as to properly direct the water and leftover foam that drips from the now clean[ish] cars). When the timer goes off, the machine asks the car owner whether or not they would like to purchase more time and most people do because three minutes (or a minute and a half, or somewhere in between those two) is not really enough time to wash one's car (the average wash goes on for around 8 minutes on the timer).

There are three bays at which customers can wash their cars but it seems to the man with the silver sports car (who comes to this car wash at least weekly, if not daily) that there is almost always one washing bay out of order but that said out of order bay seems to alternate every couple of weeks. And the case of the alternating out of order washing bay came to his attention after five separate occasions on which he had washed his car in a certain bay in the late evening and by the next morning (as he drove to work) there was an out of order sign on the bay in which he had washed his car merely hours before (printed on white paper with black lettering and taped to a thin and frayed string which was hung across the bay) and what is weird about those instances is that he is almost positive that he was the last person to wash his car in said washing bay on said previous evening and that in each instance the car wash, washing machine had been working well and thus it is confusing and bizarre to him why on the five separate mornings after his five separate evening car washes, the machine, which was working perfectly fine the night before, was closed and supposedly out of order (not to mention the question of who hung the out of order sign, as nobody that the man with the silver sports car knows or has asked, knows or has seen the shifty absentee owner of the car wash nor any employee of the car wash [if any employees actually exist, which seems unlikely]), even though he was most likely the last person to use said machine in each separate instance and they were not out of order at all.

Now the man with the silver sports car has become slightly (if not entirely) obsessed with this car wash, which as far as anybody knows is legally named "car wash") in part because of the strange case of the out of order signs on machines that (in the man with the silver sports car's humble opinion) were, now that he has really thought about each instance a lot, most certainly not out of order at all and subsequently this aptly and simply named car wash has become a big part of this man's life and has begun to take up more and more of both his time and mental capacity. The other part of the man's obsession with the car wash comes not from anything to do with the car wash but with his life, specifically his home life, specifically his marriage, specifically the bad parts of his marriage (which are slowly growing worse and worse) specifically and most importantly the fact (or at least a theory of his) that he will soon be no longer married at all and that his wife will soon, really any day now, serve him divorce papers.

He has had this fear of divorce (which stems from a deep fear of being alone which stems from even deeper and repressed memories from his childhood) for as long as he has been married, and although he has been married for more than ten years at this point and although his wife tells him (at least weekly, if not daily) that she is very happy with him and fulfilled by him and overall overjoyed with their life together and their kids and their relationship (to each other and to their kids) and their house and the city in which they live and so on, he still is deeply and stomach- upsettingly terrified of divorce and its inevitable arrival. In some sort of pathetic and mid-life-crisis-esque impulsive purchase, three months ago he sold his old car (the same one he had driven since college, the same car in which he had driven his now wife on their first date long ago) and bought the new and shiny silver sports car. And with the purchase of his new car, he started looking for a car wash close to his house because since he had just spent so much money on his new car, he wanted to make sure it stayed looking clean and shiny and silver and sporty for as long as possible, and eventually he found the car wash in question.

The man with the silver (and almost always spotless) sports car has started spending more and more time thinking about the car wash, specifically who is hanging the out of order signs and why, and in order to solve this mystery he feels as though he must go to the car wash in such a way that he can truly monitor said car wash and who is or isn't there at any time of the day. And so he has begun to try and go seemingly at random to the car wash, trying to go at times when he has never gone before in order to catch the shifty absentee owner of the car wash at work hanging up the out of order sign, and he has been doing so for about two weeks now sometimes going to the car wash in the middle of the night, sometimes at the crack of dawn, sometimes during the middle of the day and so on, but to no avail; he has seen nobody but customers at the car wash, yet the out of order sign has been moved twice in the last two weeks.

So, the man with the silver sports car will continue to monitor the car wash, hopefully closing in on its illusive owner and the mysterious "out of order" sign, while back at home his wife continues to tell him how happy she is while (most likely, in his humble opinion) definitely working with a lawyer to serve him those divorce papers, any day now.

Barber

I call in to make an appointment. The vocal embodiment of an infinity of
light beers in silver aluminum and of menthol cigarettes takes down my
name and phone number. I'm booked for tomorrow at three. I arrive early,
as always. He sees me, ignores me, goes out for a smoke, comes back in,
sips something that smells like not quite coffee from a light-blue thermos.
He wanders over to the list where I have written my name. It's three-fifteen,
he looks down at the sheet, calls my name and looks around to see who
identifies themselves with the words that he has just grumbled though his
wonderful, ashtray mouth. I raise my hand up halfway and squeak that it is
me who he has summoned; I am the chosen one; his chosen one. He looks
at me like we have never met, even though he has been cutting my hair for
about a year now. He extends a hand that is surprisingly soft. On the space
between his thumb and index finger he has a tattoo of a cross. I shake his
hand, he leads me to his chair, and the romance begins.

His chair is black cracking leather with holes that show through to the
yellow foam inside. The chair's frame is made of a smudged silver and the
chair squeals as it turns, with me in it, to face myself in the mirror. He asks
what I want, and I try not to say him, and I tell him the same as I always do.
Just a little off the top, shorter on the sides. But my hair is already short, too short
for my taste, but I keep coming here to sit in his chair and my visits are becoming more frequent. At first I came once a month, then every two weeks,
now I come once a week and am fighting the urge to come more than that.
I ask how his day is going, he mumbles a reply. The electric razor buzzes at
the same frequency as my heart as he puts the shielded blade against the back
of my head. Our empty conversation fades into the silence of the vibrations
coming from the machine in his hand. He is soft when he cuts hair. I can
smell the tobacco on his hands. He must roll his own cigarettes because

when his hands pass by my eyes I can see the brown stains on his fingers tips and the ground bits of leaf beneath his untrimmed nails. I sit in silence as he moves his hands about, clipping and cutting and snipping and caressing my head and my hair and the back of my neck. For those moments, the twenty short minutes of time that we spend together, I am his canvas and he treats me with care; with gentle touches; I am his proud creation, I am beaming with his hard work. I wear it for the world to see; *look what he has made me* I say with silent words to everybody I meet.

He trims my beard. His fingers move up and down my cheeks. This is his passion and these little movements, these touches that are somehow more intimate than they should be are why I come here more than I should. I would let him do his art on me until there was no hair left, and then I would grow it back, just for him. As he carefully circles my lips with the razor, a look of concentration on his face and a glint in his hazel eyes, I wish I was a werewolf so he would always have something to cut. I almost whisper to him that I will be his Wolf-man, I will forever be his canvas and his hands on that buzzing tool of magic will be my moon; I will change just for him; I will wait obediently in that leather chair and try not to scratch it with my claws.

It's almost over. He brushes hair from my forehead and my nose in a quiet way. His touch reminds me of when my dad used to bathe me in the sink as a child, a memory I'm not sure is a memory or just the remembrance of a story that I've heard too many times. But this is real, he is real. He puts shaving cream on the back of my neck and on the edges of my cheeks and below my beard line. I want to be coddled in that musky smell, protected by his hands. He flips open the straight razor, its glint is lightning and my breath is the thunder that follows. He jokes that he'll try not to cut me. I laugh too loud even though I've heard that joke every time I get a haircut, even though I know he won't, he is too careful, but I like the thought that he could draw my blood but that he chooses not to. The razor scrapes my skin and it stings but I like the sting as long it is he who is stinging me. I know there is no blood and I know that he is taking the greatest care, slicing each individual hair with a bit-tongue-intensity. He shaves my throat; my blood is throbbing lava. I can feel my heartbeat in my ears and the cold steel of his blade at my neck. I dare not breath. He leans forward and I can smell the cigarettes and the whiskey and the coffee on his breath, I can feel his half rolled up flannel sleeve brush against my shoulder. It's all over too soon and he snaps the razor shut, spins the chair and I get up. I tip him more than is necessary but there is no thank you. I nod as I step through the glass door. There is no goodbye, there never is. Maybe next week he will remember my name.

Breakfast

Breakfast was when we spoke. 6:30 am, black coffee in a white mug with a handle that perfectly fit around her fingers. She had red nails then, painted every night as I took my bath. And she would drink coffee from the white mug with the perfect handle and she would light her cigarette with the burner and then put a pan onto the burner and then crack two eggs into the pan. That's how she would cook; a coffee cup and a cigarette held in one hand and a spatula in the other. All the while she would talk and tell me about who the customers at the diner were the day before and who was dating who and who had been found kissing in the janitor's closet behind the manager's office and who had not tipped well and who had tipped too well and why the person who had tipped too well had tipped as much as they did and what the person who tipped too well had to hide. And I would sit on one of the white, plastic lawn chairs that we had in our kitchen and I would listen and I would play with my curls and I would try to sit up straight and not wrinkle my school dress and I would try to move my hands the way that she did and I would wish that we had enough money for me to paint my nails too. But we were poor then and she was always tired but she was never angry with me. She wasn't even angry the time I forgot my backpack and we had to ride the bus at night back to the elementary school and beg the janitor to let us in so I could get my bag and my project that I had to work on that night but had forgot at school because I had wanted to catch the bus that left 3 minutes before school ended, so I was in a rush to leave and forgot my things. I had wanted to go home to clean up the bedroom and the kitchen because I knew how tired my mother was when she got home from work and I knew how much she said it helped when I cleaned up the house and how she would smile that smile when she would get home in her light-blue work uniform and the house would be clean and in those days, I lived for that smile. And after she got home she would lie down on her bed and I would take off her shoes for her and she would have laid on the couch but we didn't have a couch because we couldn't afford one, so she would lie on the bed. All of that is why I forgot my backpack at school, but my mother wasn't even angry then, she wasn't ever angry, just tired, and even when we got home from picking up my backpack at school she still sat with me while I took my bath and painted her nails, but we didn't talk then, that's what breakfast was for. And at breakfast, after she was done telling me about the diner, she would ask me about school and I would tell her about who had been there the day before and who had not been there and why and I would tell her about who had been found kissing in the empty classroom by the principal's office and who had not done well on the math pop quiz and who had done too well on the math pop quiz and why the person who had done too well on the math pop quiz had done so well and what they had to hide. And while I told her about school, I would hold the straw of my apple juice box in between my fingers like she always held her cigarettes and I would take long drags from the straw and the straw would make these wet, sucking sounds that told us that I was only pretending to smoke and that my cigarette wasn't real but me and my mother, we would pretend not to notice.

And I remember how on my birthday, my mother would buy an extra bottle of her red nail polish just for me and how after my bath she would paint the nails on my fingers and my toes and I would have nail polish like hers until my bottle ran out and I had to wait until Christmas for another. But I would only get another bottle for Christmas if my mother got her Christmas bonus and that only happened when her boss was in a good mood and she said he wasn't usually in a good mood but I always hoped he would be in a good mood during Christmas so I could get my nail polish. And maybe if he was in a good mood and she did get her Christmas bonus, maybe I would get blue nail polish instead of red but if he was in a good mood I would prolly just end up getting red nail polish anyway because that was my mother's favorite color and it was also mine. And there were weeks when we couldn't do our laundry because my mother hadn't been paid yet and we washed our clothes in the sink and used dish soap and scrubbed our clothes and squeezed them out into the sink and then rinsed them out again and my mother said that we always had to look good even though we were poor and she always did look good and she made sure that her work dress was always ironed and always smelled fresh and never had any spills or stains on it and she always made sure that I didn't drop any egg on my school dress and if I did she showed me how to get it out by dabbing my shirt with a towel and making sure not to rub it in, but dab it. And she always looked so pretty those mornings in the kitchen with her dress already on and her nails painted red and the cigarette held perfectly in her hand and the eggs bubbling in the pan.

Now those days are gone. Now I am older. Now my mother's knees and hips and wrists are too old to hold up a tray and she wheezes sometimes and I have to tell her not to smoke and I have to go into her room and find her hidden cigarettes and throw them away and remind her that she is sick and that she is sick because of the cigarettes and when I say that she doesn't respond, she just looks down at her shoes. I'm done with elementary school and middle school and high school and I've been working now for ten years and I have a job but it's not a great job but it's a job and I get paid enough for us to have food on the table and real chairs in the kitchen and a couch but not much else. My mother lives at home with me and sometimes she cleans up the house so when I get home from the office, I don't have to look at a dirty house and sometimes she will rub my feet as I lay on the couch because now we can afford a couch but I know that when she rubs my feet, that her hands hurt but she rubs my feet sometimes anyway and she never complains. And yesterday after her doctor's appointment we got home and I was already tired, almost too tired to walk and I had to get up early again and she said she was sorry but that we forgot to pick up her prescription and I got mad and didn't talk on the drive to the pharmacy and the pharmacist was closing and locking the doors when we got there and I had to beg him to let us in and give us the prescription and I had to give him some money that we needed for groceries but he let us in and my mother got her pills and we drove home in silence and when we got home she put her hand on my arm and said sorry and her fingers were cold and I saw that her shirt was tucked into her underwear instead of her pants and I saw that she had no paint on her fingernails and I swallowed hard and I didn't cry but I wanted to. We went inside and I started a bath for her and I painted my nails while she was in the bath and afterwards I helped her dry off and then I painted her nails while she lay on the couch and then we went to bed and before I turned the lights out in her room, she said she would get up in the morning to make me breakfast and I said that it was ok, that she didn't have to get up so early, but I knew she would be there in the kitchen at 6:30 am, cooking eggs, with her

coffee cup in that white mug with the perfect handle but without her cigarette and I knew that she would ask me about who had been at my office the
day before and about who was dating who and who had not got a promotion
and about who had got a promotion and why they had got a promotion and
what they had to hide and who had been found kissing in the janitor's closet
by the boss's office and I would tell her as I twist the curls in my hair, because
breakfast has always been when we speak.

Bus stop

Beside a public park there is a bus stop. In this park, there is grass, a couple of tall and old looking trees and a hill. The hill in the park is rounded and perfectly covered with bright green and soft grass. The hilltop is square and flat and is high enough up that the city and busy streets that surround the park and the hill seem to fade away and all that is left is the blue sky and the clouds and the slight rustling of the grass and sometimes, on the best of days, the sound of laughter or a strumming guitar or soft spoken voices saying words meant only for a loved one's ear. During the summer and spring and on the hot days of fall, couples lay atop the hill on blankets beside which they have thin wooden baskets filled with wine and various picnic foods. On these warms days, the sun rays are not hard and hot but instead caress the skin of those laying beneath them with a warm and subtle tenderness. During the winter, on days when it is not too cold, this hill becomes the neighborhood (or possibly the entire city's) sledding hill and the sides of the hill are graced with lines made by sleds ridden by squealing children as parents stand at the top watching and laughing too. Half-melted snow people and the remnants of snowball fights are common place (in the flatlands of the park, between the bus stop and the hill) and there always seems to be someone enjoying themselves at this park no matter the season or the weather; whether it's the local karate school that practices barefoot in the grass, or the Saturday morning yoga class (which mainly consists of young mothers) or the old man in the beat up brownish yellow suit who brings an easel and a metal suitcase filled with paints and brushes who always paints the same angle of the hill and the mountains and the sky and the couples laying on the grass or children sledding by (depending on the season) as he hums along to classical music that plays from a tiny black radio which he always carries along with him.

But today it is cold; nearly freezing. The rain that is falling, falls from clouds the color of boredom (a light and empty grey) and feels like pure and utterly frigid death. The hill is soaking wet and void of any signs of life; even the grass which often seems so alive and lush looks crumped and miserable under the pounding sleet and sunless sky. The temperature is plummeting and it seems that any moment whatever is currently falling from the sky will turn to snow, but for now it seems that whatever sordid mix of temperature and humidity in the microclimate of the bus stop and the park is at the point where the current precipitation is neither raindrop nor snowflake but a disgusting and sloppy sludge mix of both. In the rain, lovers can dance and children in yellow rain boots can jump in puddles or float folded paper ships down the overflowing gutters. In the snow, fires can be built, flakes can be caught on outstretched tongues and playful wars can be fought. But in the sleet, in the dripping, frigid liquid sickness that is the not quite snow, not quite rain which is presently coming from the sky and ruining everything in sight, all there is to do is wallow in the misery and hope to get inside some-where warm as soon as possible.

Huddled in layers of wool and down coats and hats and scarves, hoping to be anywhere else but in this cold place, two strangers are sitting together on the green plastic bench of the bus stop waiting for the 4:38 pm bus to come. The bus is late and the sun is going down. It is a few days away from the darkest and shortest (and most likely coldest) day of the year and every-thing is muffled in a glacial and dead stillness.

The two people at the bus stop are bundled beyond recognition. In fact by sight alone it is impossible to tell the gender, height, weight or really anything about either of these people. One of these people is wearing a dark green coat and a grey hat and is shivering slightly. Beside the person in the green coat is a brown paper bag of groceries from which pokes the end of a car-rot and half of a now most likely frozen baguette. The person in the green coat and the grey hat is an old woman who is taking the bus back to her one bedroom basement apartment from the grocery store; a store at which she bought the ingredients of a soup she intends to make and basically survive off of for the next week. The recipe for the soup she intends to make has been in her family for generations and was her husband's favorite thing that she made (well it was before he died) and when she, like her husband already has, dies so will the recipe for she has no children or grandchildren or even a kindly neighbor to pass said recipe onto. She presumes that tonight may be the last time she makes this soup.

The other person on the bench is much bigger than the old woman, and is a man who works construction. He would normally drive his pine green pick-up truck to and from his job but he recently had his license taken away because he was caught and arrested for driving drunk one too many times (which in the case of his particular crime, one too many times is actually just once).

It is safe to assume that these two people do not know each other and that they have not much in common other than the fact that today they are both waiting for the bus at the same time and are possibly freezing to death in the process. Over the last couple of minutes the bundled strangers sitting on the same bench have inched closer together; driven and controlled by some type of involuntary evolutionary survival mechanism which compels them to huddle close to anyone nearby for warmth in order to make it through this cold and getting colder night. Now they are nearly touching shoulders (although the shoulder of the construction worker is at the head level of the old woman) and the warmth between them is radiant and calming. The heat between their nearly touching bodies is the only gentle thing in this storm of terrible sludge and fading light.

The stillness of the frozen flora and the carless street is made even stiller by the tension between the two people on the bench and it seems that some-one will soon speak and try to spark up some conversation, but neither of them do. If the person in the brown coat (the drunk driving construction worker) were to talk to the being beside him, he may tell her how the hill behind the bus stop used to be, in fact, a garbage dump and that this part of the city (many years ago) used to be on the outskirts of the town. The brown coated person could go on to say how he grew up in a (now long ago bull-dozed and paved over) red dirt, trailer park close by to this once and past gar-bage dump (now the hill by the bus stop where the two currently shiver and sit) and that while he was younger he would often go and watch the tractors push and stack the piles of garbage. If the person in the brown jacket were to say something, he may say how (one Sunday, as a child) he watched as a crew of workmen covered the dump with dirt and sawdust and then covered the now dirt covered garbage with rolls and rolls of sod, making what was once the dump, the hill of grass that it is today. If the construction worker were to speak (with a voice hardened and dried out by concrete dust and twenty plus years of smoking) he would go on to say how he likes to imagine that beneath what is now the grass of the city's most popular park there are old mattresses, and broken TVs and the decomposing bones of once loved and long deceased pets. He would tell the person beside him, if he were to speak (which he will not do) how he likes to imagine all these people living their light and rich lives standing atop a hill made of garbage; he would remark on the irony and poetic justice of something seemingly free and pure being built on a mound of rotting, toxic and ancient trash; he would try to make some connection between this pile of debris and the sick and horrid foundation of society today, but he won't. Instead he will stay seated on this uncomfortable bench in a sleet storm beside a woman he doesn't and will never know, until the bus comes and he can finally get home and open one of the beers that is sitting and waiting for him in his fridge.

If the old woman were to speak to the man beside her she would speak in a voice that is frail and quiet and squeaky at the end of each sentence, and she would tell this man about her family's secret recipe for the soup which she intends to make. If the old woman were to speak to the large and gruff seeming man beside her she would say how she feels that she is doing some type of disservice to her family by not having anybody to pass the recipe onto and that she hopes that maybe she could pass the recipe onto him. If the old woman were to speak to the man and the man was to speak back to her in a way that seemed respectful, she would begin to tell him how to make the soup using her family's recipe for she just wants someone to carry on the tradition; she doesn't want it all to fade into nothing with her. But she won't and although she cannot yet tell the bottom of the brown paper bag is soaked and is soft and will not be able to hold the weight of what is within it when she goes to pick it up when the bus comes and thus it will break and the contents of the bag will spill out onto the icy sidewalk and she will not have time to pick up all of her vegetables and spices before the bus leaves (nor the energy or flexibility to do so) and will have to leave her damaged groceries and her broken bag on the sidewalk in order not to miss the bus and will end up having to eat leftover casserole for dinner and go back to the grocery store tomorrow. But the old woman doesn't know about the bag and how it will soon break, and she does not intend to speak to the man beside her.

Now the man and the old woman are (physically) closer than they have ever been and the edges of their coats are touching. In the distance the yellow, scrolling lights at the front of the bus can be seen through the slush.

Cars Pass

The shovel is a soil-darkened, silver metal and has a long and smooth handle which is sturdy and work worn. The dirt is moist from the morning dew but is still heavy as it sits in a seemingly regenerating pile at the roadside. Along the road beside the dirt and the concrete and the shovels and buzzing machines, there are bright orange cones made even brighter by the reflecting morning sun and cloudless blue sky.

The worker holds the shovel and in that shovel there is dirt and with that shovel he will put the dirt into a blood red wheelbarrow and once that wheelbarrow is full of dirt he will push it around a concrete barricade and diagonally across the road and dump the contents of that wheelbarrow into a ditch which needs to be filled and flattened over. The ditch runs for a mile and so does the pile of dirt on the other side of the road from the ditch.

The worker has hands that look much older than the other parts of his body. In those hands, there are cracks and wrinkles and half healed cuts that look like they were once deep and painful, and those cracks are highlighted by and filled in with dark-black dirt. There is dust and ash and tar and chemical paint in the air by the roadside, and there is a faint, thick smell of burnt rubber and bubbling tar about.

The worker is wearing an orange vest and beneath that he is wearing clothes which match the color of the dirt, the same dirt which he has been tasked to move.

The shovel goes into the dirt and lifts carefully up and towards the wheelbarrow. The shovel repeats its movement until the barrow is full. Then the barrow is pushed to the ditch on the other side of the road and dumped. The shovel's purpose is to dig and to cut and to slowly chip away. The wheelbarrow's purpose is to hold and to carry and to dump. The worker's purpose is to push and to balance and to heave and to sweat and to bleed when cut and to work until the sun has left the sky (and sometimes even after that).

There is a radio, which is black and from that radio classic rock plays quietly enough to not by heard by the people in the passing cars but loud enough for the worker to be able to hear while he works (but he is really only able to hear the music when the cars are not passing, as the rush of wind which follows the cars as well as the sounds of the wheels on the road and the engines that make the tires turn, more or less block out the sound of the radio during the time it takes them to pass).

And this may seem like just another work day; another set of hours under the sun; more minutes rolling about in the filth, and in some ways, it is, but in some ways, it is not. This morning, at around 4:15 am, this man, this worker, this being of blood and water, received a call on his phone in his trailer and on this call, the other being of similar blood and water, was his sister and his sister informed him (the worker) that his dad was dead. Dead of a heart attack at seventy-three. Hell, that was older than he (the worker's father) ever thought he would get. And sure, this man, the father, was not the greatest person alive; not the best sack of blood and bones and water and hair. Sure, this now dead thing drank too much and smoked cigarettes on the couch in a tank top and occasionally beat the boy who would become the man who shovels dirt on the roadside, but this man, the father, tried his very best to be a good dad and to raise his children up well. The worker, as he shovels an-other shovelful of dirt into his barrow, remembers the good and bad about his father, as a mix of dirt and sweat drips down the back of his neck and runs down between his shoulders beneath his shirt.

And this man, this worker, would have taken this day of work off but he decided (after hanging up with his sister) that if he were to take the day off that he would end up just sitting around in his trailer and smoking too many cigarettes and drinking too much beer and maybe even crying a bit and so he decided to come to work anyways because at least he could work and keep himself busy while on the job instead of wallowing in whatever mess he would've found himself in.

And from this man, the worker's mouth, hangs a cigarette which is sog-gy half from spit and half from sweat and the overall humidity of the dirt tainted air about the roadside. And this man has about three days of stubble on his face and this stubble is starting to turn grey-ish silver (that is much more grey than silver) in places beneath his neck and in his sideburns and in a couple places on the sides of his cheeks. He would've shaved this morning, but on account of the call in the night and the fact that it took him a long while to get back to sleep after said call, he decided to sleep in a bit longer than usual this morning and because of his extra sleep he really only had enough time this morning to get out of bed, get dressed, get his coffee and get out the door i.e. he didn't have time to shave this morning and he usually shaves about every three days because he doesn't love to shave every day (he doesn't love the act of shaving really) and since he didn't shave today (a day that he maybe should have) he will most likely shave tomorrow morning, but at the moment (with another heavy shovelful of dirt in his hand) he thinks that he may just let his facial hair grow out and give himself some extra time to sleep in every morning.

About a mile up the road from the man with the half-filled wheelbarrow and the unshaven face, there is a little girl with a simple and pure name. This little girl is wearing a black dress and black shoes and is wearing a tiny red bow in her hair (which is in a bun on top of her head, a bun which is held up by the tiny red bow which is actually a hair clip with a bow on top of it). And that red bow is the only thing of color on this little girl's person at the moment for she is on the way to a funeral, in the back of a limo with tinted windows for, like the worker, her daddy recently died. Her daddy was driving her brother home from his baseball game last week and it was dark out and there was a low mist on the ground, and because of that mist and the reflection of her daddy's headlights on said mist the driving conditions were not good. Her daddy was a good driver and was always careful, especially on misty evenings, but her big brother needed to use the bathroom and was going on about how painful it was to hold in what he needed to let out (at least this is what she heard, she had not been in the car that evening) and so because of the urgent bathroom situation her daddy sped through the mist. So, because of said mist he (her now dead daddy) had not seen the deer prancing across the road and the deer had either not seen the car or had been frightened by the lights through the fog and had frantically sprinted across the road. So then basically, this deer ran and the car (in which her daddy and her big brother sat) collided with the deer and the deer flew through the windshield of the car and the antlers of said deer had more of less reduced her daddy to shreds; i.e. the sack of blood and bones and whatever else her daddy was, was gouged and deemed unresponsive. And but her brother had survived with but a few scratches and cuts from the broken glass as well as a minor neck injury which requires one of those foam neck braces (and her brother, at the time of the accident, had peed his pants on account of his need to use the bathroom as well as the surprise of the collision with the deer).

So anyways that was last week and since that day there had been a lot of chaos in the little girl's house, and although she didn't really understand exactly what happened nor the complexities or tragedies of life, she did understand in her own foggy, six-year-old way that her daddy was gone and that he was most likely not coming back.

She also understands that his body (her daddy's body, or what is left of it) is in a box in the car behind the car in which is she currently standing on the seat with her face out of the window, watching the trees and houses and open fields go by on the way to what her mother is calling the cemetery after what her mother called the funeral. The little girl also knows that her mother isn't in the mood for questions or any bad behavior, she has always been able to tell when her mother is in a serious mood (which up until last week had not been very often, but since last week has been more or less the norm). The mother of the little girl is seated in the same limo as the little girl is, on a bench style seat only seen in limos which is perpendicular to the bench style seat on which the little girl stands and looks out the window (a bench which runs parallel and lengthwise to said limo) and is (her mother) also looking out a window, the one directly across from her, as she leans her head on one of her hands and dabs her swollen and running mascara adorned eyes with a black handkerchief held in her other hand. The little girl knows, almost instinctively to give her mother space and occasionally hugs and kisses during this time but no whines nor complaints nor tantrums. Beside the mother (on the other side of the mother than the little girl, on the same bench as the mother but not as the little girl) sits the brother looking shell shocked and wide eyed with his neck in that yellow-white foam brace and his face a mish mash of bruises and tape covered cuts (it would be hard to say that the brother is looking out the window, although it is possible that he technically is, but since the crash it seems this boy has had a sort of blank stare with which he stares at things, anything directly in front of him but without seeing anything at all).

And so now the little girl is riding with her face out the window at the front of a precession for a man she will never see grow old; a man who will never see her stop being young and the air feels cool and coarse on her face.

The limo slows as the cars pass through a construction site and as they do, as the funeral procession goes past the man, the worker in the dirt, passing as things always do, he looks up and makes a brief second of eye contact with the little girl before she and the rest of the cars and people dressed in black move on in a cloud of dirt and noise.

And the shovel goes back in the dirt and the barrow is almost full and the day is far from done.

DAWN

It was during those couple of grey minutes between night and sunrise that we drove. An unlimited time, unburdened by the boundaries of normality imposed on most other moments. It was an in between place; a threshold; something not quite finite but most certainly there. Through the fog and early morning sparrow's hymn we barreled. The headlights of the faded yellow pick up were dimmed; engulfed in moisture; blanketed in a soil clinging haze; reduced to muffled murmurs of light; lanterns shrouded in mist. Down a sloping hill towards the salt water we coasted on bald tires and a rusted, long bent frame. As the pavement beat the dew moistened wheels, my companion's breathing slowed. Weak whimpers and whines told me she would soon be gone. I pressed my foot hard on the worn pedal, and steadied our pace.

The parking lot gravel crunched and scattered as our rig slid to a halt beside a weedy path which led to sand and sea. I strode around to the passenger door, wetness from the grey pebbles crept up the toes of my beaten brown boots. Dew and stale rain soaked my rubber soles as I embraced my beloved beast. Down a passage framed by reeds and windblown dust we walked together, my two legs supporting her four, which hung limp in my arms. Leaving shoe shaped whispered imprints in the virgin sands, we trudged in the direction of the swelling tides. On a beach soaked in a peach sunrise, salt-laden winds gently blew her fur. I was reminded of a time when she fit in my creased palm, but that was many years ago, before she had wailed at the moon, before we had first visited our favorite sandy escape. As the red sun slowly rose and I stood with her in my arms, she had howled at many moonlit nights and we knew this beach as well as our own backyard. The sun was a tangerine, half submerged in jade waters and her heart sped like those days when she used to chase rabbits and squirrels. But her hunting days were long gone; her legs and paws too arthritic to bend. We continued into the sea until my jeans were a light blue blur beneath rippling white capped sprays. In my arms, her fur was soaked but she was far too gone to notice the cold or the bite of salt in her snout. I fell to my knees as I felt her final breath wheeze out from between black lips and a pink tongue that knew my face well. The sky was violet. The sun hung low. I let what was left of my sacred hound slip into the riptide that tugged towards the endless deep. I turned back towards the day. My arms felt too light. Crusted salt streaks like dried up creek beds littered the valleys between my eyes and chin.

Death of a Father

Day in, day out. Putting food on the table. Getting paid to pay taxes, buy groceries; to buy that set of paints for his daughter or the two new baseball gloves for his sons.

This cycle of clocking in and clocking out, checking the balance of the bank account, not even looking at the mailbox which is most absolutely overflowing with unpaid bills and parking tickets and other such nasty things. This life is not what he expected it would be, although he is not sure what he thought it would be. It's not as though he didn't expect to work hard or that he didn't expect to support himself and his family, but maybe he thought it would be different, lighter somehow. Maybe he hoped there would be more time in the sun; more long drives down dirt roads in the truck with his wife beside him with her hair down and blowing in the rushing air from the open window with all the kids riding in the truck bed hooting and hollering in the warmth and roaring wind.

Yeah, maybe that is what he expected; a simpler, slower life. He certainly didn't expect what it actually is: coming home after dark (after leaving for work in the same) to an also dark house with toys and shoes and clothes strewn all over the floor and furniture. Alone in the night he comes home, to a house in which everything is still and messy and perfect and asleep.

Each night he eats his dinner cold, standing at the kitchen counter illuminated by the orange, flickering streetlight across the street from his house, as well as sometimes by the moon. All that he has built or has had built with money he earned through dirty and grueling work, sits behind him and is safe in those fleeting moments of closed mouth chewing and tired eyes.

But there is now a deep worry within him; a growing, pulsating sense of panic. Things are changing. The world is so different than it used to be.

He works as a miner as his father and his father's father did. All of the men in his family have worked in the mines that pock-mark the hills and mountains surrounding the little town in which he grew up and currently lives with his wife and their three children.

His father's father and all of those quiet, work-worn men who proceeded him both in namesake and trade were lucky enough to live to retirement age and live out their remaining days on pension; fishing in the river and making desks and tables from stumps and fallen trees. Those men put in their years with their heads down and made it out with a decent paycheck guaranteed for the rest of their lives and only a few scars and soot darkened skin to boot.

But that was a different time, he knows. Wages have raised slightly since then but not nearly enough to cover the skyrocketing cost of living not to mention the housing boom and all of those things that he is happy to buy for his children but which are certainly and endlessly financially burdensome nonetheless. His industry is a dying one and he is smart and politically plugged in enough to know it, and that knowledge of career mortality, the fact that he may not get to work and retire in the same way his forefathers did, frankly terrifies him.

This afternoon at work he heard that the mine would be closing in the next year and that there would be continuous layoffs until then. He isn't sure if that which he heard is true (he has heard rumors of an end since he started working in the mines at the age of nineteen) but he knows that it is only a matter of time before what he hears is told to him from the mouth of some company executive and at that point all of his fears will come true.

He doesn't fear for himself, no, he is way past thinking of what he wants or needs or really caring about his personal wellbeing at all. He fears the sound of hunger coming from his daughter's stomach; he fears the look on his wife's face when he tells her they won't be able to afford groceries; he fears that sick knot of dread that comes from not having enough.

There is an additional concern for him tonight though, as he stands at the counter looking out at the deep of the night. Chewing softly in the tangerine light, he thinks of salvation and what he is willing to sacrifice to achieve it. If he were asked what he would give to protect and serve and support his family, he would most definitely say that he would do anything. Now he is tasked with putting those words to the test; does he truly have what it takes to give it all up for his family; to give himself up?

In the mining world, there is a type of cracking that occurs above a tunnel, known as a widow maker. This particular geological deterioration is called what it is because when one just happens to be underneath one of these killers at the wrong (or maybe the right) time, the ceiling will collapse in, crushing and burying alive that unlucky (or lucky) someone beneath it. Now the fact of the matter is that these so called, and time proven, widow makers are jackpots in their own right, for when someone is killed on the job by something purely accidental like happening to be beneath the wrong spot at the wrong time, the mining company is legally obligated to pay the widow of the recently deceased miner said recently deceased miner's salary for the rest of her life.

And our man standing at the kitchen counter, looking out into the turmeric tinted, floating dust flecked night, just happened to spot himself his own winning lottery ticket this afternoon on his way out of the tunnels. He was walking up and out of the caverns, in which he had spent the last twelve hours jackhammering, when his boot became untied. When he stood after tying his laces, he noticed the tell tales signs of what may very well soon become the cause of both his demise and his family's deliverance.

Now taking the last bites of a meal he barely tasted he puts the dishes in the sink and stumbles over grey carpet and children's toys to his bedroom where he plans to cuddle with his wife, until dawn and whatever moments of the rest of his life remain.

The Desk at Which I Sit

The desk at which I sit is wood and atop it there are many things that I use, some more than others. Atop my desk there are pens (all black) some full of ink and some nearing the end of their lives. There is a candle that I use to ward off nasty smells. There is a cow skull, which I bought at sale price from a woman with a fake seeming British accent. There is a cactus in a light blue pot which (the cactus) I most likely water too much out of worry that I will forget to water it and will maybe subsequently kill it because of this over care.

On my desk, there is a computer and in front of that computer I sit most days, typing away at spreadsheets and emails and those mundane meaningless things that somehow also mean everything to a boss and a company and which are necessary for me to do in order to earn my wage.

I have sat here at this desk for countless hours, barely moving, with a steaming cup of coffee or of water or the occasional glass of wine (on those exceptionally brutal days). Rain or shine, snow or sleet, sky-blue blue-sky or cloud covered frigidity; I sit and type with the light from the window and the overhead bulb beating down and causing my fingers to cast small, thin shadows onto the keyboard.

Click, click, click; I am wasting away. Click, click, click; time passes by at the same rate of my fingers on these wretched keys. Click, click, click; people all around the world take their last breaths, babies are born, people are getting married, cars are crashed into each other; business men jump from the top of buildings, couples are cooking breakfast together in kitchens with blue tile floors. Click, click, click; I have lived a thousand lifetimes in the span of an eight-hour workday in front of this screen. Click, click, click; this bright light in front of my eyes is god and I must sacrifice all to it; my posture and fingers and vision and spirit; all will wane to that of the ever beaming white of spreadsheet heaven. I am an angel of the modern office and these typing fingers are my wings.

And the worst part of it all is that this is my best possible option; this cold void of unfeeling zeros and ones is something that I am lucky to be part of. I could be outside in the heat or in the callous wind grinding my fingers down to blistered bone on the hand of a shovel or atop a roof scrapping and pulling and sweating for as long as I am physically able to do so. I could be sore footed serving ungrateful pricks who pay more for a glass of wine then I pay for weekly groceries, wearing a smile that I have to practice in the mirror so that I don't show my hatred through my quivering lips. I could be out on the street, asleep on the grey sidewalk, my withered face filthy and wrinkled beside the litter and the shoe squished green gum stuck to the ground. I could be there with a sheet of cardboard pulled from a dumpster; with some sordid plea to un-looking eyes; my last will and testament written in messy handwriting with a half dead marker borrowed from who knows where trying to proclaim my humanity and insist on my sanity to those fast walking, cell phone talking folks who can't bear to glance my way.

It could be worse, so much worse for me, and so I sit in my chair at my desk in front of the screen, filling numbers into tiny boxes, little bits of me incinerating with every click.

But I'm making good money. Well not really, not compared to those that I make these spreadsheets for or those that walk down red carpets in dresses worth more than my car (which is currently in the shop) but based on my experience level and age and overall attitude I should be relishing the meager wage I receive.

And I shouldn't forget to mention the opportunity for growth I have here; the possibility of promotion and raises and bonuses and perks and incentives and company lunches and free pens and so on. Sometimes I can almost see the carrot in the distance beyond my desk; a dangling treasure meant just for me and I reach out for it, I reach out for my prize for enduring this fluorescently lit and asbestos ceiling tile adorned hellscape but I can't quite reach it yet, I'm still a spreadsheet, a quarterly report, a successful board meeting presentation away from whatever otherworldly bliss I am sure will eventually come.

DINNER

There are five people at the dinner; two couples and a single person. This single person isn't single by choice and is working on coming to terms with the fact that being single is not for one as bad as it sounds and for two not as good as people who are not single think it is. Other than the single person, who we will most certainly get back to, the two couples consist of a banker and a school teacher (making up couple #1) as well as an artist and the host of the dinner (whose profession is unclear but who [in the single person's best guess] is most likely the recipient of a trust fund which [said trust fund] the host of the dinner uses to 'survive' off of whilst doing things such as playing music or going to other countries to see 'what they are all about' as the host has surely said in the past).

The single person works as a receptionist/front desk person at a two-story office building in the basement of which there is a yoga studio. The single person operates the front desk for the whole building because there is only one front desk in the entirety of said office building and all of the businesses in said office building have sort of consolidated in a way which makes the single person more or less in charge of the organization of all of the offices in the building (as well as the yoga studio). Said organization is a job which requires much more than one single (slightly depressed) person to organize or at least requires said single and slightly depressed person to be paid a bit more for doing more than the job which they are paid to do. However, this unreasonable amount of responsibility placed on the single person doesn't make said single person feel completely unhappy because said unreasonable amount of work leads to a feeling of accomplishment at the end of each day when said single person has somehow survived another workday without some sort of catastrophe (or whatever the office building equivalent of that would be).

But anyway, the single person met the host of the dinner at the front desk one particularly busy and stressful day. The circumstance under which the single person met the host of the dinner was that the single person accidently dropped a three-foot-tall pile of papers (important alphabetized papers for a tax lawyer in the top corner office) and was on the ground trying to pick up, organize and re-alphabetize said important papers while speaking on the phone to a client of the psychiatrist who (the psychiatrist) has an office on the bottom, left corner of the office building. Said client of the psychiatrist was supposedly (according to them) having a mental breakdown. So, as (with one hand) the single person was attempting to clean up said spilled stack of important papers and (with the other hand) was holding the phone while trying not to scream as the client of the psychiatrist went on about the details of the supposed mental breakdown they were having, the future host of the future dinner party walked in for the three pm hot yoga class and looked around the desk (looking for the sign in sheet for said three pm hot yoga class) and saw the single person in the awkward position described above and instead of ignoring said awkward situation described above (like so many would and actually did), the host of the dinner helped the single person stack the papers back into a manageable pile and asked if there was anything else that could be done to help, to which the single person replied that there was not in fact anything else that the future host could do other than get the single person a better job to which the future host replied with a laugh.

And since that day the host and the single person have chatted every time the host comes in for a yoga class and their chats became longer and longer and they (the host and the single person) kind of became friends, and this friendship jumped to a new strata when, last Wednesday, on the way to the three pm yoga class the host asked the single person if they wished to join the host and some friends for dinner at the host's house on the Friday night of the week in which the Wednesday on which they spoke about the party also belonged, to which the single person excitedly (possibly too excitedly) responded yes.

And the dinner is about halfway done now, the main course has been served; well all of the food was served at the same time, in big colorful bowls made by the artist and the host in a couple's pottery class that they have been taking now for a couple of months and have been mentioning often and slyly inviting the other couple to join throughout the meal so far.

The food is decent and healthy in the bland and starchy way that much of what is considered healthy these days is. The single person knows that at the end of the evening, after every guest has left and the final drinks have been drunk and the goodbyes have been said that they (the single person) will still be hungry and will be forced to make the choice between three options; the first option being that the single person will drive back home alone and go to bed hungry; the second being that the single person will drive home alone and stop at some sort of fast food drive through restaurant on the way home and eat whatever sort of fast food they have purchased whilst in the car on the way back home; and the third being that after the dinner the single person will drive home alone and end up going through the cabinets in their house until they can find something worthwhile to eat, although in this scenario there will be not much to eat other than crackers or dry cereal because the single person has no time to grocery shop and subsequently has no food in their house and was planning on this meal to fill them up as well as save them whatever money they would've otherwise spent on a meal. After weighing the options the single person decides that the second option (the option of stopping at some greasy fast food restaurant to pick up some hamburger or burrito or something meat filled and covered with cheese along with some type of carbohydrate heavy side dish such as French fries or a four-cheese quesadilla or cheese rolls or whatever the appropriate side dish is for a burrito and a medium [which will probably be upgraded to a large] soda that [said soda] will most likely be a coke but maybe will be a root beer depending on how dry the mouth of the single person is post dinner).

The meal goes on; forks and knives and spoons clank against ceramic and artisian looking plates and bowls and cups. The two couples are speaking amongst themselves and the single person is twisting on their fork a piece of something that looks somewhat like pasta but which is not made of pasta but most likely some type of vegetable cut into a thin strip to resemble pasta. Said strip of vegetable [maybe zucchini] does not taste anywhere near as satisfying or filling or good as regular pasta and its very existence is somewhat offensive to the single person because for one they feel kind of lied to by the way this food is presented as something much better than what it actually is and for two it reminds them of all of the things that they are supposed to like and do and say and feel and worship and think that they just can't do or like for example pretending that zucchini pasta or whatever this crap on their plate is, is somehow as good or even close to equal to what it is pretending to be.

And maybe the single person is pretending to be something they are not, maybe the single person wants to not be single anymore; maybe the single person is sick of seeing other people hold hands and walk down the street together in a warmth and light that seems too comfortable and true to be real; maybe the single person is tired of going through the rounds, stacking papers on their desk, force feeding themselves during their couple seconds of free time to give themselves a bit more energy to finish the work which is the cause of their energy suck and general lack of overall enjoyment in the first place. Maybe the single person is sick of being who they are, or maybe they are sick of feeling like they are not ok to be who they are, single; alone; meant to walk down the sidewalk amongst the lovers and the falling leaves trying to not step on the cracks on their own; maybe not everybody meets that other they have been looking for; maybe there are just outliers; numbers lonely in the dark and cold not sure whether to be grateful for what they have or curse the stars for cursing them with a solitary life. Maybe things aren't fair, maybe things are just as they should be, maybe this is one of many lives, maybe each moment of the single person's suffering is a lesson; a building block for a better tomorrow; a will; a dream; a way, maybe these last couple of years have just been a bump in the road, maybe this pothole will end, maybe the single person will find someone and not have to attend these types of dinner parties minus their plus one.

And the single person sits, spinning their fork with that false thing at the end of it, twisting and thinking these thoughts about what their life is and what it may be worth, and as they sit underwater in thought they suddenly come to, like they have risen to the surface and at the surface; at the dinner table with the two couples, this single person has been asked a question by whom they do not know and the rest of the party guests and the host are sitting there staring at them with an expectant look on their faces.

The single person gets up from their chair and says that they must excuse themselves for they have work in the morning and must make their lunch for the next day before going to bed (which is a lie because they always buy their lunch on the way to work in the morning). The single person also says that they have to feed and walk and spend time with their dog who (the dog) has severe emotional issues because of abuse that (the dog) experienced when it was a puppy (which is also a lie because the single person does not only not have a dog with emotional issues that needs a lot of care but they do not even have a dog and in fact don't like dogs and can't have a dog because for one they are allergic to dog hair and for two their apartment is not pet friendly).

After their lie filled departure the single person walks across the room rather awkwardly while the two couples watch them in a sort of pity filled silence that will sure erupt into speculation about what is wrong with this single person as soon as the single person closes the front door behind them. As they are walking out of the room, their out of style, left tennis shoe catches the corner of a fancy and expensive seeming rug which is in the hallway leading to the front door of the host's house but which (the rug) extends slightly into the dining room and it is with this slightly extended bit of rug that the single person's left shoe and foot connect. The single person is able to stop themselves from falling completely over whilst they trip on the rug as they awkwardly exit a party that they most likely should never have been invited to or attended in the first place by grabbing onto the wall of the hallway beside and parallel with the rug on which they tripped. However, because of the unexpected nature of the trip the single person cannot gracefully grab onto the wall and they end up smacking (with a loud and sharp, painful sounding sound) their elbow onto the direct corner or the wall. And if all of the guests at the dinner party weren't looking at them before (which they were) they most certainly are now because for one they are intrigued by the pitiful situation that is the single person but also because that loud sound gave them some type of reason to look up. One person, the artist partner of the host, asks if the single person is ok to which the single person shamefully nods and says that they are in fact ok as they try to look not only tough but also cool and laid back (all of which they are not, specifically they are not ok at all for many reasons but in particular because now their elbow feels like it is both on fire and frozen at the same time and is almost certainly bruised to the bone if not actually broken).

The single person emerges from the house of the host with a throbbing elbow and some deep and most likely sick feeling of hopelessness that they will be alone and outcast forever; happy with only the fact that they are out of that dinner party and that they will not ever, ever have to go back. As they walk to their car (which is parked a fair bit away) they begin to realize that they will have to see the host tomorrow at work and either ignore them (which would not be professional) or try to explain away their awkward and uncomfortable behavior from tonight. Still thinking about the inevitable and undoubtedly rough future encounter with the host, the single person arrives at their car to realize that they have not only left their jacket in the house of the host of the dinner party which they just awkwardly left but that inside of their jacket are the car keys, which they not only need to get into and drive their car but also need to get back into their apartment as well as into their office tomorrow morning.

So now the single person walks a-ways back to the front door of the house at which they were just eating an un-filling dinner alone surrounded by people in love, and as they walk they are trying to think of any and every possible excuse why or how they shouldn't have to go back into the house, like how they can just walk home and leave their car and get it towed in the morning and somehow call their boss and ask her to let them in in the morning and make copies of all of the keys that they need. And as they are thinking and walking back toward a house that they previously hoped that they would never have to enter again, their elbow is swelling and red and is stinging with a dull and fiery pain that does not seem like it will be going away any time soon and with the arm that is not in pain, they knock on the front door three times and then ring the doorbell (which is one of those doorbells which glows a soft and yellow glow) and then they wait to be let back in.

Empty Acres

In the mountains, five hours and twenty minutes from the nearest airport, there is a small town that was supposed to have developed and grown much, much bigger than it once was but stayed small and more or less the same size while the rest of the small towns in the same mountainous valley in which the small town in question sits, developed into sprawling mini metropolises with all of the necessary suburban chain stores and restaurants and movie theatres and tanning salons and liquor stores and coffee shops and multi-home cookie cutter style suburban neighborhood housing and so on.

But this small town, the one that stayed small, is just that and it seems that is all it ever will be. There were big plans for this place, presentations to the town council on blocks with boutiques and breweries and houses in the hills and the plains and at the bases of the mountains that create the towering cliffs of the valley in which this small town now lays quiet, undeveloped and slowly shrinking. There were talks of skyscrapers with rooftop nightclubs, brand name five star hotels and fancy car dealerships. People bought up land, plots upon plots of empty acres on which there was nothing but weeds and dirt and the occasional deer passing through, in hopes that one day the emptiness, their purchased blank spaces would turn to gold, but they didn't. Something happened involving a corrupt town councilor and a backroom deal that was broken to the local newspaper by a hotel lobby boy acting as a whistleblower who heard said backroom deal whilst on errands in the hotel in which he worked and was shocked and awed by it and knew something had to be done. With the scandal, as well as a slumping economy, came a crashing of the plans; no more skyscrapers, no more rooftop nightclubs, no more breweries or hotels or fields turning into gold. No, the small town (the most promising of the small towns in the valley thanks to its proximity to a local ski area as well as a highway that was in the process of being built nearby, but which was also eventually scrapped because of some different but equally scandalous scandal) through human error and greed, ended up a small town and was destined to stay that way.

Now amid the time with the highest of the hype about the development of the small town, among the forefront of the most excited about said development, one of the ones preaching skyscraper dreams and the promise of riches from long fallow land, was a man, a developer, a self-proclaimed real estate and development artist. His canvas was this small town and his medium was investment from various private and public investment groups with varying vested interests in developing this once and future small town. His masterpiece, his real estate magnum opus was to be a development he planned to call something like "mountainside acres" or "pine brook" or "sunflower court" or some other cutsie but also sort of fancy and comfortable sounding name such as those listed above (and what is now called, by those miners and post office workers and longtime residents of the small town whom are not too unhappy with the fact that their home didn't turn into some extension of the ever-encroaching sprawl, empty acres). His masterpiece, a three hundred acre, three hundred home, multi-multimillion dollar project took all he had saved from his various deals around the country conducting similar (but smaller) types of real estate art pieces (as he called them) as well as, as much money as he could possibly beg, scrape, borrow (but not steal, if he could help it) from every investor, entrepreneur, millionaire, billionaire, CEO, CFO, president, vice-president, director, mayor, councilman, sheriff, chief, and/or person he could find.

This place, this "maple glen", or whatever he would've called, it was going to be his greatest accomplishment yet and would (if all were to work out perfectly) launch him into developer super-stardom and from this development he would've had the richest and the most exotic of offers presented to him on golden platters (well not literally, but actually maybe literally in certain cases). If his development were to work out, the world would hold its breath as he, the developer, would build the next wonder. Those were his dreams, he was the pharaoh of this small valley, the king of the mountains and hills; he would build this town into a colossus of modernity and with it he would earn his place among whomever he could ever want to have a place among.

But then the scandal came and the economy slumped and the sky basically opened up and let down the biggest shit storm the world had ever seen onto him and his already build but unpopulated and unsold development. And the money and the investors and the dreams of being king dried up faster than a dropper full of water squirted onto a bucket full of flaming gasoline. The people he borrowed from pulled out so fast he could've sworn he felt the ground shake and the plates rattle in the cabinets of the model home he had moved into until his home in his development was finished (which it never was or will be, in fact from the window of the model home in the half-finished development he can see what would have been his home if his dreams of being a mogul had come true. There it stands with its plastic siding and plywood walls slowly falling apart; a reminder to him of what could have been and the complete and utter decay of his reality). And with the failure of the plan he lost it all, the investors and everybody he had borrowed and scraped up money from knew he had nothing and vowed to make sure nobody would ever hire him again to develop anything, not even a truck stop bathroom (as one particularly red faced southern investor said), and they stuck to their words; he was banished; blacklisted; struck from their contact lists; cast away, and he retreated to the only place he had left which was also the place which, because of its failure, had caused him to have to retreat in the first place.

So he, the once great and most promising developer, was reduced to nothing but a man who once had dreams of something great; of being great; of building a suburban paradise and living within it as a legend. He was a shell of what he could've been and was shunned by the community of high rollers in fancy cars that he had once associated with. He more or less became a hermit in his model home, surrounded by hundreds of half-finished houses that all look exactly the same. The same house with its nearly finished siding and overgrown front lawn copy and pasted down block after empty and winding block.

Sometimes he takes to walking the empty streets imagining what kind of families would have lived in this place; in his Eden. He imagines how the mothers and fathers of each family would decorate their houses to make theirs look different and distinct in a sea full of houses the exact same as theirs. On his walks, he imagines the children in the front yards and their various bikes and dolls and toy swords thrown about the HOA recommended and weekly mowed grass in that chaotic but slightly cute way kids scatter and destroy everything in sight. He imagines the Christmas trees lighting the windows and snow filling the gutters and topping the rooves in that white and ultra-silence inducing way snow sits. He imagines fathers playing catch with their sons in the front lawns and children of all shapes and sizes riding bikes to the playgrounds and pools that are scattered across this community. The swings of those playgrounds sway and twist in a wind that seems to only affect them; the swings move in a haunting and tragic way; they are a reminder to him of the blankness of loss; the smoldering burn of pain.

This place seems like a city made to be bombed; A place that exists only to be destroyed in the worst possible way; a litmus test of rubble and black smoke and ash and collapsed in houses; manikins melted into shadows and puddles of plastic and hair. He wishes this place could have a simple purpose like that; he wishes he could have made something worthy of a vision. But there is no reason here; there is nothing to be done but walk and look into the unlit windows.

The banks won't touch the land because it would be too expensive to demolish all of the houses. The investors have no interest in this place (although they each own their respective pieces of it); there is no demand for houses in this nothing town. Nobody wants to live here, not a single soul but him and he doesn't even really want to live here, he just has nowhere else to go; nothing else to do.

And so he wanders on, shuffle footed over the perfect grey concrete of the sidewalks and roads of a place that was so close to being something special but now most certainly never will.

FALL(ING)

It's fall,

well at least it almost is.

The leaves on the aspens when he drives by over the speed limit are yellow tipped, but mostly green and healthy; only a little bit dead. Fall is not yet here but the taste of it is in the breeze. The air is thinner than it was in August and the bees buzz with an urgency that hasn't been there before. The sun is setting and light is honey gold.

The highway is long and empty and has switchbacks that make everything in his car tumble and lean to one side while he goes screeching around them (the curves). The highway is an almost cake-frosting smooth black line with a bright double yellow that just seems to glow as he speeds down it. He is moving something fierce. His windows are down and the wind and air scream past his ears.

The volume of the music on his radio is turned up as far as it can be turned up and a woman's haunting voice sings over violins and minor chords played on an old guitar. He knows this woman, the singer, and yes he did once love her (and maybe he still does).

There were days that were painted bright with snow and a sky so white that there seemed no difference between it and the ground. Those were the infinite days, or at least that was how they seemed. A roaring fire and windows that would steam up with the condensation from their breathing. Those were days of cooking breakfast on the little dark green stove they had bought together with money from a glass jar that they had saved their change in for months. Hell, they scrapped, fought tooth and nail for everything in that house and for that little wooden shelter that encased it all; they bartered and somehow made it work. It was always an uphill battle then, but it wasn't impossible and the climb was worth it for those mornings in the snow-whitened light which shown through the triangular window that looked out onto that white and onto the peaks in the distance that seemed both alien and sacred. The wooden floors were warm beneath their feet back then and there was always music, whether it was her singing floating from the bath or from his guitar that he would often play for her before they went to sleep. He would quietly strum not only for music but also for the feel of his fingers on the strings: the feel of his hands creating. His hands, those calloused things, had been so alive back then. Chipped fingernails, bleeding cuts from chopping wood for the fire, the soft touches of her hands on his, the warm skin of her thighs, of her face, of her lips...

No.

He shouldn't think of that now, but he knows he still will. But it's over, that him and her, those days in the snow. The winter was their time. The spring was pure bliss. The summer was all he had ever thought he could want. Heat and sweat on sheets that neither of them cared were getting dirty. Sun until nine and rain after it got dark. Those days he lived for the sound of the birds in the morning and when he heard those holy tunes, he would pull her close (she would still be hot with sleep and softer in his embrace) and he would turn so he could see the sun come up over the trees, which at that point were in full bloom.

But they are dying now, the trees,

and he is dying now or at least feels that way, inside beneath the skin and hair and freckles on his chest.

Well the trees won't really be dead, but they will look like they are and sometimes that is what matters.

Sometimes feeling dead is just as bad as actually being so, and sometimes, maybe, it's even worse.

He knows it is coming; the cold; the empty bottles; the baths sat in for so long the water turns cold. The stumbles and the restless nights. Withdrawal from her.

Another fall is here, well it almost is, but at times in that past life with her, he thought it might never come, but of course it did. The sun always sets; the leaves fall; hearts break; birds fly south; wolves howl at the night sky; fires burn to ash; the moon wanes to a fingernail of white light; cars run out of gas; tires pop; tears drip down sun reddened cheeks.

Somehow those sepia days seemed like forever.

He is driving too fast and he knows it. He doesn't want to crash, to crumble, to burn, well maybe he does but that's not what he is trying to do.

The wind and the music and the blurred trees and that flat road curving around into whatever lies ahead, they are what is keeping him sane. If he can stay going, if his foot can stay pressed hard on that pedal; if he can be deafened by the wind and numbed by the cold nip at the end of each breath maybe he can forget; maybe this fall will never come, maybe he will just soar on until he blinks into the horizon.

There is wind in the trees and the blowing leaves rattle like some sort of applause as he cannons by and around a curve so sharp that for a second he thinks his car may flip, but that applause and the breeze is waning and he makes it around that curve, barely.

He speeds on. The music plays and the voice of a woman he used to think holy, haunts the air behind his car like a lingering ghost. The leaves are beginning to yellow. The air is cooling down. The trees are thinning, and soon the ground will be covered in those things that were once so strong and beautiful.

Onward.

The car's gas tank is half full,

or half empty.

It doesn't matter,

what matters though, is that he will have to fill up eventually and when he stops he may not start again for a while. When he stops, he may just crumple like a wilted rose; like a carved pumpkin left for the winter on the porch; like a dead and dried up leaf. He feels rotten; less than whole; empty. There are embers in his heart; stinging thorns and painful memories that he needs to burn away. There is a throbbing in his ears and in his pressed down foot but he moves quickly on.

The light is a melted butter yellow and the trees are brushstrokes of pine green and grey. His car is a rocket that he hopes can take him away; take him to the stars or the moon or some barren meteor, anywhere but this road, anywhere that has anything to do with her or that place that they once shared, that place where she still is, but where he is no longer. He wishes there was fire coming from his tailpipe; he wishes this road led to oblivion; he wishes the sky would come down and swallow him whole.

But this road leads to a town where they (when they were a they) spent enough time that every corner, every store, reminds him of her.

He has one hand on the wheel, and one hand out the window which (the hand outside the window) he now holds straight up; reaching for something, anything that will take him, but there is nothing but sky and golden light and trees and the pain that is soon to come; everything fades to the fall that is almost but not yet here.

The leaves will fall, he knows that and so will he, the fall will come for him. But he drives on anyways and as he does he lets out a prayer in the form of a yell to whatever beast keeps us hoping for better days and makes us forget about the fall and about the winter and about the pain until it comes crawling, back, like it always does and always will. He screams to that false god of tomorrow. He cries to that splinter of hope which sticks, warm and jagged in his heart,

and he drives; flies; flees forever on; well at least for as long as his forever can be, at least until this tank and his lungs are empty.

GRASS

The grass that blows in the warm November wind looks like hair and is a thin, dying and brown. The brown of the grass (which starts about where her feet sit and spreads outwardly) is a light almost yellow brown, much lighter than her hair which is a burnt coffee black-brown and also (like the grass) blows in the wind and because of the wind and its blowing and the direction which it is blowing rather intensely, strands of her burnt coffee black/brown hair are pinned across her face. The sun is warm and the air is light and comfortable in a way that reminds her of summer, but it is winter and it shouldn't be this nice out.

She sits on a concrete step, which is built into the side of her mobile home, the only permanent thing about her home is this step. The house and the plumbing and the wires that attach to the powerline by the sidewalk and the knick-knacks she has stored on her shelves are all rootless, blown away in a moment's notice to who knows or cares where, but this concrete step is there forever (or at least it is there until it fades with rain and wind and snow into grey dust and it too blows and sifts away, but that is far from now and she will have long faded too when that day of dust does come). The step, that nearly eternal thing on which she rests is warmed and somehow softened by the low winter sun which should be covered by white and thick clouds but isn't and sits golden and smug in a bright blue sky.

She should be wearing sunglasses she knows, she has been getting migraines for a while now and has gone to many different doctors many times in failed attempts to ail her condition, and during one of those visits to one of the many doctors whom she visited (in vain) she was told (not by a doctor but by a nurse, while she was waiting for the doctor to be done seeing another patient who had, according to the nurse, a vile case of the flu and needed immediate attention) that a sister in law of said nurse experienced similar problems (i.e. migraines) and that she (the sister in law of the nurse) visited many, many doctors and that none of them were able to help with said similar problem (i.e. the migraines) and she (the nurse) went on to say that she (the sister in law of the nurse) eventually became so fed up with the so called western/conventional medicine and its/their inability to help her (the sister in law) with her problem that she went out and found some new-age/eastern-medicine type medical practitioner/healer (whatever this eastern style medical doctor identified as the nurse was unsure) but anyway this new age type doctor had done some testing (using crystals or spells or chakra attunement, again the nurse was not sure) and decided that what she (the sister in law) needed to do was to start to wear sunglasses whilst outside, stop looking at computer/cell phone screens for more than twenty minutes at a time and that she needed to drink one cup of raw grapefruit juice every morning before she ate or drank anything else and that if she did do these things, the problem (i.e. the migraines) would just disappear and not only would they disappear but she would feel better than ever before. The nurse then said to her (the woman with the medical problems similar to the sister in law of said nurse) that she (the nurse) just wanted to share with her (the woman) what she (the nurse's sister in law) found and that there was no pressure to listen to her (the nurse) but that she (the nurse) just wanted to share with her (the woman) the findings because she knew how frustrating it could be to have a problem and to not be able to solve it. The nurse also emphasized that, that which she shared with her (the woman) (i.e. the story of the sister in law with the similar problems and the supposed cure given to the sister in law by the shaman or whatever he was) was not the medical opinion of the doctor nor the office at which she (the nurse) worked and that if she (the woman) did end up taking her (the nurse's) advice on how to cure her (the woman's) problem and it didn't work, that there was absolutely no blame or liability that could be placed on said doctor or nurse or private practice, because the sunglasses/limited screen time/grapefruit suggestion was just that, a suggestion, and could be implemented but was not given in the place of the advice of a qualified medical professional (which the nurse apparently was not). And when the doctor had finally come in after subduing the violently ill flu having patient in the other waiting room (and hopefully after washing his hands or at least using some type of hand sanitizing gel) she (the doctor) said that she (the doctor) could not really say what was wrong with her (the woman) and that she (the doctor) was sad that they (presumably the doctor's office in which the woman sat) could not help her (the woman).

So now she sits on the step beside her mobile home in a ray of sunlight which is much too warm for the time of year and place on earth on which it shines down. Beside her is an untouched cup of grapefruit juice and back in her bedroom, are her sunglasses. She has tried the things suggested of her by the eastern doctor via the sister in law of the nurse via the nurse but they, as of yet, haven't really made much of a difference at all, but she knows she will keep doing those things (or at least trying to as much as she can remember to do so) because for one she can't think of any way that what she was suggested to do could hurt her situation or make her migraines any worse and for two she doesn't really know what else she can do and feels that she should do something to try to quell her pain (even if, it so far, isn't working).

Seemingly directly beneath a bright and beating down sun, sweating beneath her thin cotton dress, she squints and watches the grass blow in the breeze, hoping something soon will come to take her pain away or at least numb it a bit, and until then she decides she might as well enjoy this unwarranted good weather while it lasts.

GREEN ROOM

The comedian is not really sure why the room in which he is sitting is called the green room, because it is not green. In fact, he has never been in a single green room that was actually green (and he has been touring for years, so he has been in hundreds if not thousands at this point). The comedian has heard that originally these rooms were called what they are called because of the color which they were painted, but he is not sure if that is true and doesn't really care enough about the origin of the name of this glorified holding pen to actually do any real research. The namesake of this room aside, this particular place in which he currently sits is one of the fancier in which he has sat and waited to go on stage in. There are windows and those windows look out onto a street of a city lit by flickering neon lights. In the sky outside there are no stars but there is the occasional blinking red dot in the blackness of a passing (most likely landing, as there is an airport nearby) airplane. He is looking out the largest of the windows now and he is standing in a way that has become a cliché for people pondering their lives or trying to make an important decision, i.e. he has one hand leaning against the wall beside the window and is sort of leaning all of his body weight sideways to rest on that hand and he is just standing still and staring out; looking deeply at nothing much at all.

There are Persian rugs on the floor and there are couches that seem both expensive and uncomfortable scattered across the room. There is a chair beside a table on which (the table) sits a mirror framed by bright bulbs. Also on the table there is a tray with a couple of bottles of the comedian's favorite whiskeys and a half-finished meal that he felt inclined to eat because it was provided for free but which he only ate half of because he wasn't really hungry and was only eating in the first place to try to be polite. There is nobody else in the room not because there is nobody that wants to be there or people that should be there (like his agent or his wife or the various friends of his that live in this city in which his show tonight is, who he has invited to said show as a gesture of friendship but with whom he has no time to spend) but because he sent them out. Clearing the room, as his manager calls it, has become an unspoken tradition for him before each show and it first started because about a year and a half ago when he started headlining, he needed the space to throw up in the private bathroom attached to the green room without everybody crowing around him and asking if he was ok and asking if there is anything they could do to help. He needs the space before the show to clear his mind and to try to remember what it is like to be fighting, working his fingers to the bone for something (because he has almost forgot) as well as to remember what he has done to get himself to this point in his career; what he has sacrificed; what shitty demeaning jobs he had to work just to make enough to support himself during the day while he did open mics and little shows at night. He needs to remember and wallow in the facts of how lucky he is and maybe more importantly how unlucky he was before.

And of course, he is ok, he is more than ok, or at least he should be ok (and he hates it, and has always hated it when people ask him how he is doing or tell him how he should feel). But he tells himself how he should feel more than ever now; he tells himself how blessed and lucky and happy and overall ok and great he should feel; he tells himself that there are things in his life so great and true and wonderful (like his wife and the success which he is fully experiencing now in his career and his new house and the house he bought for his mother) that he can't feel anything but ok. But he doesn't though, not really. He is a king in his own right; a leader in his field; a visionary, genius, comedic prodigy to some. He has been critically acclaimed, he has won awards and received a standing ovation for every show he has done for the last year. He is making more money than he knows what to do with, like he literally cannot spend his money fast enough; he has bought and bought and bought and still the numbers in his bank account keep going up. He has all he has ever wanted and more; success, a good marriage, friends, laughs, houses, cars, suits, a pool, a boat, a dog, a cat, another dog, maids, people to take care of the dogs, invites to exclusive parties, boxes of free things sent to him by companies who would be honored (according to the letters that accompany said boxes of free things) for him to have, and he should be ok. But once again he is not, he isn't ok, all of this greatness and joy and wonder at what he has become has faded to a dull throbbing of grey which has become almost annoying. He feels like the world's most ungrateful son of a bitch. He knows he should feel honored and grateful; that he should live in complete and utter awe of what he has become; that he should be humbled by the love he receives, and he does but all of that doesn't make him happy.

It's bizarre, he thinks as he stares out into a black and empty sky, that everything he has wanted and worked for and sweat for and cried about and tried time and time again to get, is there not only at his fingertips but in his hands and that all he can feel is this blank numbness. It's not that he is exactly in pain, but he doesn't feel pleasure either, just a simple and ash flavored presence that is neither good nor incredibly bad. Outside, in that place beyond the windows of this room, there is a siren but he can't see what the siren is attached to and doesn't want to imagine what type of tragedy requires said siren and whatever emergency vehicle it is attached to. And if he is being honest with himself, he sort of envies the thrill of an emergency like that which the siren is speeding towards. He envies the blood and adrenaline and the panic instead of this perfect, happy life he has build up for himself.

The sound of the siren and trying to picture what it is attached to reminds him that he actually cannot remember which city he is in tonight. He looks around the room now, trying to find anything remarkable or telling of where he is, but there is nothing but the generic fancy decorations, the half-eaten meal on his plate, and that mirror with its bright and buzzing bulbs.

There is a knock on his door and this knock signals that he has about five minutes before he must go on. He moves now from the window towards the bathroom where he will vomit and hopefully not get any on his shirt, before he walks out the door and onto a stage lit by blinding spotlights and vibrating with the thunderous applause of thousands of people literally screaming his praises; all those faces in the haze waiting just for him and hanging on his each and every word.

GUARDED

The pool is a see-through, chemical green and it shimmers and ripples as it reflects bright streaks of the mid-day sun. The ground around the pool is covered with a grainy, chocolate-milk-brown colored non-slip material that feels like plastic beneath one's bare feet but does not have as much give as plastic usually does. There are white pool chairs around the pool. In total, there are twelve chairs, and those twelve chairs have been spread into groups of three which (each group of three) are spread out around each side of the pool which is (the pool) rectangular and varies in depth from three feet at the shallow end to eight feet at the deepest point of the deep end (according to measurements which are told by white tiles with black lettering on them that have been placed incrementally around the pool's edge). There is a staircase in the middle of the shallow end which has four rounded steps that lead into the water and which is bisected by a shining metal pole (well, shining at the moment because of the sunlight that is currently hitting it) which people entering or exiting the pool can use to help their respective exiting or entering. The chairs that surround the pool are made of cheap metal frames with cheaper plastic straps that are fastened around said metal frames. When around twenty of these thin and often sticky plastic straps are fastened around the metal frame, there is enough strength in the cumulative straps to hold up the weight of a lounging person. One downside to these chairs is that when one sits in one of these chairs long enough, the spaces in between the thin plastic straps (into which parts of the person's exposed skin has been squished) will leave red lines across the body of said individual who was trying to suntan and relax before being temporarily maimed.

Around the chocolate-milk-brown-colored non-slip material (that itself is around the pool) is a black fence that extends to about the waist of an average sized male (and a bit above the navel of an average sized female, and about at neck level for an average sized child at around five years of age). To the south of the black fence that surrounds the pool is an asphalt parking lot with bright yellow and freshly painted looking lines that indicate to those driving in the parking lot where to park. All of the other sides of the pool are surrounded by sidewalks. Beyond those sidewalks are roads two of which (on the short sides of the pool), lead out of the parking lot that sits behind the pool and the other (on the north-most long side of the pool) connects to a highway that is always bustling and vibrating with traffic and downshifting trucks.

The pool is part of a hotel, and is located in the parking lot of said hotel, and said hotel is one of those hotels that has an incredibly tall sign that reaches maybe three stories high and which (the sign) can be seen from the highway, which the hotel is extremely close to. The hotel is so extremely close to the highway that if there is an exceptionally loud motorcycle, or some type of car with an altered-for-noise-making exhaust pipe or really any truck, the windows of the hotel on the side of the hotel closest to the highway (which is the east side of the hotel) will shake and have been known to spontaneously shatter. This shattering of the windows on the east side of the hotel is due to (what turns out to be an illegal) closeness to the highway which has resulted in a handful of lawsuits against the hotel and because of these lawsuits the hotel has had to cut costs, and the first cost that they could think of to cut without any serious consequences was to get rid of the lifeguard at the pool. And so now, at the pool there is no lifeguard and instead there is a sign proclaiming that there is no lifeguard, and that anybody wishing to enter the pool or the surrounding milk-chocolate-brown colored, non-slip area, should do so at their own risk.

In the pool area, there is one person. This person is sitting in the middle most of the three chairs on the south most side of the pool (with his back facing the parking lot and his front facing the pool and past that the road that leads to the highway and past that another hotel). This man is not unattractive; he was an athlete in college (a rower to be exact) but he either wasn't good enough at rowing or didn't work hard enough to go pro (it depends who you ask) but what matters is that he was once in good shape (no matter if he had the skill/talent/work ethic to go pro) and that good shape can still vaguely be seen in places on his body. However, in the past few years, while most of his body has remained toned and taught, his lower stomach and the sides of his body next to his stomach have begun to accumulate not a lot but a noticeable amount of fat. And so now he is a little self-conscious about his visible belly and therefore he is sitting in his chair in a way that is not exactly the most comfortable but in a way, which gives his slightly flabby stomach the least amount of fat rolls possible, i.e. his metal framed, plastic strap wrapped chair is reclined to a point at which he is not exactly completely laying down nor sitting up i.e. his chair looks a bit like an uppercase L that has been bent slightly out of shape.

And so anyway this man is sitting in a red bathing suit which most certainly is too small for him and is wearing no other articles of clothing (unless sunglasses count as clothing, and if that is the case it is important to mention that he is wearing sunglasses and that these sunglasses are black and square framed and have smudges on the lenses). And this man in the red bathing suit is wet and greasy with a mix of sweat and sunscreen beneath a September sun in a place in which the month doesn't really determine the type of weather that occurs. In this place (the place in which the hotel and the pool and the red bathing suit wearing guy are) is almost always hot and humid. But there is a bite of cold in the breeze, that's not to say that the breeze is cold but that the breeze form of aftertaste has a sort of cold and wintery type of chill to it that is most totally foreign to this place. And because of the chilly nip of the wind, the guy in the chair has not yet gone in the pool, even though based on his attire and location one would assume he plans (or at least planned) to.

And the man is now chilled by the air, chilled enough that the hair on his arms and legs (but none of the hair on the rest of his body) is standing straight up.

The water of the pool is rippling with the push of the wind and the smell of chlorine and sunscreen seem to be the only smells that can be smelled in at least a one-hundred-foot radius around the pool.

There are sounds from the highway and there is a slight whistle on the wind. There are cars leaving and entering the parking lot behind the pool (cars packed with people, some of whom notice the man in the red bathing suit and some who don't).

And now the man, sitting in the chair, is laughing slightly and as he laughs his stomach kind of swells up and down with his intake of air and exhalation of oxygen and laughter. He is laughing at the word "lifeguard" on the sign that declares how there will no longer be a lifeguard in the pool area anymore. And what he finds particularly funny is the idea that it is somebody's job to guard his life (or at least that it would have been if the hotel hadn't been forced to lay off all of the lifeguards). And the idea of someone being paid to supposedly guard his life is not exactly funny in the same way that a good joke is funny, more he is laughing at the sadness of not having had somebody to guard his life for so long and that now while he is in a place at which there could actually be somebody there to look out for his life (guard his life, if you will) that there is not a lifeguard and instead there is a sign that tells him so and also that he should proceed at his own risk. And what is funny about the whole thing (at least funny to this man) is that he hasn't had anybody to look out for him for so long and the redundancy of the whole thing seems like a proverbial slap in the face.

The realization that there is not in fact a lifeguard and that he is there at the side of the pool taking a risk that will only affect him, makes him feel not only lonely but kind of beat down in a way that somebody who has been knocked down over again and again and is deciding whether or not to get up again can only feel.

And as this man by the pool is sort of wallowing in his loneliness and beat-down-ness, two little girls riding bikes side by side coast by. The road beside the pool must be slightly downhill (going from east to west), because the two little girls are able to coast down the road (moving slowly towards the highway and going perhaps under the highway and to the trailer park about a mile down the road and on the other side of the highway from the hotel, beside the pool of which the man in his too small bathing suit sits) without pedaling at all. And as the two children pass by the air seems a bit warmer and the light a bit more sepia and they too are laughing but not at the irony of not having anybody to look after one's life, they are giggling in that care free and fully present way that only children in the sun do. It's as if all there is, is the road and the giggling and the light breeze and these two little girls going who knows where. But it doesn't really matter where these girls are going or how far they have to go, it seems they don't care about those things. Right now, they are just coasting and giggling and moving slowly towards where the sun will eventually set.

And so now the man tries to remember when the last time he rode a bike was, as the little girls (who by the way are both wearing light blue jean overalls, white t shirts under said overalls and pink velcro shoes, with pigtails that stick straight up) pass by and down the road.

And at first he can't. He can't remember those childish things. He can't remember those endless days spent in his backyard with his brothers, sword fighting with sticks or the way that back then a piece of candy and the acqui-sition and consumption of that piece of candy was nearly his whole reason for his existence. For a couple of seconds, he can't remember when he was held close and warm, guarded and soft. He can't remember the last time he rode a bike, but he slowly begins to remember the first time he did.

The wind blows across the pool and little white capped waves form for a second. The breeze blows the chemical sting of chlorine into his nose and breaks him away from those things he can and cannot remember.

And but then, it comes to him slow like a balloon being filled up breath by breath. He and his father were out in their front yard. The grass was a yellow green and the sun was hidden and dampened by thin grey clouds that covered the entire sky. It is the fall he remembers correctly which he does, and there were still leaves on the trees, but they were yellowing and some had started to flutter down to rest on the dying grass of his front yard. The grass was long enough to reach up and tickle his shins and the back of his legs as he walked with his father and a bike that used to belong to his brother, out to the front yard of his house. His father seemed old then, much older than he had been just months before. His father was wearing a white, ribbed tank top that wasn't stained but had been turned more grey than white from being washed often, and his father was wearing dark blue jeans and no shoes and those jeans were faded in the places where his father always held the same things in his pockets, but were more or less new looking and perfectly pressed everywhere else. His father's hair was unkempt but not in the way that people today keep their hair unkempt to be fashionable, but because his father didn't have the energy to comb his hair or shave on the weekends. It must've been a weekend, maybe a Saturday afternoon because during the week his father always kept his hair combed and slightly greased over to the side and always wore his blue mechanic's jumpsuit.

The man in the red bathing suit remembers that his father's blue me-chanics jumpsuit (which, even when freshly washed, had black stains littered across it) had had a name tag on it, sown into the fabric just above the left breast pocket. He remembers that that the name on the jumpsuit had not been his father's name. He wonders who the jumpsuit belonged to and why his father didn't have his name on the jumpsuit which he wore every day to work.

And but anyway, on that long passed day in the un-mowed grass of the front lawn of his childhood home (well one of them, there were at least three houses that he lived in throughout the years of his childhood) his father showed him how to ride a bike. His father placed his hands (which were hard with calluses and never fully clean, there was always a bit of black somewhere) on the sides of his (the man wearing the red bathing suit, when he was a boy) body, right below his armpits, and his father walked slightly behind and beside him while he sat on the bike and tried to balance. And he and his father walked (well his father walked and he balanced, with his father's help, on the bike) back and forth on the front lawn. Eventually his father gave him a push and let go and the boy (well the man in the red bathing suit as a boy) coasted down the grass on his own. He stayed up for a couple of seconds and then fell down onto the grass. And it didn't really hurt when he fell because the grass was long and soft and he was not going very fast when he tipped over, but he lay there anyhow when he fell and he cried not hard but he cried as he lay on the grass with the bike half covering his body. His father walked over, not in any rush but not in an uncaring way either, and lifted the fallen bike off of the him (with one hand) and then picked up the boy (well the man with the red bathing suit, when he was a boy) and he let out one rough sounding and gruff chuckle before setting the boy down on the grass and giving him a pat on the head and then helping him to get back up on the bike.

They spent the whole day biking back and forth across the lawn, and sometimes his father let him go and he would coast for a bit and would then tip over and would lay on the grass. And eventually, after many falls and an equal amount of get ups, he stopped crying every time he fell. His father always chuckled a bit when he helped him up. His father's breath had smelled of coffee and cigarettes and slightly of cinnamon then, he can remember now.

Eventually they put the bike back in the shed behind the house and went inside. By the time they went inside, there were marks that had been worn into the grass and those marks never faded away for the rest of the time that they lived in that house.

Now the man in the red bathing suit is older, and his father is long dead. He is sitting directly beneath a sun that is hot and unrelenting, and he is sweating and that sweat is slightly greasier than it usually is because it (his sweat) is mixing with the sunscreen that he is wearing. The pool is giving off nose tingling fumes. The two little girls have long since passed out of sight.

GROCERY

They were open until ten pm and I walked through those automatic sliding glass doors at exactly 9:37pm.

Well it was 9:37pm according to my watch, which is normally correct although I cannot specifically say that it was exactly correct at the time that I walked into the grocery store, frankly because that day was a hard day and I honestly didn't really care what time it was and I only saw what time it was because I had to itch my right arm with my left. My left arm is the side on which I wear my watch, and while I itched my right arm, my left arm had to sort of cut across and in front of my body and at the same time as I was itching my arm, I was also looking down to make sure that I didn't trip over my own feet as I walked into the store through those sliding glass doors, because I didn't need any more embarrassment in my life nor any more reason to wish not to exist and therefore as I looked down at my feet and itched my arm simultaneously, I just happened to catch a glimpse of my watch and I just happened to see what time it was, although I didn't really care what time it was and I wasn't even sure if in fact the time that my watch said it was, was actually correct.

So, anyway, I walked into the grocery store because I was thinking about what I wanted my last meal to be.

It might be important to mention how that night I was planning to watch my favorite film, a romantic French movie that you have most likely never heard of so I won't bother saying the title, and eating a snack [the contents of which I will later discuss] and then [with the help of a handy dandy, everyday home chemical used to help clean/clear pipes] I planned to end my own life.

I decided that one of those cream-filled yellow cakes, some of that soda everybody always looks so cool drinking on TV and some peanut butter filled pretzels were what would make up my last meal. Oh, and I also bought some toilet paper, dish soap and toothpaste.

It may seem bizarre to buy toiletries before ending one's own life, but I felt somewhat obligated to my roommates and somewhat guilty that one of them was going to have to find me dead and deal with the subsequent annoyances, costs and overall hysteria that something like that entails. And my thoughts at the time [which were most certainly noble] were that if I chipped in on the toiletries [something I should have done regularly but had not done in months on account of my overall state of mind, which in part was the cause of my evening plans] that somehow my roommates would not be as annoyed about having to deal with my corpse and what I assume would be a mess i.e. they would say "well at least we have toilet paper, dish soap and toothpaste, now do you want to carry the head or the feet?" instead of saying "what a jerk for dying and leaving us with all the responsibility and on top of it, he never even chipped in on toiletries!" and so, I walked into that grocery store and the lights were bright, too bright I must say. See it was dark outside obviously because it was nearly ten o'clock and it was the fall so it wasn't as if it was summertime, meaning that it was a time of year and a place on earth in which almost ten o'clock pm is most certainly a time of night (or would it be time of day?) that is dark.

In the store the brightness was tangible and had a mechanical and quickly irritating buzzing sound, which often accompanies florescent lighting. And that buzzing and near-seizure inducing flickering of the florescent lighting is what lit the grocery store and is also what made the white tile floor of that same grocery store sort of shine in a way that only grocery store tile floors do i.e. they are so bright that they almost seem to be made of fluorescent lights themselves, like the ceiling (and while a floor made of light seems strangely poetic and or ethereal, in the grocery store these made of light floors are anything but that and are rather annoying in how bright they are and seem sticky).

And I was basically depressed (and by basically depressed I mean calmly suicidal) not because of some epiphanic realization about my life nor the world nor about god nor about meaning but truthfully because I hadn't had any i.e. I found in my adulthood that there was a blankness that just seemed to linger and looked as if it would never go away.

To be clear, I don't classify adulthood as the day one turns eighteen or as whatever age one's religion or society has deemed each individual's date of entering adulthood to be. I don't believe that adulthood is necessarily an age thing, and maybe that makes me sound naïve, but I think adulthood or the true mark of adulthood is when someone has to work and fend for themselves. So, a little boy who is forced to work for 12 hours a day in a coal mine is an adult. And maybe my real qualification for adulthood is that in order to become an adult one must have to suffer [or at least work hard and kind of suffer] in order to survive and support themselves. And thus, the son of a billionaire or one who never truly has to work for anything is, in effect, never an adult and dies a fat, wrinkly child.

At the point of my grocery store visit, and on the night of my suicide,

I had been an adult (as per my own personal definition as listed above) for about three and half years. And really what was so very disheartening about adulthood was how bland it was. See I was educated from three years old (when I started at preschool) until age twenty-five (when I graduated from my master's program; a program which truthfully didn't really make me a master of much at all [in fact I was so unprepared for what I call "adult life" after graduating from my master's program, that I often wonder if the name-sake of the program is in fact meant to be ironic]).

See, I see life as a sort of jump off of a building i.e. the first steps of your life [which I would call your schooling or training] are the walk across the roof of said building. You walk your whole childhood and early adulthood across that grainy, plaster of the roof, sometimes looking over the edge and wondering what the future holds for you but mainly just steadily millimetering along, oblivious of what lies forward and beneath [which, both in the context of the metaphorical rooftop and in the reality of life, is a void through which you fall for your first years of adulthood as the world blankly stares ahead, uncaring]. And so as one, or you, or as most certainly I, progresses across the rooftop of early years, the edge grows closer and somehow with the realization that there is an edge, that this pampered dream called adolescence is going to come to an end, comes denial and a sort of holding onto of the idea that what you are experiencing [this stroll towards the end] will never end. But then the edge comes and you must jump; graduate to the open air; grow up; free yourself from those constraints of ease and of the sepia of childhood. And for me this leaping, the falling off the edge happens when one is finally placed into a situation where they have to suffer to survive i.e. work a full-time job. And then adulthood is the falling. And, imagine this falling is happening at first in slow motion and gradually speeds up as you age. This falling is hard to comprehend, because so far for one's whole life they have been on flat ground, supported by the rooftop of childhood, innocence (aka stupidity and naiveté) and the work/suffering of their parents.

And so, the first few feet of falling i.e. the first few years of adulthood, is a falling without reason, a sort of stumbling inside of a vacuum; a clumsy attempt at trying to understand something you have never before done. Like birds, we, as humans, must take that leap. But unlike birds we don't ever fly. We just fall. Some of us are told our whole lives that we can do what we want and some of those told that, believe it. And when you believe that you can do anything and you jump, you believe that you will just flap and fly away, high above the city and away from all of those who doubted you, while at the same time inspiring awe and love and lust in all of those that see you as they watch you finally claim that greatness you have had just dangling over your head for your whole life.

But even those who think that they can fly, in the fall, have to realize something; that everybody just falls and that at the bottom of the fall is a sidewalk and that sidewalk is hard and cold and grey and nobody really knows what lies beneath that sidewalk. However, what is known is that you won't figure out what is beneath that sidewalk until you have splatted across the top of it and some tiny bits of what you used to be have sort of seeped down in between the cracks. In short, no matter what, we all fall and we all land, often face first on the hard ground. And that ground does not move for anybody, and once the rain has washed our filth and blood and brains and bits of bone away there is barely a mark; barely a semblance that we were ever really here.

So, that's what life is, that's what we leave; a splat which is soon washed away and/or covered by many millions of other splats on a surface that is so unconcerned with what we think is important.

And I was one of those fools who thought I could fly. I thought I would soar. I was told so many times I had the world ahead of me; that I could do anything I wanted; that I was destined for greatness; that I would do something; that I was special. But I wasn't, and maybe it took me longer than most to realize that, but I did and I fell off that ledge like everybody else, and I have been grasping for it ever since. And three and half years of grasping and twisting and trying not to look at that ever-approaching ground, was too long for me, and that is why that day, after buying my last meal at the grocery store, I killed myself.

My life played out in a sort of sad and ever worsening repeat, like someone stuck in the same day over and over but somehow that day was just different enough that you couldn't just go through the motions or put yourself on an auto-pilot. My job was difficult enough for me to have to pay attention at it, but dull enough for me to be both exhausted and completely drained at the end of each day. By the arrival of each long-awaited weekend, I was too tired to enjoy myself or participate in any activities that I would've liked to participate in because by the end of the week I was so tired from working that I would end up just sleeping away the entirety of the two days of the weekend. And the falling continued with no sweet end in sight, until I decided for myself when that all too comfortable looking end of days would come.

And walking into that store, my throat was kind of sore from screaming into the pillow on my bed. My hands were dry enough that pretty much each of my fingers had a serious (and near bleeding) hang nail on it and as I walked into the store each movement of my hands resulted in one of those hangnails catching on the fuzz or grain or loose strings of my plain, off white, button down.

What I mean by that is that not only mentally, but also physically, each step was painful and I just wanted it to end.

There were beautiful women in the store, four if I remember correctly. And I walked past one of them as I went towards the section where they sold those yellow, cream-filled cakes and as I walked past she smelled like grass and rain and flowers and fresh in a soft way that made me want to curl up into a ball and sort of melt into the floor. I just wanted to be done. It wasn't that I had been rejected by this woman (I had never spoken with her) nor had I been in a recent breakup nor had I had that hard of a time finding girlfriends throughout my short life, it was more the fact that whilst growing up I had expected to quickly find a person with whom I could share my life. And with one failed relationship after another on my love track record, I eventually realized that not only was I not going to find a somebody like that somebody I had hoped I would find, but that the kind of internal-emptiness-filling somebody whom I was looking and hoping for did not in fact exist. And so, my hope for salvation in the form of a soulmate, like the idea that I could do anything with my life, was based on a completely fantastical and untrue desire. And as I walked past the woman, it wasn't that I wanted to be with her, I was way past hope or romance, it was that just being in her presence made me sad about things that could've been or people I could've known or feelings I could've felt. She was looking through the avocados, picking them up one by one and squeezing them to presumably tell if they were ripe. And as I walked past she glanced up at me and smiled a half smile with her lips (not showing any teeth) and she was pretty in a kind way and had freckles on her cheeks and black hair that was cut right above her shoulders and she was wearing a royal blue sun dress. And I drowned in that dress and in her scent (which was vaguely rose-esque when up close) and I wished I could hold her close or that she could hold me close and tell me, whisper to me so close that her lips touched my ear and say that everything would be ok, and that she was there now and that I now had someone. But by that time, I was already gone, a shell of somebody barely able to move their feet against the squeak-inducing tile of that brightly lit place, and I did not return her smile.

And so, I shuffled through the store picking out the items I needed and balancing them in my arms. Finally, when I had collected all of my items (the yellow, cream-filled cakes, the peanut butter pretzels, some soda that seemed less cool when in the store in a plastic bottle than in a glass bottle on the beach [which is where I had usually seen it] and the toiletries for my room-mates) and had seemingly walked up and down every isle in the store more than twice, I made my way to the cash register.

In this particular grocery store, there were three checkout lanes (labeled for some reason with the glowing numbers 1, 3, and 4) but there was only one person working (as far as I could tell in the entire store). The line had fifteen people in it and sort of wound up the cereal aisle. I stood at the back of the line, my arms bulging from the weight of my grocery items and my eyes feeling ready to close. Ahead of me in line were the four beautiful wom-en I had seen when I walked into the store as well as eleven other people of various sizes, races, genders and shapes, all of whom were on their cell phones but one (not including me, I wasn't on my phone because my arms were full and also because my phone was nothing more than a sad reminder of my lack of a social life and a constant anxiety provoking tool because I would feel what they call ghost vibrations tens of times throughout the day and would quickly check my phone to find [almost always] that nobody had contacted me after all). It wasn't that I could see everybody's phones but I could see their heads and their necks and they were all were crooked down in a way that is only done when one is trying to look at their phone and is aim-lessly scrolling through whatever type of feed they prefer to scroll through when bored or frankly at any time that they are not entertained by the world around them.

The only person in line not on their phone was a rich looking older wom-an with a face full of make-up and plastic surgery and it seemed that the only reason that she was not on her phone like everybody else was because she was too busy yelling at the poor, sole employee of the grocery store.

The employee of the store was a boy in his mid-teens with mild acne, red greasy looking hair, and braces wearing a bright red visor and apron over a white t shirt and jeans, that with the reflection of the fluorescent lights and red cloth, seemed to make his hair and his skin look even more red and greasy. The boy was visibly sweating as he tried as fast as possible to ring up the items of the first person in line while still being polite and while still wearing that expected [and likely required] customer service smile (which looked absolutely ridiculous and out of place in the context of the amount of stress the poor boy was endur-ing and the harsh words the old rich woman had for him.)

and so I waited, wondering what on earth all these people had to live for, wondering how long I had left to live, wondering when (if ever) I would make it to the end of that line and out of those sliding glass doors, wondering when I would be able to walk home, under the moon to my last meal and final night, alone.

HIGHWAY

The highway is so straight it looks infinite.

In the distance, the highway meets with a vast and a hypnotic blue horizon. The sky is vast and blue in a way that makes the sheer vastness and throbbing, oscillating blue of it look like an optical illusion.

The road is one long, coal-black strip of asphalt split into two lanes with one double yellow line and it is framed by two white lines that create a border and the edge of said road. His bright red convertible and the road are the only things with colors different than that of desert sand and that veil of azure that absolutely dominates any viewpoint. As he drives down the highway, the hills which stand an unmeasurable distance against the backdrop of endless blue, seem not to move.

Were it not for the fact that his speedometer is pinned at a constant of 100 mph and his foot is strained, holding down the pedal, and that wind is whipping against his face and making his hair stand straight back, he would think he was sitting in place. The road seems to stay in the same place and there are no trees or speed limit signs or people or gas stations or birds to give him any context of how fast he is moving, how far he has gone, or if in fact he is really moving at all.

The air is so hot and dry. He feels like he is floating in a sort of oven.

He is the only moving thing in sight. The sun is directly above him and even its brightness seems to be swallowed up by the deep of the blue which seems to be ever growing and almost omnipresent.

In his car, which has a full tank of gas, there is a leather, black suitcase (that matches the color and texture of the bench style seats in the car) and inside of that suitcase (packed as tightly as possible) are all of the man's belongings. The suitcase is in the passenger seat beside him and the backseat is empty. This man left everything but what he could carry in the suitcase (which once belonged to his long dead father) behind, and set out onto this road at a time that seems like weeks ago, but which could have been as recent as this morning.

The sky and the unmoving desert sand and the soft edged hills in the distance make time pass in a way that feels like no time is passing at all. It seems like the world has held its breath in this place and has given pass to the sky. Here the sky and the blue and the cloudless infinity is king and time shirks its rigid head in the other direction. This place looks as if it was placed on pause long ago and that whomever, whatever, placed this place on pause has forgotten to press play again.

The man is alone on the highway.

There is not another car in sight, and in fact he cannot remember the last person or car he has seen or voice he has heard or perfume he has smelled. All he knows now is the beating down sun, and the dry sand and the sound of the flapping wind in his ears and that blue, and that blue. Always the blue, always there but not at the same time.

The blue is everywhere and nowhere.

He knows the blue is a mere reflection of sunlight and a product of chemical reaction and that what he sees, all he sees, is merely the effect of some twisted illusion, but that doesn't make it any less consuming.

The faster he goes, the longer he speeds down this road, the more he is lost in that sky, the less he remembers where he has come from.

Finally, after countless hours or days or months or maybe just minutes he sees a sign. It has been so long since he has seen a sign that at first it looks foreign and alien to him; something that should not be there in the desert. With a white background and blue hand painted letters the sign proclaims an upcoming attraction unlike anything seen before. Unlike other signs proclaiming roadside attractions, this particular attraction sign does not have devaluing numbers of miles until the destination listed on the sign, the sign merely says that there is an attraction upcoming and that this attraction is unlike anything ever seen and has an arrow pointed onward, towards supposedly where this attraction will be; towards the horizon and the end of the road.

The only thing he has to look forward to, the only thing that gives him any reason is that sign.

With sight of the sign the man presses his foot harder on the already floored gas pedal and looks squarely to the horizon. He will see that attraction and he will be the judge of if it is truly unlike anything previously seen.

Driven by a man leaving many things behind, the red car, in a sea of light brown sand, coasts down a long and straight road towards an all-consuming sky and an attraction that is sure to be worth seeing.

HOUSE

The house is two stories, has dark brown (espresso bean brown) painted siding and white (coffee creamer white) trim around each of the windows. The house has a lower deck and an upper one too, both of which look out onto slightly rolling hills that are mainly covered with houses painted the same shades of brown and white as the house in question. The house has four bedrooms (one of which has been converted into a home office for the father of the family that owns and resides in the house in question). The master bedroom (which has its own bathroom) is occupied by the mother and father, the second largest room is occupied by the eldest child (a boy) and the final bedroom (not counting the bedroom that now acts as an office) is occupied by the youngest, second, and most likely final child of the family (a little girl, who at the moment is wearing a bright blue princess dress and is sitting on her bed with a plastic crown in her hands, weeping).

Between the house in question and the houses on either side of the house in question, i.e. the neighboring houses of the house in question, there is twenty feet of space on each side. There are nine feet and eleven inches, leading up to a fence on either side of the fence that physically represents the property line of the house and belongs to the house in question and the house next to the house in question respectively (two inches are allocated, well one inch from each side, to allow space for the fence). The fence is made of wooden planks and is painted the same dark (espresso bean brown) as the siding of all of the houses in this sprawling neighborhood. In the nine feet and eleven inches of space that exists between the house in question and the fence that separates the property of the house in question from that of the neighbor's house, there is grey gravel that (the gravel) is all uniform in shape, size and color (the grey of the gravel is a chalky, dead skin type of white-ish grey). In almost the exact middle of the space between the house and the fence on the left side of the house, and the exact middle of where the gravel starts and ends (widthwise) there is a plant that has managed to poke up from beneath weed cloth (that itself is beneath the gravel) and then through the gravel itself. The plant, the only un-manicured speck on the property, is a light green that gets even lighter when in direct sunlight. This plant, which is more than likely just a weed, has a purple, spiky looking flower on it, stands about six inches tall and has begun to attract bees.

The front and back lawns of the house in question are mowed every Monday by a company of men who mow all of the lawns of all of the houses in the neighborhood. There are enough lawns in the neighborhood that the men have enough work to fill their entire week (except Sundays, which they take off for rest) before they have to loop back around and mow all of the lawns again. Today is Sunday, and because of that there are two things happening; one is that the sound of lawnmowers buzzing (a sound that is almost always present somewhere in the neighborhood) is now nowhere to be heard (as the lawnmowers and the weedwackers [both the people and the machines related to these terms] are in their respective homes [which are most certainly not in this neighborhood] resting) and thus there is a sort of eerie silence that has fallen like a sheet over the neighborhood and in this silence it seems as if everything; the houses, the gravel, the sidewalk, the air, are all standing completely still, afraid to disturb this uncanny peace, and two; because it is Sunday and therefore (as per the schedule of the lawn mowers) it has been almost a week since the grass on the front and back lawns of the house in question have been mowed, and therefore the grass has taken on this cowlick style of sticking up every which way and looks like the hair on the head of an un-showered man who is on the verge of some type of psychotic break. And this unraveled grass, these thin patches of wild green, seem exceptionally untamed when juxtaposed against a house, a neighborhood and a world in which things are supposed to be just perfectly so (or at least look that way).

The little girl in the bright blue princess dress with the crown in her hands is not crying because of something that most other children would cry about (such as a broken toy or because of something wanted but not gotten) no, she is crying because of, in some ways, the feeling in the house.

And that feeling in the house, that whispered truth, is much like that of the street outside and of the grass on the front and back lawns, too quiet and slightly unraveling in a chaotic way.

The little girl's room is on the bottom floor of the two-story house.

Above her room, the master bedroom sits and within that master bedroom are her parents (her mother is seated on the bed and her father paces the space between the bed and the door to the bedroom. Her parents are speaking to one another in that hushed but forceful and sharp way that people who are fighting but don't want their children to hear, speak. Through the floor, the words are muffled, but the tones and the quick words followed (on the part of her mother) by sobs and by sighs and angry sounding protests that are more grunt than anything else (from her father) can still be heard and, more importantly, felt. And each subsequent angry and sad sound adds to the overall already tense feeling that has at this point permeated like a gas leak through the entire house. And she (the little girl) is on the bed and she is crying, not because she has done anything wrong (at least not that she can think of) but because she doesn't want her parents to fight anymore. She is tired of those muffled yells, those slamming doors, those looks that seem to pierce through the white painted and sparsely decorated walls. She wants everybody to get along. She wants her mother to get home earlier from work. She wants her father to not spend so much time in his office smoking cigarettes and watching a TV that blares out static heavy sports broadcasts. She wants her brother to come sit by her, to make up stories with her like he used to before he got so quiet and starting spending so much time in his room. Above her weeping, she can hear her father's carpet softened angry footfalls (she knows his hands are clenched into fists and that his face is red) and she can her mother crying in a hysterical way that borders on hyperventilation (she knows that her mother's mouth, when she cries this hard, is open wider than normal and that her mother's hands are pressed hard against her thighs as she sits with her legs crossed on the bed). She knows the way her mother is sitting even though she is not in the room upstairs in part because she has seen her mother sit that way before but in part because she (the little girl) is now seated in the exact same way, mouth open wider than normal to allow more air into her lungs as she cries, while she presses her hands hard down onto her thighs.

Upstairs there is a living room with a rarely used fireplace and a daily used TV that is hung above that fireplace. There are couches that are spread out in a horseshoe shape around the TV and in between the couches there is a trunk that is filled with blankets but doubles as a table and footrest when it is closed (which it currently is). The floors in the upstairs are a light-hardwood and the floors in the downstairs are a grey carpet that may have been white at one point but which have been grey for the entirety of the little girl's conscious life. The master bedroom is connected to the living room by a door that is currently closed but that is often open. From the living room, there is a hallway that leads to the front door of the house which opens onto a small front porch, a porch which has three steps that lead down onto a grey gravel path that perfectly slices the front lawn in two. Across the hallway from the living room there is the kitchen. The kitchen has a window that looks out onto the fence and over that fence to the neighbor's house, which is a mirror image of the house in question and thus has the kitchen on the other side of the house and therefore when one stands in the kitchen of the house in question and looks forwardly out at the neighbor's house, they can see directly into the kitchen of the neighbor's house. In the kitchen (which is small in comparison with the rest of the house) there is a sort of enclave in which a table sits and at which the family will occasionally share a meal (and on which currently there is an apple with three or four bites taken out of it). At the end of the hallway that starts at the front door is the office of the father of the family that currently owns and resides in the house.

In the downstairs of the house (in which the little girl is still crying but now in a lesser way, a way in which she is still shedding tears but now the tears have switched from the tear equivalent of rapid fire to more of a slow faucet drip style), there is another sort of living room directly beneath the upstairs living room. This living room is set up in more or less the same way as the one directly above it, but doesn't have a fireplace. The downstairs TV is on the floor instead of hung on the wall (like its upstairs counterpart) and there is only one couch and no trunk on which to place one's drink or food or feet. This living room is used predominantly by the children but is occasionally used by the father of the house to watch football games with his friends on the weekends (occasions during which the mother will take both of the children out for dinner and a movie to give both herself and the children time away from the ruckus and noise caused by the father and his friends as well as to give the father some space to watch the game).

On one side of the downstairs living room there is a door that leads to the little girl's room, this door is open. On the other side of the living room there is another door which leads to the bedroom of the brother, this door is closed but not fully, as there is a gap that is about an inch and a half wide between the frame of the door and the door itself. And from the inch and a half gap, yellow light pours out in a single beam onto the grey carpet of the downstairs living room.

The family, at one time, owned a dog and that dog was something pure and red-nosed and sweet and the whole family was sort of brought together over their love of that dog. But one day while the mother was at work and the children were at school and the father was in his office smoking cigarettes and doing whatever he does in that office, the dog somehow got out of the house and (according to what the veterinarian would say later that day) the ecstasy of the escape from the house and the overall wonder of being out in the world excited the dog so much that its heart exploded and it (the beloved family dog) slumped over, mid run, on the left side of the front lawn of the house just inches away from the road and because of the velocity of the dog running and suddenly stopping, the body of the then dead dog had skidded with some force to the very edge of the lawn. And the dog had been found by the older brother and the little girl as they came home from school, and at that point the dog had been laying outside for the hottest part of the day and looked like a stuffed animal that had had about a quarter of its stuffing taken out, i.e. the dog did not look good when they (the children) found it (the dead dog) and the image of this deflated looking animal corpse is something that both of them (the children) will be able to see crystal-clearly for the rest of their lives. And but anyways although the dog has been dead for at least a year, there is still a decent amount of dog related toys and knick-knacks around the house including but not limited to; a dog bed in both of the living rooms, a box of unopened dog food in the pantry, and at least (but most likely more than) a handful of grey-white dog hair on every piece of furniture.

The upstairs and downstairs decks of the house both look out onto the same suburban monotonous sprawl and on the lower of the decks, the son (the brother, the eldest sibling) sits with his legs splayed to either side of him on the grainy and slightly splintery boards of the deck and with his back leaning against the espresso bean brown siding of the house, smoking a joint that is burnt down to the point that it is getting difficult to hold it without burning his fingers. The joint (which is now singeing the fingertips of the eldest sibling of the house), was stolen from his father's office by this eldest son for (as the son and the father only know), the father is not smoking just cigarettes in there.

The son was able to become aware of the fact of what his father was or was not smoking in his (the father's) office, one day after school when he saw his father speaking with an upper classman in the parking lot of the high school. The son had been surprised to see his father at school because he (the son) usually took the bus back to his house after school, but he had been happily surprised and had (incorrectly) assumed that his father was there at his high school to pick him (the son) up from school and so the son had strolled over to his father's car with a kind of half smile and had been about ten feet away from his father's car when he realized that his father was handing money over to the upperclassman and that the upperclassman was handing a plastic baggie filled with what looked like moss over to his father. And the way that both his father and the upperclassman had nervously looked around and anxiously moved to grab the thing that one was handing the other, had alerted the son to the fact that what his father was doing at the school was (while still surprising) had nothing to do with him (the son). And but anyway he (the son) had continued to stroll up to his father's car (as the upperclassmen had sulked, like a retreating fox, away) and he (the son) had asked him (the father) what he was doing at his (the son's) school and if he (the father) was there to pick him (the son) up and the father had responded affirmatively but in a guilty and sort of sheepish way and in a tone that seemed unsure if he (the father) had been found out. And so, the son and the father drove back to their house, and on that drive, back to the house there was not much said and at a couple points the son glanced over at his father and had been able to see the corner of the plastic bag poking out from the father's pocket and inside of the car during that drive there was a certain earthy and pungent smell and also during that drive the father was visibly sweating.

And back then (about two years ago, when the dog was still alive, on the day that the son saw his father at school) he (the son) felt young and hopeful and sort of fresh. He had not truly been aware of what was going on outside of his existential bubble and even within that bubble he had sort of just moved around aimlessly and in a care-free way that only young, half cognizant people can do. But after that day, seeing his dad and that upperclassman, he has grown and aged (to him) what feels like a decade, i.e. he feels older, more adult, less hopeful. Since that day he has felt more and more numb and kind of far away from everything. The enormity (a word he doesn't know) of everything and the complexity and intricacy of things just overwhelm him and make him feel small (and although the above is exactly what he feels, if asked to and if he were in the mood to describe his feelings he wouldn't exactly be able to put them [his feelings] in such a concise way).

So, but now he is on the deck and his feet are bare and the wind is lightly blowing the bottoms of his feet and passing through the spaces between his toes and the joint is almost out and the sun is low in the sky but is still quite far from setting. He feels that emptiness and a kind of detached awe as he looks out at the neighborhood in which his family lives. The same house, over and over again, like this whole place was puked out of some house making machine and plopped down onto all the hills, onto all the valleys, onto all the empty spaces, until everything was filled with front and back yards and espresso bean brown siding and grey gravel paths leading to front doors and white trim and kitchens that look out into more of the same kitchens and muffled whispers and dead dogs and a sky that is never fully dark.

It's all a blur of sameness and the bland taste of stale air.

He started smoking stolen joints about a year ago, on a boring Sunday like today when he had been just sitting in his room staring at the wall and had somehow been reminded of that day when he saw his father at school and had decided to see what else his father was hiding and he knew that his father was not going to catch him in the office because he (the father) was busy upstairs, talking in harsh and sharp whispers to his (the son's) mother. And so, he had gone into his father's office and had found some things including a dark-wooden box with a carving of a frog on the top of it and inside of that box he had found tens of joints and he had pocketed a few of them. And then he had put the box where he had found it, which was in the top drawer of his father's desk, under a bunch of papers. Then he had gone upstairs walking as quietly as possible as to not disturb or interact with at all his parents, and had taken from the cabinet above the stove a box of matches and had skulked back down to the bottom deck, where his parents never go even when they are not fighting, and he had lit up the joint with a match (after trying a couple times to light a match he had finally succeeded) and he had inhaled rather sharply and had coughed and coughed. He had coughed so loud that he was surprised his parents hadn't come downstairs to check on him (but they had not) and eventually had went back upstairs (again as quietly as possible) to get some water for his then sore and scorched throat and after getting water he had gone back to the deck and had proceeded to try and smoke the joint again and had slowly figured out how to smoke it without coughing.

And but that was like a year ago now and he has been smoking joints every Sunday, and really as much as possible, since that first day. And each month he sneaks into his father's office to steal about a handful of joints and he is not sure if his father is aware of the missing joints and is just letting him smoke them with the assumption that he doesn't tell his mother about what he saw his father doing at the high school, or if his father just has no idea that the joints are missing. And but it doesn't really matter anyway because he hasn't got in trouble yet and he is pretty good about hiding the evidence of his newfound habit; he always has gum in his pocket and he flushes the butts (or as kids at school call them, roaches) down the downstairs toilet and where he smokes on the bottom deck is a place that is mainly used for storage and a place that can be accessed by his window (from which he has removed the screen) and so he can pretend to be in his room and then climb through the window and onto the deck and be mainly obscured by bikes and extra lawn chairs and whatnot that are kept down on the bottom deck, so basically he is pretty sure that he is not going to be found out and even if he is it doesn't really matter because he is not sure if his parents would care if he was found out.

And the reason that he has continued to smoke the stolen joints is because they make him feel a little bit lighter and the emptiness that has begun to make him feel like he is sort of sinking into the ground most of the time dissipates a bit when he is high and sitting on the deck.

And below the bottom most section of the deck, well not directly below but diagonally below and in the line of sight of the top deck, there is a rectangular patch of grass that is colored differently than the rest of the grass in the back lawn and below that rectangular patch of grass the dog is buried and was buried there by the father on the night after the dog was found by the children on the front lawn. The father used a shovel to cut a rectangle out of the grass and then set that rectangle of grass on top of the grass beside where that rectangle of grass had been and then he dug a hole that seemed deep enough to him in which to place the dog's body, and then he set the dead dog (which at that point was wrapped in a white towel and starting to smell) down into the hole and then he put the dirt that he had dug out of the hole back in the hole and put the rectangle of grass back on top of where it had once been and patted down the grass with the shovel that he had used to dig the whole. And that grass had grown back into the ground but ever since that night that grass has been a yellow-green, instead of a deep green like the rest of the grass in the backyard of the house.

Well so now the little girl has now stopped crying but is still breathing in that way that one must breathe after crying hard and she has placed that plastic crown back on her head and is looking in a mirror that is hung on her wall and is trying to use her hands to flatten out creases in her dress as she tries to return to a normal breathing pattern and her brother is on the deck and his head is swimming but not like a swimmer, more like someone seated in an inner tube on one of those lazy rivers at a water park, and the parents are upstairs and their fight is still ongoing (as it always is) but they have stopped speaking, it seems there is nothing more to say, for now.

And outside the sun is hot and the grass is growing out of control.

The House by the Sea, Where Your Grandmother Used to Live but Which Now Sits Empty and Falling Apart

The sea was calm there and its color was a light blueish grey; the color of grout. Those days there weren't many people on the island, and the wide, seemingly endless beaches were empty but for picturesque white, tread-less sand and the occasional pitter pattering gull.

In the room, closest to the water, there was a piano and you remember your grandmother playing it as you and your father sat on the salt-and-sand-caked, time-worn hardwood floor and listened. Each pressed down key was perfectly timed and melancholic in a soft and ancient seeming way. The notes on the white-yellow keys were played with both intimate knowledge and care by fingers gnarled and multicolored with age and arthritis and seemed to be kept on beat by the metronome of the foamy waves folding down onto the sand outside.

The piano, your grandmother once told you, was older than she was and at that time you couldn't believe that. You told her that she was the oldest thing you knew and she just smiled and brushed your hair behind your ear and spun you around so that you could see the sea through the window and told you that what you saw out there; that glistening infinity stretching out to meet the line of sunset-reddened horizon was the oldest thing that ever was. She went on to explain how it would continue its endless push and pull; its wet, oscillating breathing long after any of us, everybody you or her would ever know, were long gone.

And that may have been the first time you realized that the things and people and places you loved would eventually be gone; that all you knew but the sea would wane and slowly give in on itself. This is when you learned that we are born of some great dust and salty winds and that no matter who we are, each and every body and soul will eventually be pulled out and away by those reaching fingers of time. This is when you learned that we all slip away in the undertow of all of our days; we all dissipate into that golden void where the ocean meets the horizon; we all disappear at that sacred threshold of water and sky.

But you suppose you already knew about the eventual passing beyond sight that we all must go through at some hopefully far way point in our lives. You knew about grey hair and cancer and peeling paint and floods; you knew about decay and how things fall apart.

In fact, that is why you were there in the first place; why you and your father were there in that little house by the ocean surrounded by green-gray shrubs and sea grapes rustling with snakes and lizards and insects and beasts with eyes that shone wickedly in the night. Yes, you were there to take your grandmother away. It seemed everybody knew it was her time to fade or at least that the fading for her had begun. Well, you guess that the fading begins at the beginning of everything; as in the first gasping breath, the first clenched fist, the first view of the world through blood crusted, half opened eyes. You suppose the fading is always going on; that the slick in-and-out of the crashing days and decades brings the end on and on. But your grandmother at that point, so long ago now, was declining, as your father said, and fast at that. It was as if the faucet of her eventual demise had been turned from a slight, dripping trickle to on full bore.

It started with a fall and some bruising. It continued with a broken hand which she couldn't remember the cause of. Then there were more falls and more broken bones and more bruises the color of squished blueberries. Your grandmother was weak and it scared your father, you could hear it in the tone of his voice and in the way he tapped his foot as he spoke with her on the phone each morning asking how she was doing, no really mom, no bullshit, how are you seriously (he would say).

And then what your father called the final straw happened. One night your grandmother wandered out into the night, naked except for a pair of bright yellow plastic shoes. She walked all night on the beach, goose bumped in the sea breeze and white light of a crescent moon until a man coming back from fishing saw her in the scarlet light of the dawn and covered her with a yellow fisherman's rain jacket (which coincidentally matched her shoes).

After that night, your father said to your mother and his sister as you listened, crouched down and hiding in the kitchen with your little brother crouched beside you, that it was time for your grandmother to move in with you; that she could no longer live alone; that she had finally become a danger to herself.

You understand that what your father was doing then was out of care and was really the right thing to do, but that didn't make it any easier; it certainty didn't mean that your grandmother was happy about what was to come.

You never knew your grandfather, he was long dead by the time you were born and by the way your father still tenses up and gets red in the face any time your grandfather's name is mentioned, you are kind of happy that you never did meet him. From the time that your grandfather died all those years ago, your grandmother lived alone: fixing her own plumbing, climbing onto the roof when palm fronds would fall onto it, teaching piano lessons and playing bingo on Wednesdays. She was incredibly self-reliant and once got so mad at a rogue palm tree in her view of the ocean, she went out and chopped it down with nothing but a hatchet and a bottle of rum (the hatchet was for chopping and the rum for drinking). So, you couldn't and you still can't really blame her for not wanting to be taken away from all that she had and moved to some far away and admittedly less beautiful and wild place.

When you and your father arrived to help her pack up her things she kissed you in the way she always had and brushed your hair behind your ear, leaving a greasy, dark-red smudge on your forehead and the tickle of some musky perfume dancing at your nostrils when she pulled away. However, she said nothing to your father when she saw him come through the door.

On your first day on the island, you and your father drove to the hardware store to buy cardboard boxes and tape and a pair of scissors (because your grandmother had recently lost hers) as well as a soda for you which you drank on the way back to your grandmother's house as you looked out the window watching the green trees flash by and the single white cloud in the sky stay in more or less the same place.

The packing progressed. All of the cabinets were emptied and so were the dressers and closets. Each piece of empty furniture was loaded into the back of an orange truck by two sweaty giants who wore belts around their big bellies and smelled like a chemical kind of smoke when they walked by.

When all was moved out but the piano and a single suitcase in which some of your grandmothers clothing, jewelry and her toothbrush were packed, you and your grandmother went to the beach while your father finished up with the men and the truck.

You knew then that your grandmother was fading. There was a scent about her like she hadn't washed herself in days; there was around her a subtle but undeniable stench of decay. You had seen her moving slower than normal as she packed her soft dresses into the boxes you had helped your father fold and tape into place; you had heard her mumble nothing to herself and forget the names of things you knew she knew. You knew then, even at your age that these were some of the last days you would have with your grandmother in the way that she truly was before the fading consumed her. You knew that when you loaded up into your father's car and drove out of the grey gravel driveway, away from that empty house and the sea, pieces of your grandmother would fall away with every passing mile and that these pieces would never stop falling off of her until there was nothing left to fall; until she was back to that sacred sand in the wind that we all become and come from.

But that night she was still her; she still smelled mostly like she always had and she still brushed your hair behind your ear as you both watched the sun drip down the sky like some slowly melting thing. You must have fallen asleep out there on the beach with your head on your grandmother's lap and your bare feet with their painted blue toenails in the sand.

When you awoke, it was dark and the stars were as bright as you had ever seen them. Your father was there then and he and your grandmother must have made up because you could hear them softly murmuring and passing a glass bottle of dark liquid back and forth between them. You sat up then as the sea breeze kicked up grains of sand which gently raked across the skin on the back of your neck and made you shiver.

You told your grandmother then that you were scared. You told her you were afraid of the dark and all of those things that lurk and move within it, just out of sight. She chuckled a deep and wet laugh and held you tight as she brushed your hair behind your ear. Then she leaned close and her breath was a hot, sticky rotten sweet and she told you that she was scared too and that it's good to be afraid of the dark. She said that those not afraid of the dark are not being creative enough.

Your father then scooped you up with his big arms in a way that he wouldn't be able to for much longer because of how small you were then and how big you would soon become. Then you all went inside to hear your grandmother play her piano before it, because it wouldn't fit in your parent's house, and everything else would soon be left behind.

JARS

On a shelf in a rarely used backyard shed there is one (among many) glass jar with a silver, metal aluminum screw-on top screwed onto the top of it (the glass jar). On the side of this jar there is a piece of butter colored, not quite white but certainly not yellow, painter's tape stuck, and on this painter's tape, written in a scrawling but easily legible script with a black permanent marker, there are three words detailing what is contained within this jar. There are about thirty jars in total stored on a high shelf above the window in the shed, all labeled with this same painter's tape and all containing various workman type work materials such as screws of various sizes and with various shaped holes and heads, as well as nuts and washers of various diameters.

And as I sort through these jars (sitting here, still wearing my suit from the funeral) although I am yet to see all of them, I can guarantee that there is not a single screw nor washer nor nut out of place. I can remember my father, when I was much younger (a boy of maybe eight) taking me out to this very shed and lifting me up (my father placed his work worn and callused hands around my waist to do so) and showing me all of his rows of jars. I think he was proud to have something so clean and orderly in his life; little bits of metal that held no consequence to anybody but him, which he could organize and clean and control in any way he wished. I think these jars gave him a mental deep breath to be around; an internal sigh that reminded him things could be simple and contained.

His life as a child (most of which I heard from my mother and his sister, my aunt, both of whom are now long dead) was filled with yelling and beatings from his father with a belt, and crackers with ketchup for dinner. He once mentioned to me that he attended eight different elementary schools because his father would so often get fired from a job and get into a fist fight with some person from whatever job he had just been fired from and his father would basically be given the choice to leave town or go to jail. And so, my father moved around a lot as a kid and witnessed or was the victim of (as far as I understand) weekly, possibly even daily, beatings up until he signed up for the army at the age fifteen, lying about his age and not looking his father in the eye when he walked out the door (according to my aunt who had moved out a year later).

Even though my grandfather was a monster, I wish I had known him or at least that he had known I existed before he died. There is an emptiness in my head; there is a dead branch in my family tree which I feel shaking in the wind where my grandfather should have been. I wish I could have sat on his lap as a child, I wish I could have watched him grow old, I wish I could've been there at his death bed to tell him I loved him. Sure, he did terrible things and those things haunted my father and somehow haunted me but I still miss that beast I never met. Maybe I think I could've fixed him or made him soft or sane or something better. I don't know and I guess it doesn't matter now, my grandfather is dead and he died never having met me or knowing that I was ever born and my father is dead (freshly so) and in this shed where I now sit, he too sat for countless hours organizing his jars as perfectly as he wished everything else could be.

LAKE

The reservoir is liquid black, even as the hot sun beats down upon it.

Close to the shore (but not close enough to the shore to make out the cracks in and the stain of the wood on the square deck while standing on the shore and looking out), there is a dock anchored in place by cement blocks which were sunk into the sandy depths fifty feet below where it (the dock) slightly bobs atop the thick seeming water.

On the shore, the sand is white in a way that is dull and sort of fake looking. This sand was moved here by dump trucks and it took over 100 dump-truck-fulls of this fake looking white sand to make this beach. This sand was not made by the breaking of shell and stone by the endless tide of some wet entity so large and vast that even in this day in age, we still can't understand it. No, this sand and the body of water beside which it sits is man-made and even though it is supposed to look as real as possible, there is a sense of falsity that passes over anyone who sits upon that liar; the sand and beside that empty vastness; the manmade reservoir.

And so even though these things are not real, or maybe they are real but are most certainly not what they seem, here there is still a semblance of that quiet and mystery that accompanies bodies of water.

There is no telling what lies beneath the surface of the water. The sound of the small waves crashing (when listened to carefully) sounds like the release of a long held breath.

The boy is young; young enough that he is not fully aware nor present in his body. There are cuts and little bruises that pepper his shins and forearms from adventures had in the woods or in the backyard of his house during which he was so caught up in said adventures that he sort-of forgot that his body could be injured and bumped into or ran into things that caused his minute injuries.

The boy is wearing a navy-blue bathing suit that extends to about halfway down his thigh. His skin is naturally tan and he has hair that is the perfect in between of blonde and brown and therefore difficult for people to classify in terms of color, and that hair which is hard to classify in terms of color is curly and some of those curls hang down over his forehead but are not yet long enough to cover his eyes. Besides the darker nature of his features, his eyes are a hazel-speckled-blue. That blue within his eyes is sometimes the brightest thing in the room. His nose is round and beside his rounded nose there are reddish freckles dotted across his cheeks. His toe nails (with the help of his mother) are recently trimmed and are now (along with his feet, up to his ankles) buried in the sand. He is sitting with his knees to his chest and his arms folded around those bent knees, enjoying and sort of wallowing in the feeling of the sun on his shoulders as he watches the slow exhale of the waves twist and turn in that holy place where water meets the earth, where liquid meets solid and mixes into something soft. And as he watches the waves he moves his feet beneath the sand, movement that cannot be seen above the surface; a secret subterranean echo of twitches and sand tickled toes.

The man (the father [or as his son calls him 'papa'] of the boy) has darker skin than his son, is much hairier, and lays beside the boy on a white towel which is whiter than the sand but not whiter than the single cloud in the sky. The towel is the kind of white that is technically white but not white in the clean and puffy way which things like the cloud or say an ideal pillow on a bed are, but is a greyish white in a flat sort of way.

The only person (other than the father and the son) on the shore is a lifeguard. The lifeguard is a woman (who is young compared to the father on the sand but old compared to the boy with the buried feet). She wears a red, one piece bathing suit and a straw sunhat which covers her face in shadow. She wears glasses and in her left hand she holds a book, which she vigorously reads. The book has been read so many times that the cover is tattered and bits of this tattered cover are flaking off with her each and every movement of the book and those flakes of the tattered cover are the same shade of navy blue as the boys shorts and they (the flakes of paper from the cover of the over-read book) slightly twist and flutter in the wind like snowflakes as they fall from the fifteen-foot-high, white painted wooden tower on which the lifeguard sits (cross-legged), and although this book has been read many times over, it is the first time that this current reader, the lifeguard, is reading it.

Today is a day like many others, hot and long and for some hard. The father has taken the day off of work and the son is skipping school (with the permission of his father) and so the day is less hard and because they are doing things that they enjoy, less long and somehow in the enjoyment of the day, while the heat is still there, it (the heat) is somehow less abrasive and when the sun shines on the bodies of the boy and of his father it feels less like a curling iron and more like a warm, caressing hand. That is to say that today is a good day, at least for the boy and his father. Well, that's really to say that today is a good day, for now.

The boy has been taking swimming lessons since the beginning of the summer and it is now almost the end of the summer (well, school has started for the boy, so the scholastic version of summer is officially over but the adult and climatological sense of summer is not yet done) and since his father has taken up more shifts to make a bit more money in the past few months, he (the father) has not yet seen him (the son) swim. And in some ways, the reason why the father has not yet seen his son swim this summer is as listed above, but another sort of unspoken reason (a reason possibly unknown by the son and a reason shamefully known by the father) is that the father does not know how to swim and watching his son do something he cannot is both a new and terrifying experience for him.

The dock, alone in the water, reflected in the blue of the boy's eyes, bobs beckoningly. The glistening liquid awaits. Glory in the form of fingers finally reaching wet wood and affirmation in the form of loving watching eyes and the thumbs up sign on both of his father's work worn hands is just a couple strokes through that water away.

The boy stands, picks up his feet one by one from whence they were buried (leaving an imprint like the nostrils of some giant animal in the sand) and gives his father that universal look that all children often give their parents, a look which can be only translated as "watch what I am about to do (insert name that child calls their parent here)."

The father opens one brown-irised-eye and looks on as the son, heavy footed-ly trudges to the edge of the water, looking back at the father multiple times to make sure that he (the father) is watching him (the son) show him (the father) what he (the son) has learned to do this summer.

The lifeguard is captivated by her book in which two of the main characters are facing off in a sort of duel style battle and it seems (based on the foreshadowing in the previous chapters) that one of these main characters of her book may not survive this fight. As the lifeguard reads, she chews three pieces of pink bubble gum (which are now combined into one giant piece inside of her mouth) and as she chews and reads, she uses her hand that is not holding the book to twist a piece of her jet black hair (most of which is hidden beneath her extra-large straw sunhat) and as she twists her hair and intently reads her book, she occasionally pops a face-sized bubble with that gum and subsequently sucks the stringy remnants of the popped bubble back into her mouth to be re-chewed and reformed around her tongue in preparation for yet another bubble (and although she is consciously popping bubbles, she is only doing so half-knowingly because most of her attention is going into the creation of a mental image of what is going on in the book that she is reading). What can be sure is that she is most certainly not paying attention to what is going on beneath her white tower nor to whom is within the waters of the reservoir.

The son glides through the water like a paddle held still beside a steadily moving kayak, that's to say that the boy has learned well this summer and he is quickly closer to the dock than the shore. The father is proud and shows it (as expected) with a double thumbs-up, a motion to which the son replies with an external wave and an internal glow that were it (the boy's internal glow) to have a color, it would be a coal-burn orange.

The father stands up on his white towel and puts his hand on his forehead to create enough shade for him to see his son sitting on the edge of the floating dock, way out there in the deep. The dock, with the boy atop it, bobs. The son extends a dripping arm and with a slightly drier hand (using even drier fingers) beckons him (the father) to come join him (the son) on that floating thing.

The sand beneath the father's feet, as he strides from his towel towards the water, is grainy fire and his ears throb with both pain and anticipation.

He, the father, steps into the water, which is cold and smooth feeling. The ground beneath the surface, the wet sand, is velvet to the father's burnt feet and the coolness of submersion calms the pounding in his (the father's) ears.

The son sits with his legs (up to the back of his knees) off of the edge of the dock and into the water and with the rest of his body supine on the slightly damp (perhaps cedar) of the dock, looking up at the only cloud in the sky, which now (the cloud) seems a bit sharper in shape and greyer in color than before.

The father is now waist deep and getting further and further in every second as he moves awkwardly in the water and closer to the dock and his son.

The sun is hot on the father's back and the black water of the lake is cool on his skin in ways he could never have imagined.

Besides baths (of which he has not taken many) the father has never been fully submerged in water before, and even in the bath (which was a rare occurrence in the first place) he had the safety net of porcelain and the wall of the bathroom to keep him from going under, but now (in a lake much, much bigger than a bathtub) he is net-less, unrestrained by the white of a tub and is loving the feel of the muck between his toes as he stumbles on.

As with many (or possibly most) bodies of water there is a drop off point a certain amount of distance out from where the waves crash on the shore. And what this drop off point is, is exactly as it sounds like it is; a point in which the slowly deepening depth of the water (that has until the drop off point been mildly sloping down) simply drops off from around maybe 5 or 6 feet to all of a sudden 20 feet.

The lifeguard, in her tower of wood, is three fingers deep in her own fine, jet black hair and is fully engrossed in the book that she is reading. All other bodily movements or really anything besides the words on the pages which she is devouring with all she can devour them with are almost non-existent. Her bubble gum and it's popping, the earth and its spinning, her fingers and the hair in which her fingers are tangled, her lungs and the air they need to keep her alive; all fade to a low pulsating grey that simply does not matter. All that matters is the fight, and that fight is happening in her book. The two main characters involved in the fight are now fighting and they are trading blows rather equally and it is really too close to call. All she knows is that she must read on.

The son on the dock, via the sun in the sky, is now completely dry in all of the places on his body that are not submerged in the lake. His eyes are closed and his whole body is the gooey kind of warm that can only really be achieved by laying face up and letting the sun hit you directly.

The father has begun to slip.

The drop off point in this specific reservoir is now directly beneath his feet. The slope is slick with muck and silt and greasy underwater reeds. Below the surface, the father's feet are sliding now. In the air, his pallor has gone three shades lighter. He is pale and rigid with fear. But the rigidity is beginning to fade, and the panic is setting in. He is now up to his armpits and is sinking fast. His arms, which are strong but not toned with muscle, are held above the water in some type of instinctual and unconscious vain attempt to make himself float. As he sinks more, his chin is now level with the water and his neck is craned as much as one's neck can be craned, he flails and tries to keep his head above the water. His arms are now moving in a classic help me fashion and all he can muster is a muffled gargle before his head bubbles beneath the surface.

The fight in the book has progressed to the point where one of the main characters has been disarmed by the other and he (the disarmed main character in the lifeguard's book) is now dodging sword blows and scampering wildly, trying to both get out of the way of his opponent's sword and to find his own. The lifeguard is reading with bulged eyes and is even holding her breath in anticipation. A light pink, un-popped bubble protrudes from her mouth as her fingers slightly shake with angst about what will happen.

The son, with his eyes closed and his other senses heightened because of it, hears the muffled gurgle of his father beginning to drown, and sits up straight up just in time to see his father's thrashing fingers disappear below the surface of the lake.

The son pushes himself up onto the dock and stands erect, then dives deep into the water using a technique he learned earlier this summer at swim-camp.

The sunlight from below the water, as the father sinks (now fully and completely engulfed), looks feathery. There is no sound but that of trickling water and of the father's heart pounding in his own ears. The cold bites his legs and he blinks his eyes to try and adjust them to the deep of the lake.

In the farthest point of his vision the father can see the chain which holds the dock in place as well as a shape moving quickly towards him.

The air in the father's lungs is hot and stinging and his chest is convulsing in a way that means his lungs have taken in what oxygen they can from the garbled breath which he was able to take before going under. All that is left within the man is unbreathable and his vision is blurring as he sinks even further down.

The son reaches his father just as his (the father's) eyes close. The father is heavy beneath the water but not as heavy as he would be above. The son kicks his legs as hard as he can while he holds onto his father's arms, which are floating lazily above the rest of his father's now half-limp body. There are little bubbles popping out from the father's mouth, but the stream of bubbles is decreasing in both width and overall amount of bubbles.

In the fight in the book that the lifeguard is so intently reading, the main character who has previously lost his sword, has now been able to regain it as well as his balance. It is as unclear as ever, who will live and who will die.

The Letter

The letter will come today.

A medium sized, light-brown, "cushion mailer" which costs $1.89 to mail (not including the cost of the weight of the package which will be added to the overall cost) and which has on it, a red tab that has *pull to open* typed and printed beneath that tab; that is what the letter will look like. In a lot of ways, in size and in shape and according to the post office's record database, what he is waiting for as he stands at the sink is a package. But in his head, he thinks of it as a letter. It doesn't really matter whether what he is waiting for is a package or a letter or a parcel (as his father would have called it), what matters, at least to him is what is inside of this letter or package or parcel. It's what is inside that will change things so much for him, it's what's inside that will determine his fate. An affirmative or a negative, that is all it will take and he will be able to know what the answer is within the first few words of what he assumes will be a typed letter which he will take out from within a package. And so maybe that is why he is thinking of what he is waiting for as a letter instead of a package, because although what he is waiting for is technically, 100% a package, within said package is a letter and said letter is what he is actually, anxiously waiting for.

He is standing at the sink in the kitchen.

There is a rectangular window which looks out onto his front lawn (which is un-mowed) and also looks across a dark-grey, leaf-covered, asphalt-paved, neighborhood street. Past the road he can see the children of the neighbors who live directly across the street, playing in their front yard. There are two children in the front yard of the neighbor.

One of the children is a girl, who he assumes must be between the ages of three and five, although he never can really tell the age of young children or anybody for that matter. The girl, who is in the front yard across the street from his house, is wearing a white dress made of a material which is light enough to move in the breeze that is blowing through the neighborhood (which it is doing as he looks out the kitchen window), but is heavy and thick enough (the dress) to not be see-through. The little girl is kneeling on the grass about a foot away from the street and is rubbing a bright-yellow, freshly-picked, dandelion on the top side of her left forearm. The dandelion (as it is rubbed on the girl's arm) is leaving a faint yellow streak, although he can't see it from across the street, he knows what the yellow streak looks like and he also knows that it feels slightly sticky in a dry and clumpy sort of way. He knows the feeling and color of dandelion streaks on skin because when he was a child he used to rub dandelions on his arms with his brother and they would pretend they had been given superpowers by the juice of the dandelions and they would wrestle and roll in the grass in their front yard of their old house until their father would call them in to do their chores, (but that was all a long time ago for he who is standing at the kitchen sink). He wonders if the little girl across the street in the front yard of the neighbor thinks she has superpowers from the dandelion's juice and he wonders what her superpowers would be if she could choose one and he tries to remember what his superpower was back when he would play with his brother and he can't quite remember what it was, but he can remember that his brother's (superpower given by the juice of a dandelion) was the ability to fly.

The second of the two children, is a boy and is most likely between the ages of ten and twelve. The boy across the street, is wearing a paper crown that is crayon-colored in with what looks like a silver that is a bit lighter than normal pencil lead. The boy across the street also has a stick and is using the stick like a sword to fight off invisible monsters.

The man in the kitchen is distracted by the dripping faucet of the sink by which he stands. The sink is stainless-steel and inside of it there are flecks of coffee grounds and bits of crispy, overcooked egg left over from the dishes and pans he used during breakfast, a meal for which he had two cups of black coffee, which he made with a French-press hence the coffee ground residue in the sink that would not have been present if he had used a coffee machine, and (for breakfast he also had) scrambled eggs on a piece of nine-grain-toast with butter, the butter was on the toast not on the eggs although as he ate his breakfast some butter rubbed off on some of the eggs and he didn't hate the flavor and he thought the next time he makes eggs, he will put some butter on them (the eggs).

The sink has been dripping for about a week. He doesn't mind the dripping, except for in the night when it (the dripping) seems to amplify through-out his house and he can hear it (the dripping) loud and clear even if he closes this bedroom door and puts his pillow over his head. And he hasn't been sleeping well lately and he thinks his poor sleeping of late is, in part, thanks to the dripping faucet of the sink, but his inability to sleep of late is mainly because of the letter and how anxious he is for it to arrive, because it is supposed to come today.

He took off work to wait for the letter, but he has decided that it was a bad idea to take off work because now he is just standing at the sink and feeling anxious about it and although he finished breakfast, he is feeling a bit hungry again, but he doesn't want to eat eggs again. He wishes that he went to work so he would have something to do instead of stand at the kitchen sink and wait and eat more than he probably should.

And then he starts to think about the letter but not about the fact that it is arriving today but about what it actually says and how what it actually says will change everything. He thinks about how, if the words in the letter are affirmative, how things will change.

If the words in the letter are affirmative, he will have to leave this place. As he begins to think about leaving, he is not sad but he isn't happy either, he just feels a slowness. When he thinks about leaving that slowness seems to spread through his whole body, until he is looking at everything in the kitchen with as much attention as possible, because if the letter is affirmative then this, right now, could be the last time he stands in his kitchen. And what if he forgets parts of the kitchen, like where the forks go or the color of the cabinets (which is a light, robin's egg blue) or the sound of the drip of the faucet of the sink he currently stands in front of. It's not that he enjoys these things or has even really thought of them before. The thought of having to leave, all of a sudden makes all of these unimportant things, very important to him and he really wants to remember everything he has here.

But then he thinks about if the letter is negative and if he ends up hav-ing to stay home, how these things will be all he has. And all of sudden these things which had suddenly become so important to him and which he wanted to remember and cherish, are disgusting to him. And all of sudden he doesn't care about the color of the cabinets (which is a light, robin's egg blue) or where the forks go or that terrible dripping sound that has, in part, been keeping him up at night.

And he just wants the letter to arrive and he just wants the words in the letter to be affirmative so he can get away from the dripping and everything else.

But when he thinks of actually leaving, he begins to really appreciate all of the aspects of his kitchen and of his life and he tries to kind of grab everything with his eyes and hold it in a mental bear hug, so he won't forget anything.

And while he pictures mentally grabbing and mentally committing to memory everything in his kitchen, the water is still dripping from the faucet and the children are still playing outside.

And then there is a knock on his front door; the letter or package or parcel, whatever it is he has been waiting for, has finally arrived.

THE LETTER PT. II

His car was silver and hers was a white that seemed dirty in an intentional way (both inside and out) and he left her standing beside her dirty car, when he sped away in his silver car in a swirl of rust colored dust down a road he had been down alone many times before. This time he wasn't coming back at least not for a long while (but most likely not ever).

In his rearview mirror, he saw her standing in that pull off, lazily waving the dust away with a hand that he knew was soft. She had on dark purple lipstick and her hair was crooked and multicolored from various self-given haircuts and at home dyes. Through the speakers in his car a song played quietly from a tape that she made him long ago and he listened to this tape for as long as he could see her in that piece of glass which showed what was behind him, but as soon as he finally rounded a corner and she disappeared into the dust and thin grey light, he shut off the radio, ejected the tape and tossed it out the window along with a couple strands of her hair which he found on the shoulder of his t shirt.

His car was loud and the studs on his tires made a hail sound on the asphalt as he hauled on down the road away from where he had long since lived but would no longer. The engine of the car and the crackling of the tires and vacuum suck of the rolled down windows almost numbed his face and ears and throat as he tried to verbally convince himself to haul on without sound.

Further and further back the woman stood and in her hand, that was not the one she used to fan away the dust, was a yellow piece of paper torn messily and unevenly from some borrowed legal pad and on that paper scrawled with a black and easily smudged pen was a letter to this woman from the man who at that time was driving away as fast as he could but before that moment had spent much time and sacred little moments with her.

Behind her was the sea and it shimmered in a summer sun which suddenly felt less warm and full than it had just minutes ago. On her face, there were sunglasses covering up half of her cheeks and which hid from the world her eyes, which (if anybody had seen that day) were deep and wide and cold like a wet and dark night beneath a cloudy, starless sky.

In that letter (which he left in her hand before he forever pulled away and into that cloud ahead), there are words of his and of hers and there are memories of times they spent together like the time they walked together in the snow and they both ended up with cold feet but they were still somehow happy and playfully throwing snow at each other into the deep of the night, and there are mentions of fights they had and of nights they spent dancing in his attic room beneath a September moon that was full and was a silver white in the haunting way that only the moon can be. In the letter, he let her know of his pain or at least tried to and wondered if she was a cure or a cause of it. In the letter, there were drips of the mornings they spent together in bed and out, drinking coffee on the porch of that old house that held so much weight and darkness.

He drove away, and as he drove, his throat (although numbed by the wind and the vibrations of his car on the road) tingled and burned. As he fled, foot down and eyes trying to stay dry, that feeling in his throat spread its twisting fingers deep into his chest and shoulders and behind his ears. Tentacles of ache spun as he tried to move on hoping that whatever panic, whatever deep and holy gloom was now creeping within him would slowly fade as he kept south and away from that pull off and dirty white car and that girl with whom he had cried and laid and stepped into the frigid and spinning waves of that grey and vast sea.

He left that place and he left her, leaving only a letter in her hand, some holes in the wall from where his pictures and posters once hung and a closet emptier than anything she had ever seen.

He was not sure there would be a response to what he had written, he was not sure she would ever speak or write or think of him again, and so he dragged on down towards a desert and some peaks that he would have to brave before he could rest again, and even when he did cross those places of dirt and rock, even when he did eventually rest he knew that when he was laid down for the night, instead of sleep only memories and more splinters of her and that grey place would come as he stared naked up at the ceiling fan or whatever thing there would be to stare angstily at on the ceiling of whichever beat down room he would eventually rent for the night.

LIGHTNING

There is a lightning in my head; a thunderous throbbing and there are swirling, squiggling sparks when I shut my tired eyes. The sound of the fluorescent lights in this room fills my head; that dreadful and sickening buzzing vibrates the liquid and mass between my ears to the point of what seems like a boil. My hands, which appear blurry and unreal as I look at them held in front of my face, tremble and there is a cut on the back of my hand from where I don't know. My bed is ice and the sheets are hard with cold as I try to crawl across this thing; this cushioned and lonely place of rest, that is much too big for a single person like myself, looking for water or something to quench my desert mouth and its wretched thirst. My body is bruised and beaten and there are places that ache and creak and crack with each and every slow movement of this vessel which at this point never really seems to be fully awake or mobile. The kitchen is but ten paces away but seems much further and the coffee and the cups in the cabinet are sure to be but a straining reach away. I know the water will only take minutes to boil, minutes that seem to take dragging hours and eternity as I sit and squint at the kettle trying to will it to heat up faster. Caffeine, my drug of choice (well one of my drugs of choice, the one I feel the least guilty about consuming) awaits and I know that it and a solid breakfast and a glass of water and some ibuprofen and possibly a hot shower are the only things that will cure this stinging, flashing fire behind my eyes. But I can't get out of bed; the thing I need to get out of bed is out of my bed and in order to get it I need to leave my bed, but I can't do that without this thing. I need my remedy; my boost; my will and my way to escape the tingling soreness and the reaching claws of sleep and laziness. I feel at the dry and sleep-scum caked edges of my mouth a craving for the deep black color and that hot, acidic tickle of my medicine slipping down my throat and seeping across my bones. What will soon be steam and the preparation from which it will twist calls to me from its place in the kitchen and I can almost hear the rattling of the silverware in the drawers.

There is an earthquake in my head; a wretched shaking of the windows and walls, and I may have the cure; the antidote to my pulsating and pixelated world if I can just make it to where my savior sits still and perfect in the cabinet.

LIGHTS CHANGE

He recently changed his alarm from six am to six fifteen am.

Those fifteen minutes are sweet and somehow make a large difference in his morning.

Although he has less time to get ready now, it seems as though the time is slower and just a tiny bit easier; he has had more rest and can feel it in his movements. Six am feels like the crack of dawn (and is often even before that as the days get shorter and darker) but six fifteen is much more manageable (even though lately as he gets up and gets ready for work, the house is dark and cold and outside is even darker and colder).

It seems there are no stars these days, at least not that he can ever see. With the changing of the time from six to six fifteen something changed within him, the strict rigidity of his daily routine and of those tasks he must do to keep himself sane during the daily grind began to fade.

He stopped showering in the morning, he has started showering at night if he showers at all (which he has been doing less and less as time has dragged on since the day he changed his alarm). He has stopped shaving and he now has a quarter-inch-thick, stubbly, reddish-brown beard which is patchy on his cheeks but more or less full everywhere else, especially on his neck in fact (if he cared about the way his beard looked, which he doesn't) he may have to trim the hair on his neck more often than that on his face because of the difference in thickness. He has started to wear the same clothes each day and has stopped packing a lunch or really bringing any food to work with him at all. He expected, when he stopped bringing a lunch and snacks, (that he previously thought were sources of energy throughout his day) to feel more lethargic because of the removal of said supposed energy giving supplements but has yet to really feel any difference in his energy or lack thereof at all. He also expected to feel some hunger pains or stomach spasms or to have a dry mouth or a gurgling gut; he expected to be hungrier and to feel all of those aches that come with hunger, but he hasn't felt any of that really.

With all of this change he merely experienced an internal blankness. He feels as if the inside of his body is painted beige.

He now has so much extra time in the morning due to the fact that he is no longer showering nor shaving nor packing a lunch and because he just picks up his clothes from wherever they were left on the floor when he took them off the night before. In the first couple days of having all of this extra time in the morning (even with the additional fifteen minutes of sleep that he has been getting thanks to his changing of the time on the alarm) he didn't really know what to do, so he just lay in his bed and looked up at the ceiling which was nearly invisible in the blackness of the night. He has never been able to fall asleep after having been awakened (especially when that by which he is awakened is something as jarring and shrill as an alarm) and so while one may think that he would simply fall asleep while lying there in the dark of his white walled room, he simply cannot and thus ended up just simply staring into the never-ending dark in front of his waking eyes.

And actually, the sound which his alarm makes isn't really as shrill or jarring as the sound of a conventional alarm clock. His alarm clock came with the option for him to program in a song and then use that song as the sound of the alarm instead of the painful beeping of most other alarms. And he did use that setting and he programmed his favorite song at the time into his alarm clock and was actually kind of excited to wake up for work the next morning because he would be waking to his favorite song instead of that fetid beeping which he has been waking up to for as long as he has been waking up to anything (these were the days when he was waking up at six am). And but on the morning of the day after the night on which he programmed his favorite song into his alarm, his awakening (while less rude and jolting than normal) was still rather uncomfortable and jarring and overall not really enjoyable. He was still pulled, as if by his ankles from a warm house into a frigid snow, out of sleep. Even with his favorite song playing beside his head, he was still not really very excited to wake up. And over time, in the last month or so since he set his favorite song as his alarm, not only has he continued to feel not very excited to get up but that song (which he did once truly adore) has become something which makes him shudder. Having that song as his alarm has made said song not only no longer his favorite but having to hear it every morning in the way he has to hear it has completely and utterly ruined the song for him, he hates that song now and no longer listens to it.

In fact, the other day as he was driving home from work and listening to the radio, said once favorite, now hated song came on the radio station he was listening to and as the song started soft and slow, he has the sensation that he was being torn from sleep even though he was already awake. The sound of the song gave him that horrid feeling of being awakened and having to get up and go somewhere he would rather not go, day after day. That night he changed his alarm, and set it for fifteen minutes later than it had been before.

And so now his alarm clock is a thorn in his mind in the morning and he can't really enjoy his favorite song anymore, in fact his once favorite song is now painful for him to hear. And this morning when he woke up he simply didn't get out of bed. He didn't bother to call in sick and he didn't even bother to snooze or stop his alarm, he just lay there in bed staring up at the sunlit ceiling. He lay there for hours, unmoving, listening to his alarm come back on every ten minutes, that wretched and twangy sound of that mix of notes and soft voices which used to be something nice but is now so not.

At around nine am he got up and walked to the bathroom, naked and foggy eyed. Maybe he should've called into work to let them know he wasn't coming in but he didn't and he didn't really care if he lost his job because of his so called unauthorized absence, and as he walked on the lint and hair littered cheap wood floor of his apartment to the gritty and sticky stained floor grey tile floor of his bathroom, he couldn't really think of a single thing that he did care about.

And there was a certain freedom in being completely devoid of passion for anything; a sigh of relief in not caring whether or not he had a job, if his alarm was still buzzing in the background, if he lived or died. There was a simple silence in his head; a moment of clarity, nothing mattered and that was good.

Things went on and he brushed his teeth and as he spat a dollop of half bloody, half toothpaste spit into the sink he remembered that his fridge was mostly empty and that he needed eggs and coffee and orange juice and turkey for his sandwich at lunch. He also needed more toilet paper (as he was on his last roll) and coffee filters and soap for the kitchen and maybe a chocolate bar.

So, then after finishing brushing his teeth and lazily looking at himself in the mirror for longer than he maybe should have he got dressed in the clothes that were waiting nicely for him there on the cold floor beside his bed and stumbled out of his front door onto the street, headed to the grocery store.

The store is only a ten minute walk from his house and although he usually drives there he decided not to do so this morning because for one he knew his car was low on gas and he didn't want to spend the money to fill the tank and for two he figured he wasn't in any rush since he wasn't going to work and really had nothing else to do for the rest of the day other than eat and sleep and maybe take a long, hot shower.

The sunken looking sky above his neighborhood, and maybe the whole world, was a white dirtied by a clinging brown haze. The sky looked like the snow on a city street three days after it has finished snowing, filthy and slushy and really good for nothing but soaking one's socks and being a real pain for everybody trying to go about their business as usual. In contrast with the wintery sky, it is hot out and muggy like a rarely cleaned steam room at a gym.

It's not that he really minds the weather or notices the color or particular dreariness of the sky, but the fact that it looked cold out but was actually rather hot and humid upset him a bit because he was wearing thick wool socks and as he walked to the grocery store his feet began to sweat and he could feel his toes become clammy and he knew that when he got home from the grocery store and took off his shoes that there would be a thick and grainy type of smell from his feet that he would have to somehow deal with. Along with the wool socks he is wearing a thick jacket, that would usually be a good fit in terms of temperature for a day which looks like today but because of the heat he is practically boiling in his jacket. He doesn't want to take it off because he doesn't want to have to carry it but having it on is a throbbing, slow sort of agony even with the zipper down.

He is almost to the store now and the sky is a swath of burlap stretched across the top of the earth.

There is a stoplight and he is there now, waiting on one side to cross to the other. There is a button which is a silver and reflects a warped image of his torso back at him as he looks down at it and reaches to press it. He never really knows if this button does anything because no matter if he presses the button ten times or not at all his is pretty sure that the light will take the same amount of time to turn. He thinks with a removed sort of indifferent distain, that the button is there to give the illusion to the person who is waiting at the light that they have some semblance of control over what the stoplight does; that button is there to give the little impatient thing the idea that they have the power; that the city and all of the beeping, exhaust spewing cars will turn on a dime or not for them. But he, the detached man waiting blankly to be allowed to walk across the road, isn't fooled by the ruse of the button. He knows he has no jurisdiction over the flashing red, yellow or green; no say in the color of the clouds.

And the worst part is that there are no cars on the street, no traffic anywhere in sight. It is the middle of the morning in the middle of the work week in the middle of a city in which there is very little unemployment. There is nobody around, yet the lights still change every minute; unaware that they are doing so for nobody much at all. He is here now and there is a neon orange hand held forward towards him, telling him to stop and wait. But there is no traffic to wait for and no danger in crossing the road, just structure in place for the sake of order; robotic, unfeeling systems operating at their best capacity, organizing an empty city, making sure that there are no crashes between the cars that are not there.

And across the city in the office buildings and the houses and the mechanic shops and the traffic control centers and the prison guards in their offices cased in bullet proof glass, the people whittle away like gears on a machine built without an off switch, and now today the man who recently changed his alarm decides to walk across the street even though the machine that he is supposed to listen to, that blinking slave to instruction, says he shouldn't.

THE MACHINE

The machine which makes the assembly line is made of a raised metal shelf in the middle of which is a constantly starting and stopping, black and ancient seeming belt (ancient seeming in regards to the worn-down look of the black [now grey] color of said belt). Said belt has crates upon crates of bottles that are slowly filled, checked for cracks, labeled, capped and finally packaged into the backs of idling semi-trucks that (the trucks) are then sent off to deliver said freshly packaged bottles to grocery stores and diners and airport restaurants and gas stations and other low to medium quality food establishments that sell whatever it is inside of these bottles (which, the stuff within these bottles, is a brown sticky-sweet liquid that is marketed as refreshing and thirst quenching but is not only not either of those but in fact leaves the mouth of whomever has drunk said beverage dry and gummy in a sickly way).

The assembly line is waist high on him (and on most people who work in the factory, due to the fact that most of those who work with him are his same age and height and class and all have the same beat down and prematurely old looking faces, posture and overall demeanor). While at work he has the option to stand (with his feet atop a black mat that is supposedly put on the floor to add a certain amount of comfort for his feet and cushion between him and the concrete floor but which doesn't really do much for him in terms of comfort at all as, if he chooses to stand up [which he does about every other day], he feels extremely stiff and sore in his legs and feet and sometimes [after a twelve hour shift] his toes will even begin to tingle and go numb) or to sit on a backless stool (which is somewhat more comfortable than standing for the entirety of the day but which [sitting on the stool] results in him ending up in a hunched over position for most of the day, which itself (his hunched position) leads to him having severe back and neck pain at the end of the days on which he has chosen to sit). That's to say that there is not really a good option for him in terms of his position while at work; i.e. no matter what he does (sit or stand, slouched or stiff) at the end of his shift (which is scheduled to be twelve hours but often goes for at least an hour [if not three] longer) he will be basically beat to shit and nearly unable to walk.

His job is to pull a lever down, hold said lever down for no more than three seconds but no less than two, and then pull said lever back up. He is paid to pull the lever down and when said lever is pulled down so comes down a square column onto whichever crate of bottles is directly below said column and directly in front of him and the lever. The square column (that moves up and down with the lever) holds bottle caps and when lined up correctly with a crate-full of bottles, places said bottle caps onto said bottles in said crate. In the no-more-than three, no-less-than two seconds during which he waits to pull the lever back up after putting it down, the caps are placed on the bottles. When the lever is raised up, the square column raises revealing caps on all of the previously uncapped bottles, then the belt moves one notch down the line. The job of guy next to him (who is one of the oldest men working in the factory) is to check that all of the caps on all of the bottles in each crate are attached to the tops of the bottles correctly and that there are no extra caps in between the bottles that accidently fell from the square column. The man next to the man who pulls the lever has a dangerous job because if he is not careful and quick whilst looking for stray bottle caps (which are more common than not in each crate) his fingers can get caught in the grid of plastic of the crate and broken or ripped off or torn apart as the unforgiving assembly line moves down another notch.

During the time the man who pulls the lever has worked at the factory (which amounts to about four years) he has seen over twelve people get their fingers caught in the grid of the crate and pulled apart as the belt moves on; those who lose fingers at the job are sent off with an extra day of pay in their pockets and a pink slip and are replaced with a new fresh-faced and ten-fingered worker within an hour. Those who lose fingers rarely ever come back to work at the factory and the very few who do leave within a couple of days. It seems that the loss of a finger is the breaking point for people at his factory, once they have been maimed by the assembly line, they can't seem to commit themselves to the monotony of lever pulling or cap snatching (as its colloquially called) knowing that great pain and extremity loss is potentially around every corner.

The lever puller considers himself lucky that (for one) he has all of his fingers and that (for two) he has never had to work as a cap snatcher and that (for three) he has a job, unlike so many people out there, outside the factory walls.

He gets two ten minute breaks per day and fifteen minutes for lunch. Those workers who are not cigarette smokers rarely get full breaks or lunch because the supervisors (who are always carefully watching) don't think it right for someone to do anything but eat, use the bathroom, or drink a cup or two of coffee or water during the breaks; i.e. there is no tolerance for sleeping or just sitting and staring into space. That is unless you are smoking a cigarette, somehow the supervisors (who are always watching) allow the workers to smoke the entirety of one cigarette during the breaks. Thus, the workers who have worked at the factory for long enough to catch onto the rules of the breaks, all smoke cigarettes and the smartest of the workers (a group in which the lever puller is included) smoke the brand of cigarettes which take the longest to burn out (a brand which coincidently is owned by the same parent company of the company that owns the bottling factory).

During his breaks, the lever puller, stares off into a sky which is most often grey with clouds and haze and smoke, but instead of seeing what he is looking at he sees white letters on a red background. These dirty white (nearly grey with age and filth) letters, while he is pulling the lever up and down, hang right in front of his face on a sign with a bright red background that reads *"hold lever down for no more than three seconds, but no less than two"* and are so ingrained in his head that it is these letters that he sees when he closes his eyes and in his dreams during the few hours he has to sleep.

He can't really remember a time when those letters weren't present, they are everywhere he looks. After many hours on the line, staring at the sign, the letters sometimes start to change shape or rearrange themselves into gibberish and when the letters start to move about and make sounds and scream little high pitched screams, he takes one of his ten-minute breaks and smokes one of his slow burning cigarettes while staring at the blank and empty infinity of sky beyond the smokestacks and the powerlines.

Today is a good day so far, the sun is for some reason low in the sky and is shining perfectly through a skylight onto the back of his neck as he pulls the lever down, waits, and then pulls it back up. The letters are behaving themselves, they are staying in place: silent and tame as they should be, for now at least. He thinks he has been at work now for around four hours in this hot, moist and dark room but it is nearly impossible to tell as there are no clocks on the floor of the factory and watches are not allowed. The walls of the factory are made of brick and the roof is made of a rusted and rippled metal which creaks and cracks in the wind rain and snow. In the ceiling there is a single skylight (as per a fairly new government regulation which states that factories must have at least one window) and sometimes, if the sun is low in the sky, sun will shine through onto the floor of the factory; a beam of golden dust in a rectangle of brick and darkness and sweat, as it is doing today. But most times the skylight dully glows, a simple reminder to those inside the factory that there is something outside of those brick walls, although even with that reminder it is too easy to forget.

And today is good because he has the sun at his neck and the warmth from that sun is something he had almost forgotten. Sometimes the monotony of the lever pulling and the slow heartbeat-esque thumping and cranking of the belt wipes his mind clean of all but the letters, the hot darkness and the slight burning in his lever pulling arm that (like the letters) seems to permanently haunt him. But the warmth of the sunshine on the back of his neck, on a patch of dry and aching skin, reminds him of grass and of wind and of days spent in the sun and these little, holy, blurring moments in a mind full of ash and letters. The warmth takes him away (be it ever so briefly) from the factory and the lever and the clank, clank, clank of the turning machine.

Another crate of bottles passes onto the old (in age, but newly hired) cap snatcher beside him. The old man searches the bottom of the crate for misplaced caps and finds one stuck in the bottom of the plastic grid of the crate. The old man reaches into the bottom of the crate but he reaches in too late, his aged body not agile enough to snatch the cap in enough time, and as the old man reaches the belt moves on trapping not one but two of the old man's fingers beneath the grid of the crate. The old man fingers, under the weight of one hundred bottles filled to the brim and capped, do not stand a chance and are easily crushed to a pulp of pulsating blood and splintered bone shards.

The lever puller cannot look toward the old man for he has to pull the lever but he knew as soon as it happened what was happening, he has heard that crunch of breaking bone and the slow squirt of hot blood many times before. There is nothing he can do for the old man, soon a floor manager will come to take away the old man and give to him an extra day of pay, a pink slip and a push down the road. The lever puller is sure that within an hour another man, hopefully a younger man this time, will be beside him snatching the caps from underneath the bottles.

And maybe he (the lever puller) will one day be moved to the position of cap snatcher, maybe he too will get hurt somehow, maybe his letters (those twists of grey plastic) will someday eat him alive or maybe he will keep smoking his slow burning cigarettes and staring up at the sky during his breaks until he simply just fades away, maybe he will keep pulling that lever down, waiting, and pulling it back up, until he simply falls apart into dust and swirls about in the humid air, and is replaced (within the hour) by another.

The Man on the Radio

At 8:47pm on a Tuesday in late August, three people from the same family in three different locations around the same city are listening to the same radio station through different radios. On that radio station a man is singing opera.

One of the people in the family listening to the radio is the only son in the family and he (the son) is seated on, with his legs hanging over the edge of, a balcony that is attached to a porch, both of which are made of burnt reddish stones held together with a grey and grainy concrete. On the porch, there is a circular, green-black metal table with one, also green-black metal chair, beside it. On top of the table is an ashtray, which is square in shape but has a circular indentation made for the reception of ash and cigarettes within it, although at the moment (8:47pm on a Tuesday) the ashtray is completely clean (as the son's father would often say 'the ashtray is clean enough to eat out of', although the son nor the father nor most other people would ever actually attempt to eat out of the ashtray even when it is as clean as it is now).

The porch, on the balcony of which, the son sits, is attached to an apartment owned by the son and is on the 8th floor of a 14-story building that (the building as well as the apartment as well as the porch as well as the balcony) has a wonderful view of the city in which all of the family members listening to the radio in various parts of the same city reside.

The son heard, earlier in the day (at work) that the sun was supposed to set at around 8:59pm, and although he has this time in mind for when the sun will disappear from view, he is sitting on the balcony because he intends to watch the sunset, and although it is not yet (technically) time for the sun to set, the sunset has begun.

The day was cloudy in a way in which the clouds did not exactly cover the sky but were present in any direction one looked. The clouds today were not those sun-blocking, flat looking, grey blankets of rain but were those castle-esque bubbly and towering white clouds that look soft, inviting and somehow regal in a heavenly and otherworldly sense.

Beyond the lights and the street sounds and the catcalls and the bass-heavy music and the subway-rattles from beneath the ground, there is a sky and in that sky, directly in the forward line of sight of the son, there is one of those cotton-cathedral-in-the-sky types of clouds. And because of the sunset (or more, because of the colorful precursor to the actual and literal setting of the sun) the rightmost side of the massive cloud in the sky is glowing a mouthwateringly and awe inspiring shade of gold.

The son on the balcony, staring at the sun-lit, vaporous, colossus in the sky, is wearing a tailored, royal blue suit with a pearl-white button down shirt. He is barefoot and the air between his toes feel exceptionally cool and refreshing because his feet are still somewhat damp from being crammed into shoes and socks inside of a fancy but nonetheless stuffy office all day. Earlier in the day the son was wearing a skinny tie that matched his suit in both color and texture, but that tie is no longer around his neck and is laying, carefully folded on the back of the green-black metal chair, beside the table on the porch.

The son's radio, which is stainless steel plated and has a three-foot-long [also stainless steel] protruding antenna that extends up towards the technicolor sky, sits beside the son (on the balcony) and on the other side of the son (the right side to be exact) there is a slightly-blue-tinted, tall, glass cup that contains a clear liquid, which (the cup) is half empty.

The radio plays a man singing opera but the station (or possibly the recording of the man singing) is fuzzy in an old timey way, i.e. the sound is the audible equivalent of sepia. There is little to no background music and the man on the radio's voice is deep in a full-bodied way.

The song reminds him of a memory (or maybe it is a fantasy wished for, for so long that it has become easily confused as memory) of his currently long dead mother seated on the lap of his currently still alive father in the backyard of the house in which he and his sister grew up. And in this memory/fantasy there is music playing and everyone is wearing summery clothes and the sun is soft and warm and the green of the grass and the red of his mother's painted nails and lips seem to be electrified in a sort of melancholic and slightly haunting way.

Meanwhile, while the same radio station plays on a light, creamy blue colored radio next to a kitchen sink in a house in the upper-middle class suburbs across the city from the son's apartment building, a woman (the daughter, the sister of the man on the balcony) leans forward with her elbows resting against the edge of the basin of the sink (which is a vintage, white porcelain). The kitchen is attached to the living room of the house though a door-less doorway and the living room connects to not only the kitchen but to the area of the house which contains the bedrooms as well as the front door to the house. The living room connects to the bedrooms via a hallway that has the usual upper middle class style framed pictures of the two children that live in the house in their various school pictures throughout the various grades that they (the children of the daughter) have already passed through, as well as the almost prerequisite, professionally taken photos of the family in all white clothing standing on too-green grass on a vacation to a warmer and much more aesthetically beautiful place than the city in which they live. There is also (at the end of the hallway, next to the closet that contains the hot water heater and beside the door that leads to the master bedroom in which the daughter and her husband sleep) a picture of a couple (the daughter and her husband) on their wedding day, in which (the picture) the daughter and her husband look both much younger and also much happier than they do now. The living room connects to the front of the house and the subsequent out-side world through a tall dark, wooden door.

There are two windows in the kitchen of the house in which the daughter lives and one of those windows is directly above and centered around the kitchen sink in front of which the daughter stands and on the edge of the basin of which the daughter leans.

The daughter is drinking a glass of medium price and medium quality white wine from a wine glass which she holds in a slightly trembling hand. She is thinking about smoking a cigarette but she won't because for one she doesn't have any and for two she quit smoking cigarettes ten years ago when she was pregnant with her first child and for three because she knows that if somehow she did find a cigarette and decided to un-quit that when her husband came home that he would make some comment on the fact that she smelled like cigarettes and even though the comment that her husband would hypothetically make would not be nefarious in intent, she would take it that way because that is just where her marriage is at this point.

Basically, both she and her husband are waiting for reasons to be mad at each other, because they already are (mad at each other) but don't really know why. Basically, both she and her husband are feeling like something is wrong between them; their marriage is stagnating; standing still; starting to rot and mold from the inside, and they are both desperately looking for reasons why this is happening and are picking these petty fights and are making up these supposed offenses in order to try to explain and justify to themselves why their marriage has reached this place of stagnation without any real problems that either of them can think of.

But her husband is still at work or is doing (something with) somebody after work and she is still thinking of a cigarette but not in a way that means she wants a cigarette, merely she is thinking about the feeling of smoking a cigarette and of how nice it was to just sit outside on the stoop of her house that she lived in when she was in college and smoke one of those cigarettes as she watched the sunset.

The wine smells slightly sour (but that's how it is supposed to smell) and she takes a big sip that stings the back of her throat and makes her stomach tingle.

Her glass is half empty and the bottle (from which the liquid in the glass came) is beside the sink (and is also half empty) and anyways she has another bottle in the pantry above the fridge that she could (and might) crack open later tonight if her husband doesn't come home before the sun goes down (which it should be doing soon).

Her children are asleep in their respective rooms and the sprinkler in the front yard is on and the water that is spraying from the sprinkler looks like it is made out of gold because of the light that is hitting it from the sunset behind her house. The glowing droplets shoot out in slow motion pellets of liquid and sheen. There is something pure about sprinklers and as the radio (which is still playing the man singing the opera which, the song, is now swelling to the crescendo) plays on she remembers and thinks deeper into that memory of her mother and father in her sepia sun of childhood and she remembers that in the background of that memory that there was a sprinkler going in the grass behind the table at which her parents sat (her mother on her father's lap).

The crickets outside provide a sort of deep beat to the opera music and the glass in her hand reverberates with her heart that is beating rather slowly.

Across the kitchen from the sink there is a window that looks out onto the side yard of the house and in that side yard there is a tall tree with grey, thick, bark beside which sits a faded and frail looking wooden bench on which she (the daughter) has never sat.

She takes a big gulp of her wine and closes her eyes to embrace that sweet and rancid sting. That bench beside the tree is the Sunday she has always wanted but has never had. That bench beside the tree is a picnic on a perfect red and white checkered picnic blanket that her husband has never planned. That bench beside the tree is the trip to the country that she has never taken. That bench beside the tree is that light blue sun dress that she has never worn because she doesn't feel pretty anymore, well it's not that she doesn't feel pretty its more that she isn't made to feel pretty and is treated by her kids and by her husband as something extremely important but not pretty.

And but that is why she doesn't feel pretty or happy or really anything but lament filled and void of feeling besides lament when she looks at that bench in the yard because sometimes she has been treated like a thing for so long that she starts to think of herself as a thing and that thing that she thinks of herself as is old and is tired and sometimes wishes to just be thrown to the curb so it (the thing that she has become) can finally rest. And really her children treat everything and everyone as things and she can't really blame them because they are not fully formed and they are still learning what respect and what compassion are, but her husband should know better than to just grunt a thank you when she has made dinner even after she has worked a full day.

That bench by the tree is the promised tomorrow that not only will not come but has never and will never exist.

The man on the radio has finished the song with a held note so deep and heart-wrenching that the hairs on her arm have stood up and in response to the emotional end of a song that she never really intended to actually listen to, she has drained the rest of her wine glass. And now with a shaking and worn hand with blood red painted nails, she reaches for the bottle by the sink as she continues to blurrily look at the bench beside the tree and think of what could have been and compare it to what sadly is.

The song is over, but the radio show is not and tonight this show is showcasing a particular male opera singer from a certain time and place, whom, the opera singer, has a certain amount of clout among other male opera singers from the same certain time and place but not much (clout or fame) among many others.

This man on the radio was young when this particular recording was recorded but he is old now. He (the father) now sits in a room that is kept at a womb like warmth and that smells faintly of mothballs and cleaning supplies in a converted apartment building (on the other end of the city as his daughter's house) that now (the apartment building) acts as a retirement home. He (the old man, the father, the singer, the man on the radio) has lived in this retirement home now for around five years and the room is finally starting to feel comfortable. When he first moved into this place (or more when he was first moved into this place) there were smells that he could not get used to and the room always somehow seemed out of order and eerie in a way that he could not quite put his finger on, but that eerie-ness and that out-of-order-ness is now gone and he is not sure if those feelings are gone because he has finally accepted and gotten used to this place or because he is now too sick and forgetful to really be able to notice what he used to.

The man on the radio sings in a melancholic and slow way that makes the man in the room's arm hair slightly stand out and goose bumps spread across the back of his neck.

The old man's room is perfectly square and there are no paintings or post-cards or pictures or posters on the walls. The walls are painted a yellow that (according to the interior design team that interior designed the rooms of this particular retirement home) is (the yellow of the former singer's room), supposed to be both calming and gender-neutral (the former is to make the residents of the home calm [obviously] and the latter is so those who work at the home don't have to deal with choosing rooms for their respective male and female guests according to the respective [supposed] gender specific colors and can [the retirement home staff] just throw the new arrivals into whichever room happens to be un-occupied because [since all of the rooms are painted yellow] all of the rooms are for everybody and therefor for any-body and even furthermore suited for quick and painless [on the part of the retirement home staff and the residents that die in their sleep] turnaround).

The old man's room has a window that would be looking out onto a vast cityscape and a sunset that is now in full bloom, but the curtains (which are a slightly lighter shade of yellow than the walls) are closed and if you asked the old man what time of day it is he would most likely think it was the morning.

In the room, besides the yellow walls, the window and the lighter-than-the-walls-yellow-curtains there is a bed, a desk, two chairs and a TV and in the short hallway between the room and the larger hallway that connects to the rest of the retirement home, there is a bathroom inside of which there is a toilet and shower. The desk is made of plastic painted to look like it is made of wood and the chairs in the room are black with green-black cushions that (the chairs) are beside the old man's bed and are for visitors of the old man (of which the man has many and frequent; including his son, his daughter and his two grandchildren). The TV is mounted on a steel platform that itself is screwed into the wall on the top right corner of the wall that is opposite the man's bed. The bathroom of the man's room is white, unlike the walls of the rest of the room. Everything is white in the bathroom except for a stainless-steel pole that is screwed into the wall beside the toilet to aid the elderly while using the bathroom. The shower has a chair in it for the man to sit down in while in the shower, in case he feels faint or sick or just tired during the shower.

The bed in the old man's room is one that can fold up and down (using electricity and a remote that hangs within the old man's grasp). The bed has crispy, almost crunchy, white sheets and a thin knitted blanket that is also white and is folded into fourths and has been placed on top of the old man's feet which (the old man's feet) are always cold these days. The rest of the old man is beneath the sheet and beneath the sheet he is wearing white socks with grey soles that go halfway up his calves, navy boxer shorts that are worn and saggy to the point that the elastic waistband has pretty much disintegrated and a white t shirt that is slightly yellowed around the collar from age and dirt and sweat and just overall overuse. The sheet is pulled up to just above the old man's (white t shirt adorned) navel and his arms (which are frail but still have the hints of what used to be slightly bulging and well maintained muscles) are on top of the sheet and are holding a matte black radio (with a too-large-looking antennae) on top of the sheet and are (his arms) balancing it (the radio) on the man's (not fat but saggy and soft with old age) stomach.

The song on the radio (sung by a much younger and much more alive version of the man who now rests in a slightly inclined bed) is from one of the sadder albums that the old man made and reminds the old man of a time when he and his long dead wife were in the back of the house that they had lived in together when the children were young and during the time that he had released this sadder than usual of albums. He in part released this sad album because he had been distraught during that time because he has suspected that his now long dead, but then very much alive and rosy cheeked, wife had been cheating on him. And he had been right and it was in fact that morning in the sepia sun of yesterday that he had found out how terribly right he had been.

He had been outside smoking a cigarette and drinking coffee with cream and two sugars in it out of a cup the color of which closely matched that of the liquid inside of it and he had been reading the arts section of the local newspaper and looking to see if inside of that arts section there was a review of his new album (which there had been and the review had been complimentary) but he hadn't been able to read the review that morning because his then alive wife had come out in one of those sundresses that always made his fingers ache for the touch of her and she had sat down in the seat across from him with her legs crossed and she leaned forward and she took the cigarette from his mouth with one milk white and red nail painted hand and she had taken a long drag of his cigarette from a mouth that was adorned with thick lips that were painted the same color as her fingernails and in her exhale along with the smoke and the slightest hint of something sweet like cherries, a confession, well more of a matter of fact statement, had slipped from her mouth and his suspicions had been confirmed.

And he had cleared his throat and he had put the newspaper down and he had taken a long sip of his coffee (even though it was nearly too hot to drink) and he had sighed. And he had begun to try and say something in response but he wasn't really sure how to respond and at the moment of the first sound of the first word of his response the back door of the house had flung open and the children (the boy and the girl, his son and his daughter) had come tumbling (as children do) out onto the grass and his now long dead wife had hopped up onto his lap and had placed one of her hands on the back of his neck in an effort to demonstrate to the children that everything was fine even though everything was not and between him and his then alive wife it never really would be (fine) again. But there was no need to involve the children in the mess of their marriage at the time and he understood that so he went along with his wife on his lap and he hated himself for sort of leaning forward into her embrace and he sort of melted inside anytime she touched him and her soft and always hot to the touch skin made him want to drool and even though he was mad and hurt beyond belief he had played happy and had watched as his daughter turned on the sprinkler and continued to watch as his children played in the falling water.

And things were good then even when they were falling apart. The sun was warm and the sky was clear of clouds and birds and planes and haze. And the backyard was filled with laughter from the children and warmth from the space between his body and his wife's and music, his music, sort of stumbled out from the kitchen where the tape of the new album had been playing and even though he felt broken and somehow frozen even in the mid-morning sun he had felt also, somehow, whole then.

And the song which played that day is now playing on the radio.

The son on the balcony has finished whatever clear liquid was in the glass beside him.

The sun has begun to set and the colors that were once pastel are now vivid and red and the sky before him, beneath him and all around him seems to be aflame. And the song on the radio reminds him of that day that his sister taught him to play in the sprinkler and of the way his parents looked, so happy, whispering to each other as they shared a cigarette, his mother on his father's lap. And as the sunset looks like a bomb blast stuck frozen in the sky, the son thinks fondly of those times in the backyard when life was simpler and he longs for simpler times like those as he absently swings his legs that hang hundreds of feet over the side walk.

And the daughter has finished half of her second glass of wine and is still blurrily staring at that bench beside the tree and her husband is still not home and her children are still asleep and there is still another bottle of wine in the pantry above the fridge and her fingernails are still painted red like her mother's were that day long ago. She remembers the sun and the water from the sprinkler and how sweet her parents looked together at that table beside the lawn. And she remembers her father looking pained and she thinks the pain most likely came from being so happy that he just couldn't really contain himself. And she takes the radio from beside the sink in one hand and her glass of wine in the other and she clumsily walks out the front door of the house, barefoot, headed towards that bench to lay on her back with her eyes closed and listen to a song sung by her father that reminds her of better and easier times when the only concern in the world was how fast one could run through the sprinkler and if one could avoid the water.

And as another crescendo is reached the old man, listening to his younger self come through the radio on his lap as if through a fold in time, takes a rasping breath that is not followed by another.

Morning

There is a room.

Inside of that room, in the upper middle section of the west-most wall there is a window. That window is slightly open (about a quarter inch open to be exact) and this window is not the kind of window that folds out to open but is the kind of window that sort of slides onto half of itself to open, and is currently slid in the way described above to the size of opening also described above.

Outside the window there are trees and these trees have white bark with dark grey wrinkly looking scars and grooves throughout and across them. And on these trees with the white, scar covered bark, leaves hang from the tips of thin and brittle branches and these leaves are a butterscotch orange yellow that gives whomever is lucky enough to look at them a mouthwatering tingle in the same way that seeing (or hearing) an ice cream truck does. That is to say that the candy leaves of these trees are beautiful and delicious in such a way that their very beauty and deliciousness transcends sight and is able to touch other senses the way only truly beautiful and delicious things can.

Now, inside the room, which contains the window that looks out onto the honey leaves of the trees, which, the trees, are now slightly swaying in a breeze that is most likely crisp and bites with a cold nip, there are two lovers and these lovers lay in a bed on the floor of the room. The floor is covered in a dusty grey and shaggy carpet, and which, the bed, is a queen size and is sort of slouching in the same way that over worn shoes slouch, i.e. the bed is pushing out on the sides.

But the lovers in the bed are not worried about it (the bed's) slouching, nor the trees, nor the wonderful leaves, nor the spinning earth, nor nothing really at all but the moment and the warmth that accompanies it. All that matters in this room is that soft white light that is falling, in an almost love struck tumble, through the window and into the room. And in the room the air is warm and sweet in a subtle way. And to the lovers the bed is more comfortable than it usually is and each breath is longer and deeper.

And the lovers are not making love, not now at least. There was love making before, passionate but careful and enjoyable for both parties in a superficial and understandably instinctually satisfying way, but now they lie, still naked in the morning light, the covers pushed down to cover just their feet and this moment, this unmoving eternity of warmth and tenderness, is everything.

One lover is curled around the other's body and the heat, the something special between them and within them is buttery and nearly visible.

The room and maybe the whole earth is silent but for the slight crinkle of a couple of falling golden leaves as they twist and flawlessly fall to the ground.

One or both of the lovers, for a brief second; for a brief lapse in their sleep slow perfection, fear for the fleetingness of this moment, yes, they will have to get up eventually. This daybreak will end; the sun will rise higher and the light will change. Flame will turn from yellow to orange to blue to soot to ash and be swept away with nothing but a breath or a gentle wind. Morning will turn to noon which will turn to afternoon which will turn to evening which will turn to night, all before today becomes something else entirely. The moment that at once seems like forever and no time at all is sure to end, but that thought like the moment and frankly everything else passes from the head (or heads) of the lover (or lovers) who was (or were) thinking it, and things fade as they do, back to something kind and pure, at least for now.

And as the lovers snuggle closer, their toes touching beneath the blanket at the bottom of the bed and the rest of their bodies fresh in the fall air, the wind picks up and more saffron leaves twist off and fall to the dew-wetted ground.

THE MOUNTAIN

The country town in which the girl lives is tiny (population 750) and flat with the exception of one small mountain, which the back yard of her family's house just happens to back up onto. Now some may call this mountain a hill but the townsfolk have decided that this is a mountain on account of its height and the rock face on the north side (that looks very much like a cliff and what kind of hill has a cliff on it) as well as the scraggily and grey trees that cling to the side of the steep rocky sides of the mountain. Her father was an astrologist (before he got sick) and her mother loved the stars (in fact they met at an astrology convention) and they bought the house with the mountain in their backyard so that at night they could look up at the stars, undisturbed by the light and noises from the town around them. The girl was once told that she was conceived on that very hilltop during a meteor shower, although she is not entirely sure as to what "conceived" means.

The girl is called a girl and not a woman because although she is not really either, she feels much more comfortable being a girl than a woman because the pressures and responsibility of being a woman are scary and entirely unappealing to her. She is eleven and has bruises the color of the skin of a smashed pear on her shins from always playing outside; climbing trees and pretending that she is the queen and that all of these pick-up trucks and beat down looking people in the town and in the whole world are hers to command and protect. Her reign is a soft but strict one and she often gets sap on her hands and splinters in between her fingers as she climbs up the trees on the mountainside behind her house.

She never knew her mother as she (her mother) died in childbirth, giving birth to her (the girl) a fact which she does not know (she has always been told that her mother was sick and simply passed away) and her father has raised her on his own ever since.

There is a path that winds up to the mountain top. That path is made of a light brown dirt and from afar looks like a thick, dust filled vein on the mountainside. She and her father have often taken that path to the mountain top and have together looked up at the blackness of space and those cold specks of long dead lights, shining from an infinity away.

But her father is sick now, some wicked thing has mangled his body so that his hands curl up towards his wrists and his speech comes out slurred and slow. He sits now by the window where she has pushed his bed and looks out that window at the rain falling (when it falls) and the birds in the trees on the mountain side when it is dry. Her father has an IV and a monitor that beeps all the time and keeps her up at night, but even in that sleepy state she takes care of him and prepares herself breakfast (she used to prepare him breakfast but he no longer really eats anything but fluid from the needle in his arm and mush which comes in glass containers and smells a sticky sour sweet, like rotten mangos in a hot and humid place). And she does her homework at her father's bedside talking to him as she does; keeping him alert and present for she is afraid that when she doesn't speak and that when she is away at school or outside in the trees, her father is slowly letting go of this world and fading into whatever grey there is beyond our final wet breaths.

She sits now beside her father and his feet are palsied and tangled up so that his toes are curled down enough to almost touch the bottom of his feet, well she can't see his feet now (they are beneath a thin white blanket and covered up with light blue compression socks, but she knows those mangled things are there and it pains her think about it). It pains her to think about her father and his slow, twisted demise; it pains her to think about the mother she never knew, about that woman who bore her and of whom she is half but whom she will never lay with or hug or smell or hear singing in the kitchen.

There are aides who work for her father while she is at school but those aides look at her father with a practiced smile behind which she knows is a certain amount of disgust and numbness. She sees that uncaring touch in the way the nurses feed her father; they spoon in bite after bite of that grey-yellow mush even when her father is whimpering and the dribble drops down his chin. It's as if he is just an animal to them, some pathetic and dying beast; some misshapen burden with whom they must deal, and the worst part is that he is what they think he is. Her father and his distorted limbs make her sick. She does her best to look at him with love, to wipe the milky beads of sweat from his brow with a smile and to treat him with respect but she has begun to despise coming home and having to be around that sickness, that rotting smell of eminent death, that feeling in the air of pain; of vultures circling above, cawing their shrill and evil sounds.

She has started to come home from school a different way; a longer route that takes her over the mountain. She has started to climb the tallest and thinnest looking trees; she has started to hang her legs off of the cliff edge; she has started to howl like some rabid animal at the sky. It's not that she wants to be hurt, but she likes feeling alive; she craves the blood pumping in her ears and that throb in her chest. She needs that rush of air in her lungs, she needs to sprint and jump and spin and fall and get up again. The girl is young and alive and all of this time staring at someone so void of life has driven her nearly mad.

And now her father is sleeping and in his sleep, he is coughing up this black-yellow phlegm and that phlegm is sort of bubbling from his mouth and down onto the grey hospital gown he now wears instead of clothes. She could wipe that goop from his mouth and shirt with one of the white paper towels from the roll kept beside his bed but she won't, she figures that there will be more coughing and phlegm and sickness leaking from the body beside her. So, she turns her chair to the window and looks up at the mountain where her now dead mother and nearly dead father were once young and in love, and she wonders how the stars will look tonight and if her father will be awake and aware enough to look at them with her from that place that will soon most certainly become his deathbed.

MILK

The table is made of wood.

The wood is a light brown and has darker brown striations running through it. On top of the table there are crumbs and thick cracks and bits of food that have been ground into the wood over time. If one were to run their hand over the table, it would not feel completely smooth, it would feel rough in a soft way, callused but cared for. The table is in what the housemates call the 'nook', a multicolored alcove that has two protruding benches connected to the walls. The benches are painted a light blue. The benches have obviously been painted many times and there are scratches in the light blue paint of the benches. In the places that the light blue paint has been scratched away, red paint shows. The whole kitchen could have been painted red at one time, long before they all moved in, nobody knows for sure how many layers of paint lay beneath what is visible. The kitchen is now painted in many different colors, painted at different times by different iterations of the same type of renter of the house; post grad creative types trying to leave their mark on an old beat up house before they move on, into another old house, into another in between place, into an old, beat up world. Some past residents have made a wall in the living room into a blackboard, some others have painted egg shaped birds above all of the doorways. There are housemates that had a kiln in the basement and that kiln forever burnt the smell of baking clay into the house; a light but earthy scent; almost un-noticeable; but always there. The housemates that are in the kitchen now are yet to leave their mark on the house, aside from the mud stains on the grey kitchen floor from one of the housemate's work boots. The mud can be washed away and if it isn't it doesn't really matter because the floor is so dirty with age and filth and mud and food spills that it's impossible to tell the difference if there is some extra mud that hasn't been washed away. The current housemates have yet to make their mark on the old house or on this old world, but they may in time.

There are two windows in the kitchen which look out onto the backyard. One of the windows is open about an inch. Through the opening in the window, a spring breeze slips into the kitchen. With the spring breeze comes the smell of a neighbor mowing their lawn, the smell of fresh flowers just beginning to bloom and the faint smell of ash from something being burned further down the block. The hint of ash in the wind has a chemical taint to it, hinting that what is being burned is trash; bits of chocolate bar wrappers; empty beer cans and plastic wrap that has run its course. It's the kind of smell that accompanies a fire which burns black and twists like a blackberry bush up towards the sky. It's a smell that stings and lingers.

One of the housemates sits at the wooden table in the nook eating an apple. The apple is green and average in size. There is a brown spot on the apple which the housemate is trying to eat around. The apple is the crunchy kind, but not the crunchiest apple that the housemate has ever eaten. The housemate is happy that the apple did not turn out to be one of the grainy ones, the kind of apple that tastes like wet sand and is not satisfying or enjoyable to eat. The apple that the housemate is eating is juicy and the housemate is slurping as they crunch on a large bite.

There is another housemate across the kitchen, standing by the stove. The housemate by the stove is very aware of the crunching and slurping sounds that are being made by the housemate seated in the nook. The stove sits atop an oven that has a dirty, black door with a rectangular see-through slot to look inside when one is cooking something. The stovetop should be white but is covered in spilled tea and bits of egg shells and burnt eggs that have leaked out when a housemate has cracked an egg on the side of a pan but all of the egg hasn't ended up in the pan, it has ended up partially in the pan and partially on the formerly white stovetop. Of the four burners on the stovetop only three work. Of the three working burners one only works sometimes if it is moved directly above where the propane comes in. The two burners on the right side of the stove are the best bet. The housemate by the stove is cooking eggs. The eggs have already been cracked into the pan. The pan was originally red on the bottom, but the drips from what has been cooked in the pan over the past six months have permanently stained the bottom of the pan a dark-brown. The inside of the pan started out as black and is still black, but is currently covered in oil and uncooked eggs.

There are three eggs in the pan. The housemate is trying to cook them just so. The housemate wants the eggs to be runny in the middle but crispy on the outside.

The housemate at the table in the nook is having a hard time eating around the brown spot in the apple.

There is music playing in another room that connects to the kitchen through a door-less doorway. The music is being played through old stereo speakers and it is too quiet to make out the lyrics, but is loud enough to be recognized as music. The song playing through the speakers is on repeat, although neither of the housemates care enough to change the music, and it is too quiet for them to really notice that it is the same song being played over and over, although if they were to listen close enough to the music and realize that the song was in fact on repeat, they would most likely, not bother to change it.

The housemate that is cooking the eggs has become distracted by the dishes in the sink. There always seem to be dishes in the sink, although all housemates say that they always wash their dishes after use. All housemates also agree that whomever is leaving the dishes in the sink, without naming names, needs to wash their dishes. There have been many different plans put into action by the cleaner one of the four housemates to get the messier three housemates to clean their dishes. There have been days of the week assigned to various housemates, days which each housemate must perform a certain cleaning task. That action plan was a failure because it seems there are no consequences if one of the housemates decides not to do their assigned cleaning duty. There is no feasible punishment for the other three housemates to enact on the other housemate who has neglected their duty, so the house remains dirty and the cleaner housemate of the four remains perpetually passive aggressive about the amount that they have to clean up after the dirtier three housemates. The housemate currently by the stove is the clean housemate in the house and the housemate seated in the nook is one of the three remaining dirty housemates, although the housemate seated in the nook would classify themselves as the cleanest of the three dirty housemates.

While the housemate who is cooking the eggs is preoccupied with washing the dishes, they forget about the eggs that are cooking. The yolks of the eggs cook though. There is a chrome toaster in between the sink where the housemate is washing the dishes and the stovetop where the housemate was cooking the eggs before they were distracted by the dirty sink. A piece of burnt toast pops up and out of the chrome toaster and onto the grey, stained floor of the kitchen. The sound of the popping-up toast breaks the concentration of the housemate who was trying to scrape some type of translucent orange crust off of a plate. The housemate puts the plate back into the sink and steps over the burnt toast to check on the eggs. At this point, the eggs have been overcooked and the yolks are completely dry. Not only are the yolks dry and broken, one side of the three-egg blob is way more cooked than the other. The side of the eggs that has been sitting in the pan is flaking and brown and the side that has been facing upwards is loose and gooey. There is a faint burning smell coming from beneath the pan that the housemate is using to cook the eggs. The eggs themselves aren't burning but the pan is covered in burnt egg drips and the residue of various pan overflows and those stains that now look like the remnants of a lava flow coating the pan, are what is smoldering and causing the faint burning smell. The burning smell coming from the stovetop is different from the burning smell of the trash that is drifting in the open kitchen window; the burning smell of the trash makes the nostrils sting; and, while the burning smell from the stove gives less of a stinging sensation and more of a clogged, suffocating feeling.

The housemate eating the apple has decided that it is too difficult to eat around the brown spot and has convinced themselves that the brown spot can't really cause any harm. As the housemate at the stove is sighing about the overcooked eggs, the housemate at the table in the nook is eating a bite of apple that mainly consists of brown spot and is not unhappy with the flavor or the texture. The bite of brown spot apple tastes a bit earthier, riper in a sweet and sour way that is not completely unfavorable.

In the background the same song plays quietly on repeat, neither of the housemates register the music although it is loud enough to be heard albeit not understood.

The apple of the housemate that is sitting at the table in the nook is about halfway eaten. The housemate is feeling adventurous and bold after braving the brown spot and surviving. The apple eating housemate has decided to eat the entirety of the apple, seeds, stem and all. The housemate crunches an apple seed in their mouth, then winces at the sourness and spits it out, half chewed, onto the light-brown, wooden table.

The housemate by the stove hears the housemate at the table spitting out the apple seeds and tenses because they know that they are going to have to clean those seeds up off of the table later.

There is a golden colored button on the back of the nook-seated house-mate's green pants and as the housemate quickly leans forward to spit out the sour apple seed, the button scrapes a layer of light-blue paint off of the bench, revealing a layer of red in the shape of the scratch.

While the housemate in the nook is spitting out the seed, the housemate by the stovetop has given up on the toast and the eggs that they were previously trying to cook and moved towards the trashcan with the overcooked, dry yoked eggs in the pan in one hand and the burnt, floor dirtied toast in the other. Using the toast to pry open the white plastic lid, the housemate dumps the eggs and then the toast into the trashcan. Inside of the trashcan, there is an empty milk carton. With the pan in one hand and toast crumbs falling onto the floor from the other, the housemate by the trashcan looks at the housemate sitting in the nook and asks

Did you finish my milk?

The housemate at the light-brown wooden table, finishes a bite of apple that consist of two thirds non-brown spot and one third brown spot, and responds,

Yes, I am going to the store later today.
I figured I would just replace it then.

The housemate holding the pan, by the trash can, sighs and turns back towards the stove. The housemate holding the pan by the trashcan mentally asks themselves if the other housemates will ever learn, will there ever be a time when each housemate respects the others' food? The housemate with the frying pan and no milk asks themselves if it is unfair to assume and expect the other housemates to not eat or drink other people's food or drinks but the housemate knows that no matter the answer, their food will still be consumed by the others. The housemate had been looking forward to having a tall glass of milk with their toast and eggs, but the milk is gone and the toast was burnt and the eggs were overcooked. The housemate by the stove decides that they will make eggs and toast and just have water, even though they wanted milk, even though they had their heart set on milk, even though they have always had milk with their eggs and toast since they were seven and their grandmother served them toast and eggs and milk, but the milk is gone, what else are they supposed to do? The carton of eggs is light grey and has three eggs left in it and is in front of the chrome toaster closer to the sink than it is to the stove. The housemate by the stove opens the light grey egg carton and takes the last three eggs out of it, cracking them one at a time into the now empty pan. Most of the eggs end up in the pan but some drip down the side of the pan and onto the stovetop, adding to the light-brown tint of what used to be white.

The housemate by the stove tastes copper and feels a throbbing, dull pain in their temples. Milk might have helped get rid of the metallic taste or quell the growing headache, but there is none.

At the table, in the nook, the housemate who is seated on the light-blue bench has eaten over three fourths of the apple and has decided not to eat the seeds because they are sour but has decided that the brown spots are not so bad after all.

Through the door-less doorway the same faint song plays through the speakers, neither of the housemates seem to notice the music.

Through the one inch opening in the window the smell of the trash burning has grown stronger, swallowing out the smell of the flowers that was once on the wind.

THE OFFICE BUILDING

The office building (in which he works) is a cold grey brick on the outside and inside there is dark grey carpet on the floor, white paint on the walls and styrofoam-esque ceiling boards in the ceiling that (the styrofoam esque ceiling boards) are white with flecked bits of grey with the occasionally blueish-grey fleck. There are fourteen floors in the building (the top three of which are reserved for executives only, a position which he is most certainly not). He works on the seventh floor in the middle of said floor, meaning that he has no view of or from a window and from his cubicle (when he stands up) he can see only more cubicles and other people working in them. The entire building (with possibly the exception of the three top executive floors, which may be lit differently) is lit with often flickering fluorescent lights that are placed (in his opinion) too frequently across the ceiling.

He is lucky (at least that is what he has been told) because he has his own cubicle, his own four (well three and a half) walls in which to wallow and hang up to four personal items and store his belongings in during the week (but not during the weekend). He supposes that he is grateful for his place and for his four walls (well three and a half walls) to himself. Although if he is being honest with himself and to himself about his cubicle situation he wouldn't mind having a cubicle-mate (like most others in the office do) with whom he could make little jokes throughout the day. He would love to have somebody to complain to whilst at work about the grind of the work itself and the often painful and bizarre interactions he has daily with the other employees at the office. But he doesn't and he supposes that he should be happy with having his own space (but he really is not, at least not fully, if he is being honest with himself, which he really tries hard to be).

Well now it is 9:48am on a Thursday (his least favorite day of the week) and he is already thinking about food, which is never a good sign. He often daydreams while at work, but he tries to keep his daydreams about places and people, and especially not about food because if he begins to think too much about his food, then he will end up eating his lunch early (which is never good because if he eats his lunch early then he will be hungry for the last couple hours of his workday which [said last couple of workday hours] are always the longest and worst especially if he has eaten early).

His lunch today consists of a salad which itself consists of lettuce, diced tomatoes, diced cucumbers, some type of cut up nut (possibly almond, although he is not sure and frankly he can barely taste the nuts anyway and puts them into his salad only for the added crunch) a sliced chicken breast and some cheese which he grated on the top of the salad after he had placed it into the tupperware which he uses to bring his salad to work. Also, for lunch and snacks throughout the day he has two protein bars (which he considers the human equivalent of animal feed, but which he eats every day because they keep him full for longer and cheaper than anything else) and an apple (which is bruised on one side and which he plans to eat at 3 pm, two hours before he gets to go home, to give him that extra sugar boost that he will need so much by that time). As he thinks about his lunch he remembers how last night (he was very tired because he had been up most of the night before because he has started having dreams in which he is in a cubicle which has four actual walls from which he cannot escape no matter how hard he tries) he was forced to stay late at work to finish up a group presentation (which he must give later today) and how when he was making his salad he realized that there was no more salad dressing in his fridge and he was too tired to go to the supermarket to get more dressing and so he ended up just making the salad without the dressing. He, until this very moment, forgot that he didn't have any dressing for his salad, which makes the whole idea of eating his lunch that much less appetizing and makes his hunger for something good and for anything but what he already has that much stronger and deeper.

So now he is thinking of food but he has only been at work for less than an hour and that is not a good sign because that means he is most certainly going to eat his food earlier than he should and subsequently the whole day will end up lagging and sort of limping slowly on (which is the opposite of how he would like his day to go).

While he is daydreaming of food, the food about which he is daydreaming is certainly not the food that he has brought with him for lunch. The protein bars and the salad and even the apple (a snack which he used to enjoy) all taste worse than bland to him. In fact, the thought of eating what he has brought with him to eat not only doesn't make him hungry, but makes him nauseous.

No, he is not daydreaming about his simple (dressing-less) salad nor his animal-feed-esque protein bars, what has captured his attention (and what will subsequently ruin his daily eating schedule as well as possibly his whole day) is a sandwich.

And oh, dear lord, that sandwich is going to be something special. Each day after work he makes his dinner for the next day as he eats his dinner for that day (which was made the day before, and so on). It is always the same thing that he makes and although he eats it every day this dinner sandwich is always so satisfying and basically the best part of his day. For the bread, he buys a rosemary sourdough which he toasts as a first step of his meal prep. He then applies (to the bottom piece of golden-toasted toast) a thin layer of a garlic mayonnaise and an even thinner layer of pesto (which he makes himself each weekend by blending together fresh pesto from his garden along with some olive oil, some crushed garlic, and a pinch or two of pepper). On top of the pesto and mayonnaise (which when mixed together make a creamy dark green which has become his favorite color) he stacks thin slices of roast beef (which he roasts himself in his croc-pot during the weekend and which he stores in the same pot in the fridge during the week and which he reheats on the stove top in a pan along with enough olive oil to cover the bottom of the pan and some salt before putting it on the sandwich) until the pile reaches the desired height of about an inch up above the bottom slice of toast. Atop the roast beef he places some Swiss cheese which he will melt into the sandwich later when he reheats it for dinner the next day. Atop the Swiss cheese (which will later be melted) he places thinly sliced mushrooms (which he sautés with a dash of dessert wine and some Italian seasoning). And finally, atop the mushrooms he places three or four sundried tomatoes (which he buys at a specialty Italian import grocery store). Then goes the top piece of toast on which he will spread a spicy-sweet jalapeño jelly. When he reheats his sandwich, the night after he makes it, he will place it into a rectangular shaped pan that opens and closes like a briefcase that is used mainly by people cooking on campfires, but which he uses in the oven in his kitchen. On the rectangular pan, he will spread butter (which is locally sourced and thicker than the average store-bought butter) as well as a small drip of honey and in the pan, he will place the sandwich and sort of squish it down as he closes the pan and places it into the oven. The use of this pan makes his sandwich crispy, and hot (and melts the cheese) in a way that he could not achieve otherwise.

It is now 10:34 am and he has spent almost an hour going over in his head the process of the preparation of his daily dinner, a time during which he was supposed to be finalizing the details of his part of a group presentation but instead he has done absolutely no work and actually, literally drooled a bit onto his white button down during his daydream (thinking specifically of the mushrooms, which he always sautés until they are crispy on the edges but soft and warm in the middle).

And with his sandwich he often makes sweet potato fries (which he makes by cutting an already baked sweet potato carefully into eight pieces and lightly frying said pieces in a pan) as well as some Brussel sprouts which he steams and sprinkles with balsamic reduction and garlic salt.

Now it is 11 am, he has thought about the Brussel sprouts for nearly a half an hour and the way that the balsamic reduction is (in his humble opinion) the perfect mix of sweet and salty.

And now he is late for the meeting in which he (and the group of people with whom he has been working on the presentation) has to give a presentation on the potential new layouts of the 'contact us' page of the company website.

In some ways, the presentation is meaningless because, as so often happens, he (and his 'team') will present their ideas to the middle management executives on the fourth to top floor (the eleventh) and they (the middle management) will add their critiques and notes and then some of those middle management executives will go up one floor (to the twelfth) to the upper-middle management executive's floor and present their notes and ideas to the upper middle management executives and then the upper middle management executives will go up one more floor (to the thirteenth) to the upper executive's floor and present their ideas and their notes (as well as the ideas and notes of everybody below them [both literally and hierarchically within the company]) and then one upper executive will schedule an appointment with the secretary of the CEO of the company for the next week and then (at the time of the appointment) the upper executive will take the private elevator up to the top floor (which serves as the office of the CEO) and will proceed to present the findings to the CEO. And when the CEO has had time to think over the changes (or about whatever is being discussed) he (the CEO) will send his ideas and changes and comments and critiques back down the chain, all the way back to the single cubicle of the man who has spent all morning thinking about a sandwich.

And that process is constantly ongoing and ideas and projects and whatnot are always being critiqued and approved and denied and postponed or put on the backburner to make room for something more important and it seems, at least to the man who is late for his presentation, that nothing is ever truly or fully finished here.

It is now 12:48 pm and the meeting about the 'contact us' page went well, that's to say the middle management executives were not unhappy with what the group had come up with and barely even looked up from their cell phones or computers when he came bursting into the meeting room ten minutes late. And now, as of five minutes ago, he is back at his desk and is thinking about what he could add to his sandwich recipe to make his sandwich all the better as he eats one of those tasteless protein bars that claim to be 'trail mix' flavored but taste mainly like peanuts and dry oats.

One of the results of this mornig's meeting was that he has been assigned a new project with a new group of people. This new project is to decide what shade of light blue the background of the newest company pen should be as well as if the pen should be a pen that clicks to open or spins to open. His specific job is to decide where the company logo (which is white) should be placed on the pen and whether or not the logo should be placed on multiple sides of the pen. As he looks at his computer screen on which shows a pen on which he can place the logo anywhere he wants, his stomach gurgles and he smells ash and the smell equivalent of the color of the carpet.

It is now 3:01 pm and it's time for his apple. His lunch, which he ate at his desk as he worked (as per company policy) was worse than normal on account of the lack of dressing which (the dressing) is really the only thing that makes his lunch half passable or enjoyable in the slightest (which even with the dressing is barely so). He was so tired last night (because of his lack of sleep because of his reoccurring cubicle nightmare as well as the fact that he had to stay late from work) when he made his salad that he forgot to slice up the chicken and he only ever brings a fork to work with him so he during lunch (while he was eating his chicken) he had to pick up the chicken with the fork and take bites out of it, which he did not really enjoy doing at all because it kind of grossed him out to have to take bites out of a big piece of meat and he would rather have it sliced up.

He decided that the logo on the pen should be in the middle of the pen, about a millimeter below the clip-on tip of the pen (which one could use to hang the pen from their pocket or from a page of a notebook) and that the logo should be on two opposite sides of the pen so that no matter the way the pen is rotated the logo will be in view.

Above his desk the fluorescent light (which always terribly shines and vibrates and buzzes at a frequency that haunts his dreams at night), seems to buzz and vibrate louder today than it ever has before.

The bruise on his apple has spread its mushy and brown self across one side of the apple to the extent that the apple is almost not worth eating, yet he eats it anyway and when he reaches the brown part he juts throws the apple into the waste basket below and to the left side of his desk.

It is now 5:04 pm and he is in his car. He watches the lights in the building flicker as he drives out of the parking lot and onto the highway, which after waiting for too long in traffic, will eventually take him home (and to the sandwich which has both plagued and blessed his day, and which will hopefully make his night at least somewhat decent).

The traffic is heavy and smells like exhaust, even with his windows closed. Due to the fact that it is winter the sun is already down and thus the only lights are the taillights of the cars in front of him, the headlights of the cars that pass going the other way, the streetlights (many of which are out) and the moon (which is half hidden by smog and clouds and is just a cut fingernail of white light, and which he doesn't even really notice because of his rumbling stomach and the call of that thing he has been waiting for from its place in his refrigerator).

It is now 5:51pm and he is pulling into his reserved parking spot in the parking lot of his apartment building that, like his office building, also has fourteen floors and, also like his office building, has top floors which are reserved for people much above his pay grade. But he is not thinking of that now, he is focused on the promise of what lays just barely out of reach.

His keys are heavy in his hand as he walks up the stairs to his apartment which is on the second floor and which has a view onto nothing but more apartment buildings and a grey and white sky.

It seems he cannot walk fast enough up the stairs.

The door opens with a creak and he leaves his keys in the door. He doesn't even bother to take off his shoes or his jacket as he steps into the kitchen and with one swift motion opens the fridge.

In the refrigerator, he sees nothing but half empty sauce bottles and a gallon of milk he should most likely throw away.

He turns around and on the counter, there are the ingredients of the sandwich which it turns out was never made last night, he must've been too tired and forgot to put together everything for today.

What he hoped for, what he dreamed of all day, is in fact just a lie and he really only has himself to blame.

He sits, more slides, down onto the floor of the kitchen (his shoes and jacket still on) and the white tile of the floor is cold even through his slacks.

On the clock in the stove of his kitchen, another minute clicks by.

ONE OF TWO

"'Come two, come all' they said, 'for some grand romantic adventure.' This spa could wow the likes of the god of love himself proclaimed the glossy brochure. 'This long weekend retreat will be just what we need' said I; the electrical plug with just the right voltage to shock us back into the love we once so passionately had. (Our friends) Sam and Dani (Sam being the male of the relationship and Dani being the female) had been experiencing let's say some marital strife for the past couple of years, ya know with Sam's drinking and Dani's gambling and shopping problems as well as the fact that Sam's mom didn't know about Dani until the month of their wedding (or was it Dani's mom not knowing about Sam, whatever that's really not the point), but so they went to this place for a week and a half and after that they came back more in love than ever (I mean they did eventually get divorced but you should have seen them after their week and a half at this spa, I mean oh my god they were so in love, and also very tan). And anyways me and my man tried to book a reservation for a week in advance and we got like the perfect room with a king bed and a Jacuzzi and a complimentary bottle of wine, but then my man had to do something super important for a client at work and had to be gone the weekend that we booked the trip, but we couldn't cancel the reservation because (as said the brochure) there was a no cancelation policy (the brochure went on to say how like their policy on reservations, marriage should have a no cancelation clause as well, which I had to admit was somewhat clever but it was also like really annoying that they wouldn't let us cancel our reservation for the four nights that we planned on going). And so then on the weekend when my man was supposed to be gone working with that client on that super important thing, I came back to the apartment after spending the day with my mom at the mall to find my man in bed with the super important client for whom he had needed to cancel our (as in his and mine) special romantic, relationship rejuvenating, trip to make us fall in love again. Basically, the super important job he had had to do was doing the client, in our bed. And so, I left and there were tears and there was that lousy sap running out into the parking lot in his underwear trying to explain to me how this whole thing was one big misunderstanding and so on. So, I just up and drove away and eventually I realized that I was like sort of instinctually driving towards this place where we had the reservation that we were unable to cancel and I was like oh what the hell, I need relaxation more now than I did before I saw my now ex man screwing some woman in our bed and plus the whole four days are already paid for and so I just kept on driving until I got here. Yeah, and I am just like so happy that I was able to make the choice for myself, ya know and really give this time to myself away from it all, all the drama and bullshit. So yeah that's how I got here and I know that's like a really long answer to your question of how I am doing, Mr. bartender sir, but thanks for listening so well and um by the way can I get another one of these smoothies with a double shot of rum, thanks hun!"

THE ONE WHO LEAVES

He is a master at leaving; an expert at getting gone.

There is a process in leaving; a sacred and simple release and he has this process down to a T.

He knows exactly how long it will take him to pack up and be out of wherever he is. 37 minutes is what it takes to forever and completely disappear (and that is including a shower and breakfast).

He is always leaving, traveling, arriving, unpacking, working hard for many days on end without sleep and with barely any food, then packing up and leaving again. This list of things he does repeats every two weeks and he has been on this cycle of coming and going almost as soon as he has arrived for nearly thirteen years.

He works for a company at which he manages computer systems. Specifically, he updates the processers with the newest and fastest technologies. He goes from town to desolate dusty town working in frigid, highly air conditioned rooms uploading the newest data, checking on all of the wiring, making sure all of the computers are working at maximum efficiency. He travels back and forth across the country, updating the software, and by the time he has updated all of the warehouses across the whole country there is a new set of data and a faster type of software to install, and so he makes his rounds again and again.

It seems the company he works for chooses to build their computer centers in the most desolate and boring of places across the country. He assumes this is because these empty places have the cheapest land and the least people nearby to complain about the nightmares and (alleged) cancer causing cell and radio waves and radiation that these massive computer warehouses produce. It seems a computer company like that which he works for, would have a better more technologically advanced way of updating their processing systems; that there would be some type of uplink that someone could click on and automatically send the newest update to all of the processing warehouses across the country, but there isn't. It seems that those at the top of the company are more focused on product development and on marketing and on getting as filthy rich as possible (although he can't really imagine the people at the top of the company getting any richer than they already are; it is rumored that the company he works for has more money than the government of the country in which he works, and he thinks that that rumor is an underestimate). He often thinks that those he works for, have forgotten about him and his work. He hasn't spoken with his boss in a year and as long as he keeps all of the computer processing systems up and running and as long as his paychecks keep coming, he is ok with the way things are.

The houses in which he stays are each technically different, yet are nearly the same in terms of décor, building materials used and color. The houses all have white walls, a kitchen with a grey tile floor, a bedroom with a twin bed on a metal frame and a grey desk with one (empty) drawer on the side of it, and a bathroom with a shower, toilet and a sink. There is often a washer and dryer in the hallway between the bedroom and the bathroom, but not always. Sometimes he has to wash his clothes by hand and hang dry them on the shower curtain rod in the bathroom with the bathroom fan on and the window open to aid and quicken the drying process.

When he started this job, he had a duffel bag and a suitcase which he brought with him to every new place, but he quickly realized that having more than one bag was overkill and was just a drag on his overall journey. So, he slowly got rid of all of the things he didn't need and now when he travels he has only a small square suitcase in which he has two pairs of paints, three button down shirts, five pairs of underwear, three pairs of socks, three ties and a pair of slippers (he wears his dress shoes during his travel). He also has a jacket and a pair of thin but warm gloves that he wears while at work because the rooms in which he spends all of his work days are kept at a balmy forty degrees (in order to prevent the processing systems from overheating), items which (his jacket and gloves) he also packs into his suitcase. Finally, he packs his rectangular toiletry kit (which includes his toothbrush, toothpaste, razor, shaving cream and floss) as well as whichever book he is currently reading. He takes only a single day off during his time in each new small, rundown and often nearly abandoned town and he uses that day to find the nearest book store and buy a new book (as well as to find a local pub, or as he likes to call it "local watering hole' in which to have one beer and a pretzel [if they have pretzels on the menu, which they most often do]).

When he finishes a book, he leaves it on the grey desk in the room from which he will soon depart and not be back to for at least a year (if ever). He likes to pretend that whomever cleans the house after his visit leaves the book for the next guests of the house, however he has never once seen one of his old books in a house that he has previously stayed in and he fears that the cleaner of the house simply throws the old books away (the thought of which makes him a bit nauseous and thus he has simply made himself not think about where the books go anymore).

Every two weeks he goes somewhere new.

He doesn't even look to see where he is going anymore, he just takes the manila envelope in which the tickets (and his fortnightly paycheck) always arrive the day before he is to leave and heads to the nearest airport in a taxi that is prescheduled to pick him up on the date of his departure. Today he is leaving again, and the car always comes at about 2pm.

He has a routine now, for that day on which he is set to both leave and arrive (somewhere old, and somewhere new, respectively). That routine includes waking up at round ten am, showering, shaving (an act that he enjoys immensely and which he does more for the feeling than for the actual result, in fact he thinks and has been told many times throughout his life that he looks better with facial hair or at least some scruff, but he enjoys the scrape of the razor against his skin and the warmth of the shaving cream on his face so much that he does it every day anyways), eating a breakfast of oatmeal and one cup of extra dark, black coffee and finally packing up his things.

Right now, he is at the breakfast section of his leaving day routine and is leaning against the kitchen counter eating his oatmeal and looking out the window. There is a window across the kitchen from the sink and it is this window which he is looking out of, and out of this window he can see a spikey, twisting bush and on said bush are fuzzy, plump looking birds that he assumes (if the window were open, which it is not) chirp and sing in a soft and gentle manner. As he watches the birds he feels a certain type of comradery with them; they too are travelers, they too are ones who leave and fly from place to place, never truly stationary.

He is so consumed by the hopping and slight fluttering of the little birds on the shrub right outside the window that the spoon from which he was eating his oatmeal slips from his fingers and bounces on the floor with a shrill ping, flinging bits of oatmeal about on the grey tile floor. The sound of the metal spoon hitting the floor breaks him from his trance and he sets down his bowl so he can bend down and pick up the spoon from the ground. He picks up the spoon and places it in the sink, then wipes the flecks of oatmeal from the grey tile with a paper towel that he got from a roll beside the sink. As he wipes the floor, he sees something sort of pushed up against the corner where the tile meets the wood of the white cabinet door below the sink (in that place where no broom can ever really fully clean). He reaches his dry and long index finger towards the metal thing and drags it to a place away from the cabinet where he can pick it up. With his index finger and thumb he grasps the whatever it is and holds it up to the light to inspect it.

It's a bobby pin; dark brown and crimped on one side, used to hold up hair maybe a woman's hair. The bobby pin sends through him an electric like jolt of loneliness. He has chosen this solitary life of wires and data and grey desks in empty rooms with white blank walls that will most likely never be filled with anything but dust and maybe more, newer and whiter coats of the same white paint. He has chosen this rootless life. A human tumbleweed is what he is and he has been ok with that; rolling and twisting from place to place, doing those same simple tasks for the sake of a job, for the sake of the paycheck. But he doesn't really even need a job anymore, his lodging is free and he barely eats and he is paid a very hearty sum every two weeks; a hearty sum which just sits and accumulates in his bank account. He has enough money to retire, his only real expense (besides the obvious) is the biweekly (often used) book he buys, but that barely touches his savings. He is a rich man in some ways, he has worked hard for years and has saved and saved and he doesn't really need to work, but he doesn't really know what he would do if he didn't; if he just walked away or if he decided to stay in someplace for more than two weeks.

He has been running, foot stepping forward for so long that he has grown numb to the path on which he is on and the desolation and boredom of his solitary and routine being. He has been moving for so long that he feels like he may just simply break apart if he stops; if he starts to let his roots grow.

The bobby pin is cold in his palm but reminds him of warmth. This little metal piece spurs in him images of sharing that twin bed with somebody; of waking up in the night next to the heat and soft of a sleeping someone; of having a hand to hold; of making an oatmeal breakfast for two.

One of the birds flutters its hollow bones and feathers in the periphery of his sight and distracts him from his midmorning dream. He puts the bobby pin in his pocket and reaches for his oatmeal bowl; he must get back to his routine for the car is coming and he is now a bit behind schedule.

Soon he will leave this place and tonight he will lie alone, somewhere new but not entirely unfamiliar.

THAT OPEN MOUTH OF THE DEEP

At this point the best splinters of something pure that I am able to find, are in the darkest (or what seem like the darkest) points of the night; the coldest times when anywhere but beneath the blanket is a frozen wasteland of frost hardened sheets and blank white walls that are still visibly white and blank even without the sun or lamp light. These moments are the most joyous, well some of them are, not because of the darkness nor the cold, nor the warmth beneath the comforter nor the comfort that comes from a sleep slowed mind. These seconds in space; these momentary specks of truth in a life of dark nights and dim days happen a couple times per week and they (these things of rare and soft beauty) have become something that I look forward to and depend on to go on even though their very essence; the very existence of these moments (when I think about them deeply) is extremely depressing and often causes a sort of existential rift within me.

What happens in these lint balls of happiness pulled from a pocket full of grit, is that I am asleep, and I wake up, often sweaty, often from a dream (that I won't remember) and after waking I lie there in the dark. And this blackness is not black in the sense of a color, but more an entity of black, pulsating and throbbing in tune with the sound of the crickets and the passing cars outside (always cars are passing, even in the time when my world is still and bedded down). And in this blackness, in this gaseous tar that takes over my room while I am not there to will it away, I wallow for a couple of seconds or for an eternity (it's hard to tell which, and maybe in that swirling night time doesn't matter). And but anyway as I wallow, anxiety and the worry that always follows carries in from the yesterday to the tomorrow (a yesterday that seems to drag on for weeks and a tomorrow that never seems to truly arrive) and in that sickening worry and slowly constricting mind I begin to wonder about the time.

And that time is suddenly all that matters, it is not so much what time it is but what time it isn't and that time that I so hope that it is not, that time which has made me suddenly begin to believe in god again so I can pray that the time is not what I don't want it to be, that time is six am. And that swallowing night; that open mouth of the deep continues in its blackness and I continue to lie but now stuck in an achy, bone deep fear.

On top of my desk (which is a soft wood that I poorly painted white) beside some crumpled and a few un-crumpled papers and gum wrappers, beside pens that are half filled with oil slick colored ink, beside a post card I haven't yet had the heart to open, beside my wallet and my keys and those glasses that shield me from the sun, there is an automatic clock. And this clock is black and rectangular and plastic and it is plugged into the wall beside my desk (on the other side of the desk than my bed). And on this clock (that I have turned to face the door to my room, turned away from my bed so I can't see it all night, for if I could I would do nothing but look at it and watch those lines click by) there are numbers that are red, but not blood red, no a machine like this is too cold and calculated and focused on its task to bleed or having anything human to do (or feel) at all.

No, this thing, this rigid, petroleum based tool of regiment and order is there to tell me when to wake and sleep and eat and dream and bathe and call my mother and when to work and when to shave and when to get dressed and when to put on my shoes and when to take them off and when to stare at the wall and when to lie still.

In that profundity of almost liquid seeming lightlessness there I lie and I slowly raise myself half up, to a seated position, naked in my place of rest, to look upon the face of something that will not look back at me nor speak but will haunt me all the same. And as I look at this contraption that keeps me trapped; in line with the others; beneath the hard-pressed thumb of the system. I hope to see nothing, but of course I will see something and it is what I see and what I have seen that will determine my tomorrow and when it comes.

The moment of bliss, the gap showing daylight in the blackout curtain of the grinding gears, is where I exist and it is then that I look at the clock and hope that I have more time to lie in that gaping shadow. And if I have the time, if the minutes have chosen to bend their red selves into numbers that mean I have more time to rest, I will and I do and I fall back into the darkness, into that bed, into the half-forgotten dream of many minutes ago.

If I don't, if the time is not on my side, if I am faced with the glaring six and two zeros, I place my feet on the wooden floor (that should be swept sometime soon, but most likely won't be) and I flip on the light and the darkness and the fingers of the night and the specks of throbbing weariness and of joy, slowly recede into the bright of another day that feels so much like yesterday.

PATH

The path is long and narrow and it winds up and out of sight between some battered looking old pines and the grey, jagged bottom of a small mountain. There are two walkers on this path, one old and one not as much so. The older makes the pace and the younger follows; sometimes the younger one will walk ahead but he will always fall back to let the other lead. The path is dirt and riddled with stones of grey and light brown and even some faded purple bits. There are occasional shards of arrowheads from long ago; this path has been walked upon for generations and as the two men walk the older of the two points this out to the other saying how one day he (the older one) hopes he (the younger one) will bring others up this path later when he (the older one) is gone and when he (the younger one) is old and leading the pace for whomever will come next.

These trees, says the elder, will outlast us all, as they pass beneath those rods of bark and pine and sap and water that sway in the once and future blizzards that will soon be upon this place in less than a month.

The younger man has walked this path since before he was even a man, just a barefoot boy, wild and running amongst the sprouting flowers and waving pines and once, many years ago before the older one's beard was grey and before the younger one had a beard at all, the boy fell and hurt his knee on a sharp and unforgiving rock; and he still has the pocked scar to prove he was once much smaller than he is now and to remind him to be careful; that not everything will wane in his wake.

And he is older now, he thinks he knows more than he does but he knows some and he will continue to grow strong and wise like the man who shuffles beside him breathing shallow and quick breaths like that of an injured animal. But this man, the elder, is not injured, he has just walked this path long and far and has taken many falls himself.

He too holds the scars to prove his moments of unbalance and he wears them proud and raw.

The two reach a particularly steep and slippery section of the path and as they start up it, the old one slips nearly to his knees and nearly to what could be some great injury, but the young one catches his shoulder and pulls him back up to his feet.

And they go on, upwards and rambling towards whatever lays beyond that bend and the bend beyond that.

One day the young man will not catch the older one, one day the old one will fall and the young one will not be able to hold him up, but for now the two walk together and the elder keeps the pace.

REDONE

The kitchen is in shambles.

The house is a study of complete and utter chaos in the form of drywall dust and soot from where the chimney used to be and sawdust and chips of wood and blocks of wood and nails and screws and bolts. Adhesive and silicon caulk and mortar and cotton candy looking insulation fluff poke and seep and ooze in a way similar to the way lava oozes out from every uncovered seam and crack and half demolished wall like blood and veins and marrow from a severed limb. The innards of this place are exposed, dropping, dripping, dusty and stripped to the wood and wire and concrete bare bones. The air is thick with a white grime finer and much dryer than snow and loud with the buzzing and rattling of power tools and generators and vacuums. Sparks shower out of what seems like nowhere every once and a while and thick men with tool belts walk back and forth with dirty boots and soggy cigarettes hanging from their mouths, grumbling technical terms to mainly themselves.

And she is there in the midst of it all; making coffee by what seems like the truckload, answering calls, signing paperwork, looking at blueprints (both hand-drawn and actually blueprinted) and looking (so much looking) at what the men, the workers in her home, so often need her to see; approve; give the ok.

Her husband is at work; some office job at which he has a desk with windows that look out onto something not ugly but not that interesting either (she has been there a couple of times) and at which he is most certainly not the boss but is definitely not at the lowest point on the so-called totem pole. And while this whole remodel is being done, while their place of residence is getting literally torn to shreds (well not exactly shreds, but pieces and shards and broken, ruined scraps), he is gone and she is there to sort of watch over all of the work although she is not by any means an expert on or interested in the work which she has been tasked with watching over.

It wasn't her choice to move to this place, it wasn't her choice to move at all, and while she did do it, while she did move to somewhere which she had no interest in moving to (or even really ever visiting) she did so willingly and knowing that it was a move that needed to be done. Her husband got this job offer after finally (after 6 years of night school) graduating from law school and even though this place to which they have so recently relocated was so far out in the middle of nowhere in a city as empty and as void of anything interesting as the term "the middle of nowhere" implies, he took the job because both she and him agreed that getting a job in his field and at the pay level which this company was willing to pay him was not only lucky but was some sort of blessing which had been bestowed upon them by some higher power (in which she is not sure she believes) and that not taking the job would be some sort of unlucky and more ungrateful gesture. And so, that is why they moved all the way out here to this place and bought this house (for a supposedly great deal) that basically needed to be gutted to even begin to be lived in, in any way that was close to comfortable or normal, even though not him nor her had any real interest in moving to where they now live in the first place.

She was ok with moving to where they did because for one she loves her husband and she just couldn't say no to him when he came bursting in a couple months ago with the news that he had been offered what equated to his dream job; albeit not his dream job in his dream city, but it was exciting all the same, and for two because the job she was working at the time before the move was not terrible but not great and was all together pretty boring and stale in the way that so many so-called adult things are, along with the sad fact that most of her own friends from college (and potential reasons and proverbial strings for wanting to not move) had moved away after said college ended, so basically she wasn't really leaving anything behind. Well, she had her husband (whom she loves, even though he is at fault for moving her out here to what her mother [while drunk, last Christmas] referred to as bumbfuck, USA) and a decent enough education and a subsequent degree from said decent enough education in a "desirable field" that more or less ensures her a job anywhere she wishes to have a job and she had no good reason or excuse or really any string to cut at all (other than her job which was a string she may have cut anyways if she hadn't ended up moving) and so she moved.

And she is here now, in whatever wasteland this place is; in the dust and unfinished walls listening to the whacking and grinding sounds and trying to enjoy her breakfast and read the newspaper on her computer as working men with big beer bellies and dirty coveralls tromp in and out of the front door of her home, grinding mud into a carpet that she knows she will have to replace after the remodel is done because of said ground in mud that she cannot get all out even with a vacuum each night after the grinders of said mud have long since left and her husband has returned home.

Outside the ground is frozen and rock hard and everything seems to be either dead or silent (or both). Through the glass paned front door she can see that there are no birds in the sky and that said bird-less sky is a light, grey-white that is so life and colorless that she can barely stand to look at it lest she may end up spending the day in bed again with her head under the covers leaving only to use the bathroom or scavenge the kitchen for something slightly edible and small enough that she can take back to her room to eat under the covers.

Beyond that terrible grey sky she can see on the hill up the road a house that belongs to a neighbor whom she has never met but has seen the silhouette of through a window that is lit at night and faces her house. She is not sure if this silhouette belongs to a body of a male or a female and in some ways, it doesn't matter. She has seen this silhouette, backed by a golden yellow lamp light and wearing some type of flowy and possibly nightgown-esque article of clothing, swaying to music that she cannot and most likely never will hear. Or maybe there is no music at all. Maybe this someone (whom she may never really know) is just swaying to silence; alone in the night and warm light moving to something only heard by them. She has begun to look at that house up on the hill every night, waiting for whomever, whatever that person is to come in their loose clothing and sway and twist and spin by the window. This dancing thing, this creature of movement and shadow and soft grace is what she has begun to live for and even now, in the morning of another loud and dusty day, as she thinks about her neighbor and their twisting in the night, all those sounds and clouds of toxic things seem to fade away as she is consumed by the warmth and small beauty of dancing just for the sake of it, swaying the night away.

SCRATCHES

There are scratches on the floor; gouges in wood made by wood weighed down with flesh and bone.

The gouges are black but the wood in which they are gouged is a yellow-brown. There are two chairs at the table beside the gouges and in those chairs, sit two people. The table is round and is made of a grey-flecked, white stone. The two people, who are seated in the chairs, have pushed their chairs close to each other but not close enough to each other that the chairs, or the people in the chairs, are actually touching. As they talk, the people, the chairs are slowly sliding away from each other around the sides of the table at which they, the people, are seated.

There is a woman at one of the chairs. She has shoulder length hair that is the color of pine-tree bark; an earthy brown that, her hair, has strands and splashes of black within it which somehow enhances the brown. This woman has freckles on her cheeks. According to the person seated in the other chair at the table, who is a man, who is her lover, about whom the woman has many stinging, conflicting feelings that have long since been sort of sitting unattended to but present in the space between her throat and stomach and are, the feelings, the reason, in part, that the couple is sitting at the table, according to the man there are more freckles on the right side of her face than on the left side but not by much. The man in the other seat was able to determine the amount of freckles on each side of the woman's face using kisses and soft touches to help him count, one morning (a Sunday) while they, the man and the woman, lay together in bed listening to cars pass and birds flutter; a time during which he, the man in the other seat, counted all of the freckles on her, the woman's face. But that was long ago and at that time, especially during their lazy mornings together, everything, even time itself, had seemed to be sepia toned and un-imaginably cozy. She, the woman, has bright, white teeth but her bottom, front-most teeth are somewhat crooked, a feature about which she is insecure and thus she smiles with a closed mouth but of which, her crooked bottom two front teeth, he, the man, is very fond. There is something about slight imperfections in something enchanting or someone, at least in the man's opinion, that make them, the subject with the imperfections, subsequently all the more real seeming and all the more enchanting. The man believes that a flawed beauty, is a true beauty and thus, a true beauty is the only sort worth cherishing and he, the man, believes that the woman seated to his left is most certainly worth cherishing. The woman's eyes are like peppermint tea with a scoop of honey, that's to say they, her eyes, are chilling but sweet and also, they, her eyes, are a key-lime green.

The man beside the woman at the table has his elbows on top of the table and is resting his face, specifically his forehead, in his hands in a way that, from a distance could resemble prayer. Although, if one (as many do) can define prayer as speaking to something or somebody that the speaker thinks of as holy and expecting your words to be listened to, then his pseudo-prayer pose on the table top only truly resembles prayer by the fact that he is in fact doing the opposite of praying, i.e. he is listening to the words of someone he considers his salvation, the woman beside him, and hoping that he can take in and make true what is being said. That's to say the man is seated with his head in his hands, listening to the words (of which there has been a constant stream since they sat down at the table) pouring from the woman's mouth beside him. And although the woman is indeed speaking a lot, her words and the speed and amount of time that they are being said is not unwarranted or inappropriate; the woman is merely attempting through an ongoing mono-logue (that is slowly increasing both in volume and in intensity as her speech goes on) to explain to him, the man, her innermost feelings and thoughts and wants and needs to which, all of those things mentioned above, he, the man, is attempting to listen and internalize. That's to say the woman is ver-balizing sentiments that she has held in for a long time, things that need to be said, and the man is trying hard to both support the woman as she says what she needs to as well as listen to what it is she is saying in a way that he can actually understand and eventually attempt to respond to.

On the table there are two glass cups. One cup is half filled with black coffee and quickly melting ice cubes and is being drunk in throat moisturiz-ing sips by the woman, in between her paragraphs of exasperated speech. As she speaks, she uses one of her hands, her right, to emphasize and visually punctuate her speaking points, and with the other hand, her left, she is grasping the half-filled-with-coffee glass cup, from which she is, as previously stated, sipping occasionally. The woman, as she speaks, grasps onto that cup like she needs something solid to ground her; something solid to keep her on point; something solid like the man beside her has failed to be, at least in the way she needs, and this failure is a problem that, at least in part, is what she is speaking to him about.

The table, at which the couple sits, is in a terrarium of sorts. That's to say that the room in which the couple sits, in which the table also sits (but in a different sense) is mainly made of glass. The room is a part of a café and is separated from the rest of the café by walls of glass which surround the room on all sides. The ceiling of the glass room (which itself is made of glass) lets in warm sepia sunlight that, the sunlight, allows for plants to be grown in the terrarium-esque room and thus there are many plants hanging on the walls and from the ceiling. In fact, beside the table at which the couple sits, there is a deep green ivy plant (climbing hooks that are suction cupped to the glass walls of the room). An outlier leaf attached rather haphazardly to and hanging in a bizarre angle away from said ivy plant, hangs just beside where the woman's right hand is moving back and forth as she speaks. On five occasions so far in which some specific point in the conversation needed some special emphasis she has (while using an exaggerated hand movement to sort of visually speak to the importance of her verbal point) accidently hit the leaf with said over-exaggerating hand. And thus, as the woman speaks, the renegade ivy leaf is slightly bobbing, from the accidental collisions with the woman's hand i.e. it sort of looks like the leaf beside the woman is nodding along in agreement with what the woman is saying to the man (an occurrence that neither of the members of the couple notice during the conversation because the man is looking down, trying to listen to what the woman has to say and the woman is facing away from the leaf and therefore cannot see it bobbing).

There are three other tables around the glass-walled room. In a square, the four tables in the room are evenly spaced throughout the room. The table at which the couple sits, is the furthest from the door-less space in the glass which acts as the entryway to the terrarium section of the café.

At the first table in the room (in respect to its closeness to the entry way to the door and its subsequent obviousness and visibility when one enters the room) sits a plump man wearing expensive looking, burnt-orange loafers with a golden buckle and no socks, pinstripe fitted suit pants, black suspenders (that, the suspenders, sort of bend off to the sides of the man's body around the bulge of the man's belly), a white button-down shirt and no tie. The man's sports coat (which matches the pinstripes and colors of the man's suit pants) hangs on the back of the chair in which the man is sitting. The plump man in the pinstripe suit is typing on a laptop computer and is occasionally (about once every five minutes) speaking one word affirmatives or negatives into a cell phone which rests on the table beside the computer when not in use. Other than the cell phone, the laptop computer and the elbows of the plump man in the pinstripe suit, on the table, there is a cup of coffee (almost empty) which is clouded almost beige with copious amounts of creamer and sugar. Next to the cup of coffee there is a glazed donut from which a single bite has been taken.

At the second table (in regard to the closeness to the doorway of the glass-walled-annex of the café) there are three women. One of the women borrowed her chair from the table at which the plump man sits, before the plump man sat down, because there are only two chairs allocated per table in this section of the café, and the women, these women, always travel in a fast-talking, often-giggling, party-of-three and thus they needed an extra chair. The plump man seems not to have noticed the absence of one of the chairs from his table, and he most likely would not really care if he had noticed, which he hasn't. The three women, all of whom have blonde but not dyed blonde hair, meet every Saturday afternoon for coffee and pastries as well as to catch each other up on each other's lives. Contrary to popular belief, a belief system that is rather harmfully perpetuated by mainstream movies and TV shows, women, when together, do not only discuss the men in their lives. Although men, or any type of romantic relationships with any and every gender do come up in the conversations between these three women, the conversations that these three women have do not, surprisingly to some, revolve around men or romance at all. Instead, their conversations often consist of quips, self-deprecating comments, or inside jokes that are themselves so complex and multileveled that none of the women can even remember the shared experience which caused said inside jokes. In fact, while the women meet every week, almost without fail, not much of actual substance is said during these weekly Saturday afternoon meetings. But the substance-less conversation is not boring nor useless and actually provides an extremely important escape and break from the extremely busy and energy-consuming lives of all three women. The three women's luncheon acts as a sort of return to childhood, or at least as a return to the lightness and responsibility-less-ness of childhood, which is both necessary for the adult lives of the women and is fitting because these women have been friends since they were five. Although their weekly carefree conversations are not particularly intellectual or emotional, the three women, throughout the rest of the week (between their Saturday meetings) spend many hours on the phone or at each other's respective homes discussing the intellectually and seriously emotional topics that they so purposefully avoid on their Saturday meet-ups. The three women all think of their Saturday meet-ups as a sort of cleanse and release from the hustle and bustle and wear and tear of their everyday lives, and subsequently and therefore the three women colloquially call their weekly meet-up their C and R (an abbreviated phrase that is in the company of many others in the context of the friendship and conversa-tion amongst the three women. In fact if an outsider were to listen to their conversation, the eavesdropping outsider might think they were hearing a creole-esque dialect being spoken due to all of the inside jokes and abbre-viations.) One of the women is an elementary school teacher (3rd grade) is married (and has been, to a man who is a fire fighter, for the last seven years) and is trying to get pregnant. She, the married teacher, is drinking an herbal, iced, non-caffeinated tea that is maroon in color. The second of the three women, if one were to move in a clockwise fashion from the teacher around the table, works at a local running store, is an avid trail runner herself and is training for her first marathon that will, the marathon, take place in less than two months. The third woman at the table is tragically, perpetually and often, somehow, beautifully lost. She, the lost one, is lost in a way that makes her appear free and almost outside of the laws of the natural world to most people, but not to the other two women, who know her better than anybody and understand that the never-ending stumble of her life can occasionally be a burden. The trail runner is drinking water with no ice and the lost one is drinking a something that contains more ice-cream than coffee. The lost one is also eating a donut, the same as the plump man, although hers is more than two thirds eaten.

The third table is occupied by a man wearing what can only be described as a white, linen robe the likes of which has not been worn as well or as flaw-lessly for many thousands of years. The man has thin, red-string bracelets tied around both of his wrists (which he most likely picked up on a spiritual, quest-for-the-self style journey to the far east) and is wearing a necklace, the pennant of which is some sort of tree seed, like an acorn but not an acorn, that is pierced and strung through the middle with yet another red string. The man, whose style could be referred to as "messiah chic" has a beard that is dark and hangs low enough to almost entirely cover his neck. The man's knotty hair often falls down below his shoulders but is currently held up in a messy bun top of his head, that itself, the bun, is held together by an un-sharpened, white-painted, pencil. The man is sketching, in vague detail, in a notebook with yellowing pages, a sort of blueprint to what will eventually be a thirty-foot-tall statue of what is turning out to be a goat made of pixel style cubes. The man is most obviously some type of artist and, as he often pro-claims to whomever will listen, lives, eats and breathes art. Pretentiousness and utter, remorseless and delusional narcissism aside, this man, this "artist", is regarded as a sort of avant garde genius that, according to some, will soon come to international fame.

The fourth table holds the couple, and the woman is still speaking to the man, who is resting his head in his hands. The woman's speed of speech and overall tone of voice is lowering and quieting and thus, signifying to those who know her well, she is nearing the end of what she is saying.

The second cup on the table, at which the couple sits, is filled to the brim with water which once had ice cubes in it. Those ice cubes have now melted because the terrarium room, in which the couple and the others mentioned are seated, has a glass ceiling and said glass ceiling lets in hot beams of sun-shine and those hot beams of sunshine have been basically, directly shining onto the glass of water that once had ice cubes in it. And now with the added water of the melted ice cubes and the fact that the man has not yet taken a sip of the water, the cup is nearly overflowing and has a meniscus of water protruding from the top of the cup in a dome like fashion. The meniscus of water wobbles with every movement of the table. On the glass, itself, there are beads of water running down the sides and forming a perfectly circular puddle, like a tiny moat, around the cup. With each picking up and putting down of the other cup by the woman as she speaks, the meniscus of the cup that contains the undrunk water of the listening man, the meniscus on top of the water (bulging like a bloated beer belly) moves and ogles in a slow and rippling way like jelly or Jell-O. That's to say the water cup of the listening man is near spilling over because of the melted ice cubes and the constant, albeit slight, shaking of the table by the woman as she speaks rather vigorously.

The plump man, the three blonde friends, and the bearded genius, while being focused on what they themselves are doing, are all only half paying attention to what is going on at their tables and are all secretly and intently listening to what the woman is saying to the man and are anxiously, toe tappingly excitedly waiting to see if or how the man to whom the woman is speaking, will respond.

The woman's emotionally and super serious monologue comes to an end with a plea and some tears which were obviously held back and in for as long as possible but just couldn't be held back or in any longer and with the final plea (which was whispered more than spoke) tears, the size and density of which match the drops on the water glass of the man, pop out from underneath her eyes and slide slowly, almost reluctantly down her freckled cheeks. Some of the tears fall over her auburn lips and past her slightly crooked lips and down the downturned corners of and into her mouth. The man, who has sat still in his prayer-not-prayer position for the entirely of the woman's speech continues to sit completely still but his eyes, which are a grey flecked hazel, move back and forth from one end of the table to the other in a movement that can only be described as the human version of computing and processing.

While the man computes, the woman, with a slightly shaking hand, wipes away tears with her sleeve, which is cotton and soft and is attached to a short sleeve white polka-dotted, red dress in which she looks absolutely wonderful. While the man computes and the woman wipes away tears, the rest of the café patrons in the terrarium section of the café go silent. Everyone's breathing is hushed and nobody dares move. The plump man's cell phone rings, and with a bite-full of donut in his mouth (a bite-full that he is trying to chew without sound or movement) silences the call without answering; work can wait. The only visible movement in the room is the slight bobbing of the leaf beside the woman's hand.

From the main seating area in the café, outside the terrarium room, an analog clock ticks unimaginably loud. The sound of the clock has been previously drowned out by the many voices of the people in the terrarium room but now as everybody sits in held breath anticipation, it, the clock can now be heard. The only sound, other than the clock is the pounding of each individual's heartbeat in each individual's ears.

The woman sniffles, half to clears her nose of the mucus that comes from crying and half to get the attention of the man and to remind him that she is, that they all are, waiting for a response.

With his elbows still on the table, the man un-intertwines his fingers and rubs his hands together as he clears his throat and quickly glances at the woman without moving his head. He then lifts his elbows up from the table and puts one arm down under the table, and rests it on his leg. With the other arm, he reaches for the meniscus topped water cup, but the movement of the man's elbows make the table wobble and with the wobble the meniscus atop the water cup finally breaks and water comes pouring over the edges of the cup as he reaches for it, the cup. The wobble of the table caused by the lifting up of the man's arms has made both of the cups on the table wobble. The man reaches for his glass rather clumsily because his mind is focusing not on the table but on his response to what the woman has just said. As he reaches for his glass his torso bumps the already wobbling table and makes the table wobble even more. The table is now falling and so are the glasses and the whole room is watching the glasses and the table fall in what seems like slow motion. Everyone in the room is watching, but the man. As the table hits the wooden floor with a low thud and the glasses both shatter (spewing coffee and water in most directions). The man twists his chair so that he is face to face with the woman beside him and takes her hands (which are cold and soft and painted a light red at the nails) in his (which are worn and warm and callused). As the light brown liquid that was once contained in the confines of their respective glass glasses, looking like dirty puddle water, seeps across the broken pieces and settles in the gouges in the floor beside where the table once stood, the man looks into the sweet peppermint eyes of a woman who loves him; eyes whose loving gaze he most certainly, most probably doesn't deserve, and as he looks into those eyes he begins to speak; to apologize; to break open bit by recently encased in what felt like impenetrable glass bit.

As the table rolls back and forth on the wooden floor, like a fallen but still moving top, the rest of the room quietly erupts back into typing, non-serious conversation and statue-blueprint shading as if there had never been any silence at all. The scratches on the floor, the gouges made by the weight of flesh and bone are almost completely filled in by the mixture of the couple's beverages, although the water and the coffee settled into these scratches on the floor are not a permanent fix but perhaps they will fill the spaces for a while.

As the man speaks, holding the hands of the woman and looking into her eyes with his, sun shines through the ceiling and makes the broken pieces of glass on the floor glint and shimmer.

Above the table at which the couple sits, the leaf ever so slightly, bobs.

SITTER

One of your best friends from childhood has recently moved back to the place where you both grew up. You are happy about this friend moving home because it is always nice to see old friends and most of your other friends from back in the day, as they say, have long since moved away and are most likely never returning (well maybe for the occasional holiday visit but none of these once local friends plan to come back to actually live here). Your friend (the one who has just come back home) came home to be with his mother, or at least near his mother, who (the mother of your friend) has recently been diagnosed with terminal breast cancer and he brought his family with him; his wife and two children (a boy of three or four and a baby girl).

You have met his wife twice now and she seems nice, however she looks at you like she has heard many stories about you that have warped her perception. You know that look; that judgmental stare that seems to say that she knows all of the weird and fucked up stuff you did in and since junior high. His wife seems to make him happy and you want your friend to be happy you guess, so you are ok with her for now but it is not like you two would ever hang out one on one. The kids are fine; although you are really not a big fan of kids (you are certainly not having any of your own), the boy seems fine although he is a little bit loud and seems to always be picking his nose and the baby is just that, a sort of blob that constantly needs to be coddled and loved and fed and to have its diaper changed. You don't love spending too much time near the baby and it's incessant crying and needing; you feel like leaning over and whispering in its ear that it has no idea how lucky it is to be treated so well and that its only going to get worse for it, but you don't whisper that (at least, you haven't yet). They are a bit confusing for you, the kids, all of the endless commotion and movement, and you cannot seem to remember their names or their ages and end up asking your friend or his wife over and over again what the kids names are and how old they are, and this repetitive asking and forgetting, you are sure, is certainly not helping your friend's wife's opinion of you.

When your friend first moved here, or more before he moved here, he came to visit his mother and you met up for lunch and to go with him to search for a place for him and his family to rent. He was late to the lunch because he had been at his mother's house with the rest of his family sort of going over the details of the disease and its treatment and he had lost track of time because as he put it, everybody was crying and he himself was a wreck. At the time, you understood that he was going through a hard time but you were not super happy with the fact that you had to wait at the café where you were going to eat lunch for like a half an hour and you had not eaten before coming because you had thought that you would be eating quickly but due to his late arrival you were famished and your stomach was hurting. But so anyway after lunch, you and your friend went with a realtor to a bunch of different houses and your friend was being really picky about where he wanted to live, saying how this place didn't work because it was in the basement and there was barely any light or how this place was too cramped for four people or how this place looked like a murder scene and not an apartment, and you just kind of wandered along behind him, feeling hungry and tired and annoyed and thinking that it was a mistake to have come.

Finally, he settled on a two bedroom, one bathroom cabin on a couple of acres close to his mother's house and with a view of the mountains (and with a nice hot tub in the back yard that overlooks the forest and from which one could see the stars, as the relator pointed out). He asked you if you liked the place (as if he had consulted you at the tens of other perfectly fine places to which he had said no) and you said more or less yeah, and he said that you could make yourself at home there too and you said you would, and even though he seemed like he was joking you weren't really.

So, he moved back and you were happy to have somebody to hang out with besides your parents and their dog, and you went over almost every night the first week that he arrived (until he took you aside and said that he and his family needed a bit of space and that you should not come over for a couple of days). After that night, you drove home in your dad's car and thought about how your friend thought that he was better than you and how just because he had gone to a school on the east coast and had met a nice woman and had two kids and a high paying job and so on and so forth. Just because you still live with your parents (even at your age) and work at the mini mart by the highway and you don't have your own car, he is not better than you, even though it seems like he and his wife and your parents and more or less everybody else in your hometown seems to think so. But you remember when your friend was like you and how you used to go to that empty lot beside the lumber yard after school and smoke joints behind that massive pile of logs, and you remember how he would always cough when he inhaled the smoke and how you would always be able to hold your inhale in the longest. You remember how you asked that girl to homecoming junior year and how you went with her and had a tie that matched her dress and how your friend didn't have a date and you took him along with you and your date to dinner because you felt kind of bad for him, not having a date and all. But apparently, nobody else remembers that, nobody besides you seems to remember how you were cool and your friend was that skinny kid who would always follow you around. No, it seems like he is the cool kid now, or at least that is how he acts and that is the way his wife seems to treat you. The least he could do is show you some respect and remember that you used to put up with him when he was nothing and you were the king.

So, you stopped going over every night to spend time with him and you stopped texting him to see what was going on, and you tried to do other things but then he texted you and asked you if you could come babysit for him. He went on to say via text that their sitter had gone out of town and that they had tried to find other sitters but that they had no luck and were desperately in need of a baby sitter for tonight because his mother was going to be in surgery and he and his wife were going to need to be able to fully give all of their attention to helping care for his mom and they couldn't really have the kids to take care of. Your old friend went on to say that he would have to owe you a big one if you could come watch his kids, and you liked the sound of that. And so, you texted back and said that yeah it would be no real problem to come over. He responded that he would be happy to pay you for your time and you thought that you should most likely say that you would do it free of charge but then you thought about the fact that you are actually really in need of money this month, especially since your parents have started to charge you rent for living in their basement and also because you bought a new and expensive bong which most certainly was worth the money but which pretty much broke the bank, as they say, and also which your friend had no interest in trying out when you told him about it and brought it over to show him (but that was most likely because he was afraid to cough and look weak like he always used to do, he was afraid to be showed up, once again, by you). So, you said that he could pay you and you made up a super high hourly rate that you told him you usually charge for babysitting even though you have never babysat before and he said fine and said he would see you this evening.

So now you are at his house and he is long gone, at the hospital with his stupid wife and his mom or whatever. You came over at around five in the evening and put the kids to sleep more or less as soon as you had made sure that your friend and his wife were out of the driveway. The baby fell asleep quickly after you gave it the pacifier and the little boy was a bit whiny but after you gave him a bottle in which you put a bit of juice and some whiskey, he quickly quieted down. So, you have basically been paid to just hang at your friend's house which in your opinion is a pretty sweet deal, especially since you charged him double what you make hourly at the mini mart.

And after you put the kids to sleep you smoked a nightcap, i.e. you smoked one of the joints that you brought over and as you smoked your joint (and didn't cough for the record) and stuck your head out of the sliding glass door to blow the smoke out of the house you saw the hot tub and how nice it looked beneath the night sky and the stars and you decided to go in once you had finished your joint and made yourself a drink with some of the whiskey you had used to help the little boy to fall asleep (whiskey you found in the cabinet above the refrigerator).

One minor setback with your plan to chill out in the hot tub was that you realized that you didn't have a bathing suit but you decided you will just go naked because for one nobody is awake here at the house and for two your friend and his wife shouldn't be home for a little while. So now you are naked and your clothes are piled on the couch beside the sliding glass door that leads out to the patio on which the hot tub sits and you figure that you will just go in the hot tub for a bit and drink your drink and look up the stars and just take it all in and then you will come back inside and go to the bathroom and use one of the towels in there to dry off before your friend and his wife get home and then sit on the couch and watch TV and make it look like you never were in the hot tub at all. So, you step outside and close the sliding glass door behind you and its colder than you remembered it being outside and you are sort of shivering as you walk across the cold flagstone patio to the hot tub. You fold up the top of the hot tub halfway because you think you may not be able to put the entire cover all the way back on, on your own.

You are about to get into the water but you realize that you have forgotten your drink inside on the counter next to the whiskey bottle and a plastic gallon of orange juice that you took from the fridge and you decide that you don't need your drink and that it will be more refreshing after you have soaked in the hot tub and come back inside. So, you hop over the lip over the hot tub and splash into the water and you take a big gasping breath. The water is freezing; the hot tub must not work or maybe is not turned on. Your teeth are instantly chattering and goose bumps break out across your naked body.

Now you face the choice of having to either get out of the water and face the air which was already cold and will now most certainly feel colder or stay in the water. But if you stay in the water you will only get colder or at the very best stay the same temperature, which is most certainly not comfortable. You want to go back inside and you can see the lights inside and you know that once you get in the house you will be warm again but the thought of getting up and out of the water and walking across the patio dripping wet makes you shiver even more than you already are. But being in the water is absolute misery; it stinks like chlorine and stings your eyes with its chemical stench along with the fact that you are so cold now that your toes are beginning to tingle and go numb one by one. However, you are almost fully submerged in the water, you are sunk down up until the bottom of your mouth, so that you can breath but so that everything else is beneath the water. Your head is wet from the splash that occurred when you jumped into the water and your hair feels extra heavy on your head, you think your hair might be freezing into dreadlocks of ice and dirty hot tub water.

You are naked and soaking wet in the dark alone, unsure of what to do, unsure if you should emerge and head towards the light and the unknown frigidity of the space between the tub and the house or stay where you are freezing but safe in your knowledge of the temperature.

At the other end of the house, it sounds as if your friend and his wife have just pulled into the driveway. You can see the shadows of headlights like sleepy yellow eyes in the night and you can hear muffled voices. You want to call out to your friend and tell him where you are but you remember that you are naked and that maybe you shouldn't be naked, but you are cold and want to be helped. You imagine your friend and his wife wrapping you in a big and fluffy towel and bringing you inside to warm up but you think it is too cold to move or speak. Now you watch as your friend and his wife come into their house and you hear them call your name.

So Early It's Late

It is so early that it's late.

Well it's not technically late but it feels that way to her, that's to say she feels like she hasn't slept enough and honestly that is most likely the case because she hasn't. She went to bed at around midnight last night and when she awoke she didn't look at a clock but she doesn't think she could have slept for more than three hours, i.e. she is exhausted but cannot sleep.

She is sitting on the tile floor of the kitchen of her apartment in the dark and although it is not cold out, she is. She is cold because she is wearing a long white t shirt and wool socks but nothing else and her kitchen floor, well the tile that makes the floor of the kitchen of the studio apartment which she rents (but does not own) sort of sucks ups cold from the air around it and that sucked up cold is seeping slowly into her entire body through the parts of her body that are resting against the tile on which she sits (those parts being her feet and her butt).

She doesn't know what time it is because she doesn't want to check. She woke up about ten minutes ago and, dreary eyed and with slow, stumbling feet she made her way to the kitchen (picking up a cold cup of coffee from the counter before she sat). She thought that maybe through the window in her kitchen she could get some fresh air and to maybe see the stars; but it turns out that is not possible as the stars are covered by clouds and even if they weren't, the urban neighborhood in which she lives (and the bustling, crazy city of which the neighborhood is part) generates too much light pollution for anybody in the general vicinity of said urban neighborhood to see the stars even on a night clear of clouds. Although she does not know what time it is, she decided that if it is earlier than four a.m. she will go back to sleep but if it is later than four a.m. she will stay awake and watch the sunrise or watch a movie or just lie on the couch and stare at the ceiling.

She doesn't know what she hopes for.

It would be nice to be able to go back to sleep, well a lot of different scenarios would be nice but they aren't likely and neither is the possibility of her actually falling back asleep, at least not now. It's not likely for her to fall asleep now because beside her on the floor is a cup of coffee and that cup is white and its half full of black coffee and this cup is her second cup of coffee (in terms of measurement not in terms of beverage receptacle i.e. she has drunk two servings of coffee from this cup, well one and a half seeing as the cup is only half empty at this point and she has stood up once in the last ten minutes to fill up said white cup with more cold coffee from the pot on the counter of her kitchen and while she was standing up in the kitchen filling up her coffee cup she forgot to look at the clock on said coffee pot stand or on the oven or at the clock on the wall to see what time it was). And but anyway the caffeine from her one and a half cups of coffee has permeated her body (as has the cold from the outside air and the tile of the floor) enough that there is just absolutely no way that she will be able to slow down her mind and heartrate enough to actually fall sleep again, not for many hours at least. And but then when the night comes again she will most likely have a hard time falling asleep and staying that way not because of the coffee nor cold but because of what woke her up this morning in the first place (and what in part, along with the coffee, is keeping her awake now).

And that thing, that throb in the dark, which jostled her out of the warmth of her unconscious and much needed rest, is how wonderful of a day she had the day before, i.e. yesterday.

There are no cars on the street beside her house, and this seems strange to her because she is almost always only awake during times when there are not just some but a lot of beeping, idling, exhaust producing machines and so now, when there is nothing and nobody out on the road (with the exception of perhaps a raccoon or some trash that has blown out of somebody's trash can or which has been thrown onto the street by somebody who does not believe in trash cans) she feels a bit uneasy. She isn't sure whether her uneasy feeling is from the fact that she has had no more than four (but most likely less) hours of sleep, or if her uneasy feeling is from the silence or from the fact that she has almost drank two cups of coffee on a completely empty stomach or most probably what is giving her this queasy sensation is that thing that kept her up (along with the mix of all of the other things listed above as well).

What that thing is; that needle in her side; that mix of words and sounds and pauses and eager eye brow movements is a date that she went on yesterday with a man whom she once knew long ago and has recently reconnected with after running into him at a grocery store and getting his phone number and promising to call, which she did, resulting in the date that happened yesterday.

It's not that she had a bad time on the date, not at all. She had a wonderful time and in some ways, some shallow, twisted and fearful ways, she wishes she hadn't. With the weaker parts of herself, she wishes the man with whom she spent almost twelve hours yesterday had been nasty or ugly or cold or rude or something bad; she wishes, with some of the worst places inside of herself, that she had a bad time.

But she didn't have a bad time, the day proceeded like some cliché romance movie (a movie which she would make fun of with her friends, while hoping secretly that she could ever be so lucky). The leaves were falling outside; spinning slow as they fell in a breeze that was warm and smelled sweet. The sun was out but there were enough clouds that the sun did not beat down like it does so often, the clouds acted as a sort of filter through which the rays of the sun were somehow dulled to a perfect and golden temperature. Yesterday everybody seemed to be walking lighter on their feet; people were smiling at each other; children were squealing and running about; somebody was blowing bubbles which shone and shimmered as they pulsated and popped into drips of flawlessly refracted rainbow light. The mood on the street beside the restaurant where she and the man met for the date was filled to the brim with the societal energy equivalent of a glint in someone's eye; the air was buzzing with a sort of glee. They elected to sit outside because of the rare and most welcome soft warmth that had befallen the city and as they sat at their grey-white wood table, they watched people walk past. The conversation was good and natural and he had a buttery deep laugh that made someplace in her chest quiver with a balmy attraction every time she heard it. He was strong but quiet, kind in a way that made her blush, gentle but not too much so.

And even thinking about it now, about the way his hair fell nearly perfectly down across his forehead makes her want to puke. She is not a sap. She is not some romantic; not some poet wandering the streets at dusk looking for some long-lost love from a past life to fulfil her. No, she is just a regular person, she has a day job at an office which she barely puts up with, she has a couple plants that she has to try hard to remember to water, she has a father and a mother and a little sister. She has friends, some better than others. She has bad dreams that wake her up in the night and she will sometimes sing in the shower. She isn't exceptionally beautiful but she thinks she is cute and she knows how to dress in a way that subtly shows off her figure (which she works hard on the treadmill and at yoga classes to keep up). She feels lonely often but doesn't know that finding somebody would really do anything to quell that loneliness. There have been times in the past (some of her loneliest nights) during which, even while lying next to someone in bed, she has felt stone cold and utterly, completely alone. She knows she has flaws, she isn't the best at communicating her feelings (especially when she is intensely feeling those feelings which she needs to communicate) and she can be short and grumpy and terse when she is tired or hungry or just not feeling like talking.

But all of this is kind of beside the point, her flaws and fears and dreams of failure and humiliation in the night are not why she is tired nor why she is terrified and cold on the kitchen floor in the dark. Yes, she is happy to have met the man who she met, but with this meeting (a meeting she has needed, and deeply yearned for, for so long) has come with a certain and atrophying terror. This dread; this wicked fire in her gut; this gnawing and gnashing wonderful thing that tore her from sleep is that this man and her will become something together; that they will continue to see each other; that there will be days of walking in parks that before seemed dull, but with him seem full of life and infinite; that there will long nights of slowly eating meals which they have cooked together and of laying together in her bed watching the rain run down the window pane and listening to the sirens and brick-wall-hushed yells from the street; that there will be slow mornings spent doing the most tremendous nothing of all; that there will eventually be fights and screams and glasses thrown hard against the wall; that there will be days of silence and pained looks; that there will be times when they softly kiss and hold hands in the street as they walk together to the grocery store to pick out food that they will share and eat together; that there will be ups and downs and that they will have each other; that they will become almost part of one another (as cheesy as that sounds); that they will be each other' everything and that one day (be it a year or a month or a lifetime), one of them (or both) will be left alone. She is afraid that things will go well; that this man will become her somebody; that this somebody will become the person she associates with every love song on the radio; that the love, this man, this companion whom she is, as everyone may be, designed to find and keep and hold tight will become what she looks forward to at the end of each work day; that while doing anything else her mind and heart and spirit and whatever other holy places within her (or at least bits and blushing pieces of all of those things) will be locked in bed, warm in his embrace.

And ugh, these thoughts of romantic bliss are disgusting and beautiful and so fulfilling and exciting that she thinks she will burst right now; that she will simply cease to exist, but she doesn't combust or implode of tear apart with the thought of maybe falling in love with this person; this man; this new obsession and cause of both deep anxiety and internal blow torch heat.

Yet again, she is getting ahead of herself. She has gone on one single date with this guy; this new meaning of her life, yet she has already planned out her entire relationship. What she is really afraid of is the pain she will feel if it ends; what if she isn't good enough for him; what is he isn't good enough for her; what if all this intensity she feels now fades; what if she doesn't like him after a couple of weeks; what if everything is better than she could have ever imagined anything could be and they live together and everything seems to glimmer and shine in a new sort of way and then he dies in a car accident? There is so much worry and pain in love (or whatever it is she has with this man whom she barely knows) but it may all be worth it in the end, or it will all crash and burn.

Oh well, she decides, there is nothing she can do now to quell her fears and there is no way of knowing what will happen with her or this man or really with anything else. Above the cold tops of the other brick buildings in her neighborhood she can see lava red cracks of sunlight starting to twist and reach across the sky; it must be later than four, maybe she slept for longer than she thought she did. The sun is coming up and she resolves to watch it come up and light her city, and after the sun is up; after what is dark is brightened by that big and glorious thing; she may go back to her bedroom and try to fall back asleep or maybe give her new man a call.

STEAM

After work at the bowling alley you usually take a bath, a hot one that generates steam which twists and spins into the thick and wet air of the small
and cave like bathroom of your basement and also quite cave-like apartment.
Not even the piss and mildew smell of the bathroom nor the crusty stains
on the cheap faux tile floor nor the cramped too-small porcelain-style plastic basin can take away that gentle feeling you get from sitting; wallowing;
melting into that liquid warmth. There is a calm in that tub unlike anywhere
besides maybe the deepest of sleep and possibly even deeper than even that.

Back at the bowling alley you work in a room spraying aerosol disinfectant into the required rentable bowling shoes which (the shoes) are black
and red in the men's sizes and black and white in the women's sizes; first
you place the shoes onto the countertop in front of you and with a gloved
hand (the kind of easily breakable and heavy hand sweat inducing blueish,
nearly translucent latex glove) you lift up the tongue of each shoe and point
the sprayer end of the aerosol disinfectant can towards the now widened
opening of whichever shoe sits on the counter and then you spray the disinfectant into the shoe for around five seconds per shoe and to be clear your
hand which holds the can is ungloved because your boss thinks that only one
hand (the hand that actually touches the shoes) needs a glove and that the
use of two gloves is not only supposedly wasteful in terms of using some
product when it does not need to be used but also in terms of money, i.e.
he doesn't want to pay for you to wear two gloves every time you work and
so he makes sure that you don't and if you do you not only get in trouble
but are docked an hour of pay to cover the cost of buying an extra box of
gloves even though the gloves are only three dollars per box of one hundred
pairs of gloves and your hourly wage is (not much but still is) more than that
and the worst part of the single/double glove dilemma is that the gloves
actually come out of the box of gloves stuck together in pairs and so when

you take out one glove you have to take out two and since you don't want to get in trouble and certainly don't want another hour docked from your pay for using too many gloves, you have to carefully take apart the pair of gloves and put one glove back into the box and this glove that is put back into the box is almost always crumpled and ripped when taken out again and ends up being thrown out anyway and would have been better used and ripped from use instead of ripped from having been put back in the box, and you told your boss as much and he told you that you better not question his authority and that he makes the rules there and that if he says you should wear one glove you will wear one glove and to that you said that he could take all of his gloves and basically shove them up his ass and you then stormed out of the bowling alley and don't really even care about picking up your check for this past pay period because for one it was only for a couple of shifts and for two you never want to see your ex-boss or those stupid gloves or shoes or lined up cans of spray disinfectant again.

Calmed down a bit, you are back at your basement apartment and you are starting a bath because you did still work an almost full shift and you feel like you have had more stress than normal today so in some ways you need a bath more than usual.

Downward the water pours into a tub which although now cold will soon be warm and inviting.

Engulfed and soaking in a slightly chemical and fake fruit smelling steam and slightly oscillating water you are free and good and slightly softening into something maybe better. You rest your head against the back lip of the tub and look up at the ceiling of your bathroom which is low and slightly bulging and has a somewhat whiter patch than the rest of the ceiling that seems like where there used to be a leak or some type of hole that is now fixed or at least kind of is.

From the ceiling drips collected water and that dripping water has cooled and feels cold when dripped onto your body which is warmed and has been warmed by the water that is filling up the tub.

Grappling with the loss of the day you fade into the vapor and heat. As your head spins and your body floats you think that maybe the way things ended today, the way things always seem to do is somehow for the best.

Hot and wet in water that is still swirling with a low-lying fog you think you will stay here for a while; there isn't anything to do, no gloves or things to clean, no bosses or docked hours of pay, and maybe once you are out of the bath you will make some toast with jam and butter on it or simply stumble from the bathroom into bed.

STATIONARY

He decided not to get a treadmill because the idea of running in place was for one; too on the nose in regards to the way he felt his life was actually turning out and thus he didn't really need to do any more running in place on a daily basis then what he was already doing, which in his opinion was already too much, and for two because he hates running in general. He does though, know that he needs to start to get more exercise and that is why he was even considering the option of getting a treadmill i.e. he is already kind of fat and he is getting older and fatter and he knows deep down that he needs to get in shape or else he will most likely die a lot earlier than he plans on dying. It isn't that he has great plans for the future, he really doesn't have anything planned at all; he would most likely continue to work as a janitor for as long as he could physically do so, not because he specifically enjoys the work or finds cleaning toilets and exercise machines and being basically ignored by every person that walks through the door of the gym where he works exciting or fulfilling in the least, but because it is more that he is afraid of doing anything else and especially afraid of ending up in a situation where he will not be able to pay his bills. And he understands the irony or whatever it is of his need to buy an exercise machine when he works at a place filled with them, but the thought of exercising at the gym where he works makes him want to vomit. One thing he still has pride in is the fact that he pays all of his bills not only on time but as early as the company or person to whom he is paying said bills will let him pay, and the thought of letting these people down by not paying early or even on time or god forbid at all gives him such a deep feeling of shame that just the thought alone of not paying through his bills makes him sweat almost through his shirt.

It isn't that he is super happy with the way that his life has panned out, i.e. living alone in an apartment working the night shift at a gym and sleeping most of the day, which makes him want to try to live longer but it is that thought; the hope; the midnight dream that things will get better, that he will meet somebody, that he can maybe get promoted to daytime janitor; that he can live more of a normal and better life, it is these hopes that keep him going.

The treadmill, or more the idea behind buying the treadmill or some type of exercise machine like it, is an important step for him in terms of getting his life together; in terms of grabbing his own bull by its horns, but an actual treadmill seems like a terrible and depressing machine; a sad and utterly bleak reflection of his own life, so he decided not to get a treadmill and opted for something that was (at least in his opinion) less on the nose in terms of the meaninglessness and stagnant nature of his own life and more positive in nature. He bought a stationary bicycle. He actually hates biking and how much biking makes him sweat and puff and how dry it makes his mouth, but that is biking outside. With his stationary bicycle, he can watch TV as he puffs and pedals and sweats onto the towel he placed beneath his stationary bike.

And so, watching fake detectives solve fake crimes done by fake criminals on his TV, he now heads towards what he hopes will be a better tomorrow, moving nowhere but dripping and huffing all the same.

SUNSET

You are seated on your brown reclining chair.

The chair has become an important part of your life; it has become your friend. The chair is a bit too big for you and the cushions are worn and have a kind of musty smell, but somehow the chair is still appealing and comforting to you in a run down, beat up sort of way. The chair is where you sit after work. You got that too-big-worn-out-but-still-lovable-brown-reclining-chair from your neighbor after her husband died. You are sitting in this chair when it happens again. It has been happening more often recently. It used to come and go and it was never this intense but that feeling, that urge to slice into yourself, into your wrist, it comes like a wave and it hits twice as hard as your father ever could.

At first it is a falling, but not the weightless kind, it's a heavy kind of falling and it's cold. In the falling, all air rushes past and colors blur into grey and you kind of shrug away into the chair as the it, the falling, gets worse. Soon your body seems empty, sure the bones and the skin and the muscles and the scars are still there, the scars are always there and so are your eyes, reflecting off of anything they can to bare down on you, but you still feel empty and somehow non-existent while at the same time being utterly there and so wanting to not be. Your body feels empty because whatever warmth that is supposed to be present within, is gone. That golden light at the deepest internal point of being, inside of you has been replaced with a stone laden soil that feels coarse and clumpy and wet with a soggy hot rain and that feeling of the soil comes not from outside but from inside, from a place deeper than bones, the very marrow of your being. Your insides are turning bad while you sit in your brown recliner feeling that feeling, feeling that falling, feeling that it, again. You had been trying to relax, trying to wind down from your day at work, you had put on your favorite cd and were listening to your favorite song, which is track number seven on your favorite cd, and the music was finally succeeding in calming you down after another mediocre day spent doing menial tasks under florescent lighting.

But then the neighbor began to scream, not the neighbor who gave you the chair after her husband died, the neighbor on the other side, and the screaming sort of slapped you out of your calm and made the feeling, the falling, the it, come.

Now, after the falling has once again run its course, leaving you sagging, like a boneless pile of skin on your chair, you know you have to get up and leave. You know you have to get up and go on a walk, or get on that bike that you bought and promised yourself you would use but have not used. You know you have got to get away because you know if you don't, if you stay in your brown chair, the knife drawer in the kitchen will call to you. It, the knife drawer, is going to spell your name in Morse-code-bangs as it opens and closes. Inside of you, you can hear the rattling of steel and of black plastic handles and of the sharp edges. Knives are a special kind of cold. You know if you stay in the brown chair, those knives will be too tempting, and your veins will ache for their, the knives', bite more than they, your veins, already do. You know, once the blood in your wrists start singing to be let out, to be freed, to be released from its fleshy dam, you will not be able to hold out for long.

So, you leave, you get up from your brown chair, you abscond into the still day-lit evening. You are wearing a size-extra-large white t-shirt and size-large white underwear, no socks or pants or shoes or jacket or tie, just your tee shirt and your underwear that, the underwear, is sagging a bit on the ass. And your tee shirt is big enough that is hangs over your underwear, making it look like you are naked except for the tee shirt. You walk outside, into your driveway, stepping with shoeless, cold feet over grey gravel to your car.

You get into your car and you start it and you put it first in reverse and then in drive, after you have backed out of your driveway and then you drive. There is nowhere to go, but you drive.

The light outside is peach like a melted orange-creamcicle when the creamy inside has leaked out and mixed with and diluted the orange shell, the light is like that; a cream-muted neon orange.

The sun will set soon and you decide to try and find a pull off to park your car in and from which to watch the sunset.

You drive through the empty city.

The buildings are dark and everybody has gone home. The few people that remain and that you pass by are walking in twos. All you see are couples. All that you see are people holding hands. The people in the car beside you at the stoplight are kissing and you shirk down until you can't see them anymore and you turn on the radio to try and escape from your head and from all the couples that are surrounding and suffocating you. There is nothing on the radio but static; every station, number after scrolling number reveals just more static; a scratchy white noise that pesters and pokes your eardrums. The stoplight changes from red to green and the couple kissing in the car beside you doesn't notice the light change, but you do and you speed away and turn up the radio even though all there is, is static. And you roll up your windows and you scream but it is a weak scream that you can barely hear over the static, but you scream anyways as you drive out of the city.

You are driving towards a thin, winding road that overlooks the bay and is riddled with pull-offs from which the sunset set can be watched and it is from one of these pull-offs that you wish to watch the sunset, but as you arrive to every pull-off, each one is already occupied by a car of popular color and make and inside of the car or leaning against it or sitting on the hood, is another couple. Some couples, are sharing cigarettes with glowing tips the color of which matches that of the slowly descending sun. And some couples, are wrapped in multicolored blankets, cozy and rosy-cheeked having just finished a hood-top-picnic-dinner and most likely a bottle of under-ten-dollar-red-wine. And they are all bundled and they are all together and they are all warm within the embrace of each other and they are young and in love and you are alone and the radio is still playing only static and the windows of your car are still rolled up and you are still screaming but it's a quiet kind of non-scream-scream that seems to come not from your mouth but from your heart and your lungs.

You drive and every spot is taken, every pull off is filled with another couple in another perfect-looking car with its, the car's, little bits of rust and witty bumper-stickers and broken in passenger seats and you look over at your passenger seat and it looks like it has never been sat in, but that can't be true but it must be true because you can't remember anybody ever sitting in it and all the pull-offs are full. The sun is down and the colors that accompanied its departure are beginning to fade to grey. The sky is darkening but you are still looking for a spot to watch the sunset even though the sun is already down, maybe if you do find a place to pull off you will at least be able to hear the ocean or be able to see the shimmering lights of cargo ships in the distance. Eventually, cars full of red cheeked and smiling couples are passing you going in the opposite direction and they have their windows open and leaking out from those open windows you can hear music and you wish you brought your favorite cd but you forgot it in your rush to get out your door and all the radio is playing is static.

But now you have stopped screaming and the road curves away from the coast and you are taken deep into a forest. Dark and ragged shapes surround your car on both sides and no one is passing anymore, and you are alone again but you started out alone and have always been, alone, but now in the forest that feeling of being alone is somehow deeper and more penetratingly upsetting for you. As you drive you look out and up and try to see the sky or the stars and your headlights are dim orbs almost suffocated by the reaching blackness of the trees and you can't see the stars or the sky just the hint of your car's lights and the spreading deep of the woods.

In a flash, a fawn springs in front of your car. There is screeching and there is a thumping and sliding on the road and your car is stopped and you put the car in park and step out. The ground is cold beneath your bare feet and your legs are cold because all you have on are your white underwear and that white tee shirt.

In front of the car is the fawn and it is most certainly dead, it is not moving and its neck is broken in a way that makes its head bend back over its torso in an impossible seeming right angle away from the rest of its body. Its eyes are open and they reflect your headlights and the shapes of the trees.

You kneel down on the pavement and you extend your hand out towards the fawn. As you extend your hand, it is shaking. Above there are no stars, at least none that you can see because the sky is blocked by the clouds and the clouds are blocked by the trees.

From the car, you can hear the repetitive ding that reminds you that the door of the car is open and you can hear static from the radio wafting out from the open door and from the forest you can hear crickets and the rustling of a faint, night-time wind.

SUNSET PT. II

You want to watch the sunset.

You are all set up to do so, you are seated in a lawn chair on the light grey concrete of the driveway of your one-story house in which you now live alone. You always have said that watching the sunset is something that you often do, even though it is not, but you are trying to change that fact about yourself (among many other things). This night, tonight, watching the sunset is going to be a step for you in a new direction, and that new direction is a forward direction and that is to say you are moving forward towards a better you (although you are pretty sure that you are pretty much ok already, but you guess that everybody can be improved even if they are already pretty great as they are [like you are]).

The sunset is beginning.

That's to say that the sky is colorful and the light that is left other than the colors of the sky feels kind of thin and you can hear the frogs and the bugs starting to make their respective croaking and buzzing sounds in the lawns around your neighborhood and the lights that are on in the houses in your neighborhood seem to get brighter and brighter as seconds pass (but in reality it is the outside that is getting darker and darker) but anyway the houselights are beginning to glow in that cozy-yellow way that they do. The sunset is now full-fledged, that's to say that the sky is a surreal pink-ish red and it (the surreal pinkish red of the sky) makes you think about how so many people are just going about their normal everyday tasks and errands and are not really paying attention to the sunset, which by the way is quite beautiful tonight. And you realize that you could be one of the only people in the city (at least in your neighborhood, but most probably in your city) that is actually taking the time and space in their super busy lives to watch the sunset, which (in your opinion) is the most underrated part of the day. You often talk about how crazy it is that something so beautiful happens every day and you often then say that it is even crazier that most people don't even watch this beautiful thing when it happens every day.

But you are not one of those people anymore, you are in your lawn chair with your non-alcoholic beer in one hand and a menthol cigarette in the other and you are just fucking taking it in. You are really appreciating the spectacle of nature as the car sounds and the bug sounds and the frogs sounds and some jerk's radio or speakers from down the street make some type of ignorant racquet. But you aren't part of that anymore, you are free from not being free.

There is one problem though.

It's not really a big deal, but it is bothering you and it is taking away from your sunset watching experience. That thing (that thing that really isn't that big of a deal) is that there is a tree in your front lawn and the tree is sort of blocking the sunset (and there is another tree across the street in your neighbor's lawn that is also blocking your view, but the tree in your yard is much more in the way of the sunset than that in your neighbor's yard). And as the sun goes down further and the sky becomes more and more red, you end up looking not at the sunset but more at that goddamn tree blocking the view. It's not that you can't see the sunset because of the tree but that the sunset would just be so much better if you could see the whole thing. And even when you move your chair to the other side of the driveway and then onto your lawn and then onto the other side of your lawn the tree is somehow still in your view and is just consuming all of your energy and is ruining your sunset viewing experience.

So, you chug the rest of your non-alcoholic beer and burp and then you crunch the can up and pick up your lawn chair and take it back to the driveway. Then you lumber over to the door to the garage, not the garage door but the side door (like the actual door-door of the garage, not the door that slides up and down with the push of a button, but the wood door with a doorknob and a lock). You open the door with your house key because you always keep the door locked because you never know who could be in the neighborhood and what their intentions could be. You open the door to the garage and you go inside and you get that ax that you bought (the one with the wooden handle and the stainless steel head) and you bring that ax outside with you and you close and lock the garage door behind you because you might as well be safe because who knows if you will have to go to the bathroom or something in between the time that you need the ax for and the time that you put the ax away and you don't want to risk having someone being able to go into the garage while you are in the bathroom and maybe steal something, so you lock the door behind you as you step back out onto the driveway.

The sky is now a blood red, but not the kind of fresh blood, recent cut red, it's more of a smeared across someone's cheek almost dried blood from a broken nose kind of red. And you go over to that pesky tree that has been obscuring the view this evening and you start just going to town on it with the ax.

And the frogs and the bugs and some bats seem to be all vibrating at the same rhythm and the traffic sounds of the city seems to fade a bit as you whack and whack at the base of the tree, trying to hit the same section of tree every time.

And soon there are wood chips of most shapes and sizes scattered around the lawn on which you are standing and in which the tree that you are cutting down is planted. The indent in the tree that you have made with the ax is now about halfway through the tree and your shirt (which is thin and cotton and used to be white but is now greyer than it once was) is soaked with an almost sticky sweat that smells a bit like that non-alcoholic beer which you recently chugged.

After many minutes of hitting the tree with your ax, the tree starts to creak and sway and then with a couple more, hearty swings you fell the tree and it lands with a thud between two red cars that are parked beside the curb by your house. Yellowing leaves flutter in the air above your head and around where the tree landed. For a second the frogs and bugs stop their noise and even the city halts and the sunset, in all its fleeting red-purple glory, is there in full view in front of you.

The city sounds start back up as you stand in your front yard, leaning on that ax. And the frogs and the bugs once again commence their nocturnal buzzing and you can see the shapes of bats zipping about and both of your hands are now throbbing and you are pretty sure that you have a couple of blisters on each hand. The tree is down and your view of what is left of the sunset (which is not much) is somewhat improved and you open up that lawn chair again and you set the ax against the side of your house to be put away later and you sort of jog back into your house and grab a couple more non-alcoholic beers. and you come back outside and sit back down in your chair and watch the last splinters of sunset retreat from the sky along with most light from the sun, and as the dark really begins to set in you realize that the tree in your neighbor's yard is truly in the way of a really decent view and that behind your neighbor's yard, in the yard of the house behind theirs there is a tree that is also sort of obstructing your view. And you decide to talk to them about having their trees removed or at least trimmed so that soon, in the next couple of days or at the latest weeks you will be able to watch the sunset in all of its wonderful beauty while the rest of the idiots in the city continue to go about their daily lives without even once looking up at that daily art show in the sky.

SUPERMOON

There is a brewery and inside of that brewery (which is really just a bar made for, marketed towards and currently filled with [excluding the two men by the dart board) young, hip, rich, fashionable people).

The floor of this glorified and pseudo-upscale pub is wooden and dark brown and is covered with streaks that (said streaks) are even darker brown then the wood floor already is and which (said streaks) are made from shoes and stools and dropped glass cups, which shattered upon impact. Other bars or restaurants may buff out those streaks and marks on the floor; those other places try to wax out the filth and can often succeed at doing so over and over again, but this place, the brewery or more the people who own operate and market the brewery, purposefully don't do much cleaning of the floor at all, i.e. this brewery wants to look fashionably rustic and beat down enough that people who are in the know and who are considered cool, or whatever the term for cool is these days, will come to said brewery but clean and upscale enough that the usual barcrowd of bums and beat down people who lean too far over their drinks and speak too loud and often, wont. There is a smell and that smell is earthy and slightly sour in a way that stays with one even after having left said bar, and said smell comes most likely from stale beer and sweaty, drunk bodies. This not entirely bad smell comes from overflowing cups; this smell is from stumbling people; loud and clumsy, tripping into the night.

Outside the double pained and wood framed windows of the bar, there is a moon; full and glowing and yellow like a dollop of melting butter in a pan, but none of the patrons in this place seem to notice.

The two people playing darts are both men and both of these men are thick in a muscular (but not toned) way and have scraggily beards and are wearing clean looking blue jeans and open button down shirts. They are by no means poor but are most certainly not rich, and really in comparison to the rest of the people in the bar (the tech start up, ivy league or west coast equivalent educated and young types) they are sort of poor (and even if they are not poor or uneducated or somehow less than the rest of the people at the bar they are most certainly looked down at as so by said people at the bar). One of the men by the dart board is a tradesman, a drywaller; a man who makes his living working in the dust with hands that have grown hard as the walls his makes when they are finally hung right and dried. This man, the drywaller, is also a painter and uses the funds from his dry-walling to buy the best types of oil paints he can buy and with these paints (on the weekends and during whatever few splinters of daylight he has left after each long workday) he paints (on huge eight by eight foot canvases which he hangs himself) scenes of fallow and empty fields beautiful in their bleakness and in the vivid detail he painstakingly puts into every stone and bent, dead stalk of un-plucked wheat. He has sold one painting to a friend of his mother's and he presumes that the purchase of this painting was half-done out of pity (and most certainly done out of suggestion from his mother to said friend who had pity purchased said painting). But even with the fact that he has only sold one of his hundreds of paintings (which are currently taking up nearly every inch of the garage beside the house which he rents) he still paints, and he doesn't really even paint with the intention of selling his work (although if asked he would say that selling his work is his dream and ultimate goal) but because of his need to do it. It is not really even anything to do with pleasure or creation or some sick need to be famous or great or world renowned or somehow known and accepted and loved for what he makes. No, he drags the brush against that rough and thick sheet of canvas because he needs to; the images of empty fields and of snow and rain and distant mountains too massive and far away to know anything about other than their size and overall powerfulness come to him in the night and in the haze of drywall dust in which he works. His hands move. Drywall cakes his fingers and spreads, like a reaching toxic fungus beneath his nails and inside of every crack and crevice in his body. His mind races and fuzzy pictures of those things he will soon paint, fill his head like smoke in a room with no windows on fire.

He, the drywaller, is not appreciated for his work although most houses are filled up with drywall; sometimes he wonders if people think that houses just suddenly appear out of nowhere; that somehow these mansions of brick and wood and insulation are made easily in the night, forgetting that each house, each dwelling comprises months and months of work by tens if not one hundred people working their bones to nothing; sweating and bleeding in the grime and heat and dust.

The other dart player, a man who the drywaller has been friends with since childhood. (A childhood which was spent in a neighborhood that was recently demolished to make way for a single, massive house, inside of which the dry-waller will most likely end up hanging the drywall), is a teacher at a school that will be shut down at the end of the year (and most likely also demolished to make way for a parking lot or a fancy apartment complex or maybe another mega-mansion with a fountain and a garden and a pool). The teacher teaches a class simply called computers and during his off periods (of which he has three, but not in a row) he smokes cigarettes in his car in the teacher's parking lot and stares at the sky through the sunroof in his car (which although it provides a decent view of the sky, has been broken for the entire time he has owned the car [which he purchased used] and which, as a mechanic friend of his told him, would cost more than the entire car is worth to replace).

Both of these men try to be kind to those whom they love and to those whom they don't; they both try to say "how are you" to people they meet and actually try to really listen for a genuine answer; these men try to be good (as good as anybody can be), and they are good (or at least as good as anything else). They are both on their third beers of the night and they are both red cheeked and are laughing and slightly swaying as they stand by the tall circular table that sits close to the dart board as they take turns throwing darts at the board and playfully jeering at each other, calling each other names and occasion-ally letting out a whoop of laughter that echoes across the bar and is returned by downward looks from people with upturned (both literally and proverbially) noses. The drywaller is winning in the game which they are playing and has only to hit the bullseye once more to finish the game, but the teacher is catching up; it should shape up to be quite a show down (although nobody is watching and the outcome of some amateur game of darts at some pretentious bar in a city that is slowly being bulldozed to make room for more second or third or fourth houses for the uber-rich, doesn't really matter).

Outside the brightest and biggest moon of the year (and possibly the next) illuminates the empty and cold cars in the parking lot beside the bar, as the drywaller slightly misses a bullseye and lets out a comedic-ly dramatic sigh and finishes his beer, waving at the bartender for another round.

Three pm

There is a bar in the downtown of a city.

The city, where the bar in question is located, has around eighty thousand inhabitants. Of the eighty thousand inhabitants of the city, in which the bar in question is located, the majority of said inhabitants are in their homes, homes which constitute of; houses; townhouses, houses converted into apartments, community houses and one apartment building that stands fifteen stories tall (nine stories taller than any other building in the city) and which, the apartment building, is made of a dried-mud colored brick. The bar is one and a half blocks away from the apartment building, and (the bar) is located in the basement of what used to be a laundromat but what is now a vague "tech company" that, the tech company, has no name or sign on the front door and many grey desks on top of which are computers and beside which are rolling desk chairs (these things can be see when one presses their face against the glass of the front door of what used to be a laundromat, after hours, in a failed attempt to find out what kind of tech company this tech company is exactly).

Inside of the bar there is a black clock with a cream white face and black hands which hangs above the bar on a nail against a dark green wall that, the wall, looks black due to the lighting in the bar. The lights in the bar are always so dim that it seems each color in the bar must choose between being black or white, a color which when chosen by said object, said object must be seen as. And thus, the dark green wall seems to have chosen the color black to emulate and is doing such behind the clock which, the clock's, outer border and hands it, the wall, matches. The clock is three minutes slow and although every employee of the bar (of which there are two) and every regular of the bar (of which there is one) know that the clock is slow, the clock will never be adjusted to show the correct time because, as unofficially agreed upon, according to all parties involved with the bar, three minutes

slow is close enough to the real time and not worth taking the time to correct. The black clock on the quasi-black, actually-dark-green, wall says that
the time is two-fifty-seven and thus most other clocks in the city say that the
time is three pm on the dot (or maybe a few seconds past the so-called dot).
However, since the clock is analog, by just reading the time on the clock, the
reader of the clock, if said clock in question is analog (which it is), will be
unable to ascertain whether the time displayed on said analog clock is in fact
AM or PM. Whether any time in general is AM or PM is often understood by
whomever is reading the clock, by how much or how little daylight is present
outside; i.e. if it is dark out then it, the time, is most likely PM and if it is
light out, it, the time, is most likely AM. However, there are a few cases and
a few places where and when it is nearly impossible to tell whether the time
shown on any analog clock is AM or PM, because A.) It is winter and is dark
during so many hours of the day that, for example, both five am and five pm
are times which are completely dark and thus, whomever is reading the clock
and attempting to determine whether the time is AM or PM cannot use the
degree of lightness to determine what they are trying to determine and thus
will have to use other forms of time perception such as said individual's level
of fatigue which could indicate how long said individual has been awake and
thus what time it is. However, this latter type of time perception is highly
susceptible to various variables that deem it mostly untrustworthy. Or B.)
the place in question in which the analog clock in question is located, has no
windows nor ways to see outside and determine whether it is light or dark
out, thus making it nearly impossible to determine if the time is AM or PM.
The latter, option B.), is the case with the bar in question in the city with
eighty thousand inhabitants, the latter option specifically signifying that there
are no windows that show daylight or lack thereof, and thus any bar patron
will have a difficult time determining whether the time is in AM or PM. This
inability to determine the exact time is noticed most when looking at the
clock in the bar, gives the bar in question a certain timeless feel.

Of the eighty thousand inhabitants of the city in which the bar in question is located, there are many young men. Of the many young men in the
city, there are many who live in the sole apartment building. The apartment
building, located in the middle of the city, sticks out nine stores higher than
everything else in the city's skyline and looks like an upright, god-sized, turd
with windows and a basement parking lot. Inside of the apartment building
there is one young man of note and he lives on the fourteenth floor. This

young man will eventually go to the bar, however, at three pm (or two-fifty-seven, according to the black clock hung on the pseudo-black wall in the bar) the young man is in his one-hundred-and-fifty-square-foot apartment on the left side of the fourteenth floor of the only apartment building in the city. At three pm the young man is staring at the wall. On his wall, there is white paint. It's not the kind of white paint that one may see at a hip coffee shop or at an expensive clothing store, instead it looks as if the previous tenant of the apartment, or the landlord, painted the walls with crushed up egg-whites mixed with water and milk. That's to say that the paint on the walls of the young man's apartment is chunky and is cottage-cheese-esque in texture. It seems the walls would run onto the floor and slump in piles of coagulated-cellulite-white, if it were to get too hot or even hot at all, in the young man's apartment which luckily for the young man it has not yet done.

The young man can thank the apartment building's central heating system for the lack of heat in his room because said heating system is either controlled by A.) a polar bear or is B.) part of some government experiment in which scientists are attempting to discover how cold of an environment a human being is willing to live (and pay rent) in. No matter who (or what) is controlling the thermostat of the apartment building, the temperature is kept at what the young man guesses is less than ten degrees warmer than a refrigerator, an appliance that the young man cannot afford nor fit in his apartment, and because of his lack of a refrigerator and subsequent thirst for something other than tap water to drink, he will eventually get up and go to the bar. Although at three pm, he is staring at the wall of his apartment trying to decide whether the paint looks like spoiled-milk or spoiled-yogurt (although, really, there is not much of a difference) as he eats his seventh granola bar of the day (a snack of which most of his meals consist).

While the young man is eating his granola bar, inside of the bar beneath what used to be a laundromat, there are two people. One of the people in the bar is a half-brother of the co-owner of the bar, who, the half-brother, was given a job as a bartender at the bar not because of his qualifications (of which he has none) but because of his inability to get a job anywhere else due to his criminal history (which consists of multiple drug-related offenses and one DUI). The ex-con bartender was given the job of bartender because the co-owner of the bar, who is the bartender's half-brother, felt a familial loyalty to him, the bartender, and thus helped him, the bartender, out by giving him a job.

The other person in the bar is a man with scraggily hair. Many people have a quality (most often a physical quality, but occasionally this quality can be a personality quirk) that somehow defines who this person is to other people and, this quality, is somehow all someone else needs to know and understand to be able to, in a flash, completely and tragically know and understand the person with said quality or quirk. For the man with the scraggily hair, his scraggily hair is the quality that, upon sight, can quickly define who he, the man, is. The man with the scraggily hair's scraggily hair is shoulder length, a cigarette-ash mix of grey and dark-charcoal black, stringy in the way bits of wet newspaper hanging from bare tree branches is stringy and is rarely washed. The man with the scraggily hair's scraggily hair (if one were close enough to smell it, which the half-brother of the co-owner bartender is purposefully not) smells like a sponge used to clean the floor of a middle school boys' locker room that has been left out soaking wet for a week in a humid place where mildew certainly grows. Luckily people are rarely close enough to smell what the scraggily hair smells like, with the exception of the man to whom the hair belongs although he, the man with the scraggily hair, has long grown used to and subsequently numb to the smell.

There seems to be a person in every group of people that is an outcast; a black sheep; this much is pretty much fact. And that person, who serves as the outcast in each group usually has something which none of the other persons in the group have, specifically and most commonly a physical trait such as a weight-issue; as in the outcast in question is obese and the rest of the people in said social group are not, however occasionally if said trait is not a physical trait, said trait could be something like a stutter or and a lisp or an accent that none of the other people in said social group have. Simply put, in order to become the outcast of a group, the soon-to-be-outcast must have an actual perceptible trait that makes them, the outcast, different from each and every other person in the group from which they are eventually cast out. There are however, certain types of outcasts, outcasts of the outcast-community if you will, that have no easily perceptible physical or social trait which warrants their casting out, yet they are cast out anyway. It seems these normal seeming outcasts are only outcasts when there are no other, more outcast-esque outcasts available, thus making this seemingly normal outcast a fall back type of outcast. Now the young man, who is sitting in his apartment staring at the wall, has no perceptible physical or social outcast worthy traits, yet he often finds himself alone and in groups is often the subject of ridicule that is put off as playful jabs but in reality, comes from a dominant, quasi-alpha-male complex that seems to be especially rampant among young men. Thus, and therefore because of his, the young man's, outcast-ness he is alone at three pm, lives alone and spends most of his time alone, including his birthday (which is today). Although, in this loneliness, there isn't as much pain as there is blankness; a poorly erased whiteboard of emotion; smudges of suffering. The young man's loneliness is a numb torture that isn't as much excruciating as it is throbbing; a dull yet uncomfortable and constant splinter. That muted heartbeat of something a little bit less intense then the crushing sinking of un-chosen solitude is what the young man, who is now another year older, feels as he sits and stares at the curdled looking wall.

Meanwhile at the bar, the man with the scraggily hair is on his third beer and second shot. The beer (which is light and piss like, both in taste and in color) is in a twelve ounce glass and the shot (which is a bit darker than the beer in color, resembling a blood-tainted-piss but not a super-bloody-piss, a piss with just enough blood in it to darken the color without overwhelmingly turning it red, thus making the color of the shot a piss and blood reddish yellow-brown and in fact upon leaving his body the alcohol of the shot will remain more or less the same in both chemical content and color) is in a shot glass. The exact type of alcohol of the shot is not known by the bartender nor the man with the scraggily hair, but it, the type of alcohol that the shot is, is bottom shelf and comes from a label-less plastic bottle. The sensation that follows oral consumption of the alcohol which makes up the shot, which the man with the scraggily hair is drinking in sips rather than taking the whole thing at once, is similar to the sensation of a yeast infection in the tip of one's penis; that to say it stings but not in a warming pleasant cold-feet in hot-water way but in more of a painful, I-should-probably-go-to-the-doctor-and-get-on-antibiotics way. That's to say that the alcohol in the shot is not of good quality and even for the most experienced of drinkers, a group to which the man with the scraggily hair most certainly belongs, requires a chaser. The piss colored beer in the man's left hand is the chaser for the blood and piss colored shot, and so as he sips the liquid from the shot glass he follows with a larger sip, a gulp if you will, of the beer and that is why he is on his third beer and only his second shot.

It is now three twenty pm, according to most clocks in the city. The black clock in the bar says three-seventeen. The man with the scraggily hair can't remember if the time is in AM or PM and because of the lack of windows in the bar, the man has no way of easily answering his question using his observational skills, which are minimal and blurred, so he takes a sip from the shot glass, wheezes from the sting, gulps some beer, burps (causing some foam bubbles from his mouth to fall onto his cigarette-ash-colored beard), and without looking up he asks, presumably the bartender, if the time is AM or PM. There is no answer from the bartender because the bartender is not behind the bar, instead he, the bartender, is in the bathroom (the women's bathroom) snorting cocaine through a rolled up five-dollar bill (that he "borrowed" from the cash register behind the bar) off of the stainless-steel hand dryer beside the sink. The bartender is in the women's bathroom not because of any perverted reason but because it, the women's bathroom, is cleaner than the men's bathroom. However, to be clear the women's bathroom is cleaner not because it is cleaned more often or because what women do in the bathroom is somehow cleaner than what men do (it is most certainly not) but because the bar in question attracts mainly men and thus the women's bathroom is cleaner than the men's bathroom merely from lack of use. That is not to say that the women's bathroom in the bar is by any means clean, because in fact it is still almost unbearably dirty, but it is still less disgusting and less cave-like than the men's bathroom, which is why the bartender is in the women's bathroom snorting cocaine off of the hand-dryer, instead of in the men's bathroom snorting cocaine off of the hand dryer. While the bartender is powdering his nose in the ladies' room (non-euphemistically) and the man with the scraggily hair is unknowingly asking questions to nobody, the young man is walking down the stairs into the bar.

Upon entering the bar, as is the case with most basements and bars, especially basement bars, there is a musky stench which hits almost immediately and most definitely before one's eyes have adjusted to what is presumably, almost certainly, jaundice lighting absolutely swimming with specks of what is possibly and probably dandruff and dust that can be seen when the bar is briefly exposed to sunlight while the door is momentarily open. Thus, the one entering a bar, like the bar which the young man is entering at three-twenty, is blinded and overwhelmed both in sight and smell and therefore must rely on his or her other senses. So, as the bartender is snorting and the man with the scraggily hair is saying things to nobody, the young man is sort-of feeling his way down the staircase, using a crusty railing for support, as he tries to adjust his nose, to the musky piss-beer-and-body-odor smell of the bar, and his eyes to the piss colored lighting of the bar.

The young man and the man with the scraggily hair, besides being human males and being physically in the bar, have only two things in common. The first being that today is both of their birthdays; a fact of which the young man is painfully aware and a fact which the man with the scraggily hair does not, in fact, remember thanks to many decades of alcoholism, all around poor body treatment and severe psychological issues that prevent him from leading anything close to what most-people would call a normal life, which in turn has led to his only option being to drink and live on the streets, a lifestyle that is basically expected of him. The second thing that the young man and the man with the scraggily hair have in common is that both of their fathers were named John and were called Johnny by their, their father's, friends.

At three thirty, after waiting at the bar for ten minutes two seats away from the man with the scraggly hair, the young man is about to leave, when the bartender prances out from the women's bathroom feeling splendid. In a sing-song voice the bartender asks the young man what he will have to drink and the young man says that he wishes to buy everybody a round, on him. The phrase which he just insecurely mumbled, a phrase which he has never before uttered, is something that he has heard said in movies and in those movies, the utterer of those words had seemed rather suave and cool and sexy and had eventually ended up with the girl and the young man can't think of anything that he wants more to do than to end up with a girl, but in some ways that doesn't matter. And in response to what the young man said, which itself was a response to a question that the bartender should have asked many minutes before, instead of making the young man wait while he was in the bathroom, the bartender asks the young man what kind of alcohol he (the young man) wants his (the young man's) round for everyone to be. To which the young man responds "whiskey." The young man is extremely surprised that his is initial response had merited yet another question and subsequent response because in the many movies from which he had lifted his line about the round for everybody, there was no second question nor second response, the movie bartender had just seemed to know what type of alcohol the orderer of the drink in the movie had wanted, but that is not how it had gone in the young man's disappointing real life drink ordering experience. In fact, his second response of "whiskey" was not enough for the actual bartender, as opposed to the omnipotent movie bartender, because the bartender asks the young man "what type of whiskey?" and it seems that the sing-song-y voice in which the bartender asked his first question has been replaced with a tone of impatience and teeth grinding. The young man, having minimal to no idea what types of whiskey there are, looks frantically about and, hoping that what the man with the scraggily hair is drinking in the shot glass is whiskey (which it in fact is), points at the glass and says 'Whatever kind he is having." A response to which the bartender scoffs but obliges and takes out three clean-ish shot glasses from beneath the bar and proceeds to pour, from the label-less plastic whiskey bottle, three shots full of the piss-and-blood colored, worse than piss-and-blood tasting, knife-in-the-chest-sting- inducing, liquid. He (the bartender) pours one shot for himself, one for the young man and one for the man with the scraggily hair (who most certainly does not need any more alcohol).

While the bartender and the young man have been speaking the man with the scraggily hair has been in a type of alcohol-and-mental-illness-induced stupor which renders most sound into murmurs, light into haloed, too-bright orbs and all taste into ash. The stupor is broken, as much as a stupor that deep and psychological can be broken, by the bartender passing him (the man with the scraggily hair) a shot glass. Through the fleeting seconds of partial clarity from the semi-broken-stupor, the man with the scraggily hair is able to see the young man raise his glass in a comradery-esque cheersing motion (a motion the young man also learned from the movie he stole his drink order from). The man with the scraggily hair also, during the slightest of breaks from his otherwise numb and mostly deaf existence, is able to hear the young man say, as all three of the men in the bar raise their glasses up above their heads, "happy birthday." The young man was saying happy birthday to himself in a sort-of part-ironic, part-self-deprecating and completely lonely and pathetic gesture but the man with the scraggily hair, as he often does, reads the situation and what was said, differently than how it played out in reality. Although the man with the scraggily hair consciously, on the surface, did not know that, like the young man, it was his birthday, something extremely deep down inside the man with the scraggily hair knew. The 'deep' in reference to the depth within himself of the part of the man with the scraggily hair that knew it was his birthday is the deepest possible definition of deep; not a-hole-dug-in-one's-back-yard-deep but a-throw-a-penny-in-to-the-deepest-depth-of-the-ocean-and-then-swim-down-and-dig-on-your-hands-and-knees-until-you-feel-the-molten-core-of-the-earth-deep; a core code deep. Whatever subterranean cave of knowledge inside the psyche of the man with the scraggily hair that also holds the pieces that make this man human, it was in those dark recesses of the mind that the knowledge that today was actually his birthday, was stored. And from that dark place, that deepest of caves, upon hearing the uttered happy birthday, something emerged. Hearing someone, although mistakenly, say to him (the man with the scraggily hair) something as caring as happy birthday for the first time maybe ever, broke something open within the man.

The young man takes his drink of whiskey after saying happy birthday to himself and reaches into his pocket for his wallet with which, the money inside of the wallet, he intends to pay for the three shots of below-bottom-shelf-level, piss-and-blood-colored, whiskey. As he pulls his wallet from his pocket and sets it on the bar-top, the young man notices that the filthy-looking and terrible-smelling man two bar-seats away from him, is crying. The cries of the man with the scraggily hair are not dramatic sobs, it looks as if the man is coughing but instead of the sound of coughing emerging from the mouth behind the scraggily hair, whimpers and nose sniffles emanate from the shattered thing at the end of the bar.

The young man doesn't think much of the crying man and assumes, incorrectly, that the crying has nothing to do with him. The young man looks back to where the bartender had been merely seconds before, but is met with his own reflection in the mirrored shelves holding half empty bottles, in front of which the bartender had just been standing. The young man can see, beyond the bar, the back of the bartender's foot, disappearing behind the closing door of the women's bathroom. The young man overestimates the cost of the whiskey and leaves a few crinkled bills on the bar. As he turns to leave, he nods at the man with the scraggily hair, who has one thick, milky tear rolling down his face. The man with the scraggily hair does not return the nod of the young man, instead he takes a larger-than-normal gulp of beer.

The black clock with the white face on the dark green (turned fake black) wall now reads three-thirty-two but the clock in the bar is three minutes slow.

At three-thirty-two, according to the clock in the bar, the young man is exiting the bar and exhaling a sigh that, if one were to smell it would smell like shitty-whiskey and stale air, as he wonders what he will do for the remaining daylight hours of his birthday.

At three-thirty-two, according to the clock in the bar, the man with the scraggily hair has mostly stopped crying but is, quietly, making that stuttering-for-air sound which comes after crying especially hard, in between his sips of whiskey and gulps of beer.

At three-thirty-two, according to the bar's clock, the bartender, who is the co-owner of the bar's half-brother, is once again in the women's bathroom, snorting cocaine off of the sink beside a mirror on which the name "EMMA" is written in cursive with glossy pink lipstick.

And in the following years, on the following birthdays, as time clicks on with the black hands of the white-faced-clock in the bar, the young man may begin to feel less lonely. Maybe the young man will find love? Maybe he will find friends and in that find a community that will allow him to have people to spend his birthday with, instead of spending it alone. Maybe things will get better for the young man, or maybe not. Maybe his experiences in the past year; the grey loneliness, the hours spent staring at the rotten-looking wall; maybe those experiences are all building up to something after all. Maybe there is a reason. Maybe there is a way. Maybe not. Buzzed on the single-shot of whiskey and happy to be out of that piss smelling basement bar, the young man walks slowly back to his apartment in the warm sun and thinks how maybe, just maybe, things may get better for him from here.

And as time clocks by on the clock hung on the quasi-black wall in the bar, the bartender may spend more and more time in the women's bathroom. He may one day, become light-headed from a particularly thick and quickly snorted line of cocaine ingested through a rolled-up bill though his nose off of the metal hand dryer. And with that light-headedness he may slip forward and hit his head on the metal-hand-dryer from which he had just snorted cocaine. And subsequently, he and the metal hand-dryer (the hand-dryer's front dented from the impact of the bartender's head) may both fall onto the floor of the women's bathroom. And the bartender may lay on that floor unconscious on his back, long enough that he may vomit and suffocate on that vomit. And the bartender's body, may not be found until the co-owner of the bar comes into the bar to see just what the hell is going on and why he, the co-owner, has not heard anything from the bartender in days. And he, the co-owner, may find the body of his, the co-owner's, half-brother, on the women's bathroom's floor only because of the smell coming out from under the bathroom door most pungently than anywhere else. This may or may not come to pass, but as the young man walks back to his apartment, the bartender has returned from the bathroom again and is pocketing the cash the young man left on the bar, instead of putting it in the cash-register where it should go.

And the man with the scraggily hair, may eventually wobble up from the barstool, drunk to the point of seeing in an out-of-focus black and white, and from the bar stumble into whichever alley-way he is sleeping in. And in the morning, after most certainly not enough sleep, he may be awakened by hunger pains or by a garbage truck emptying a dumpster in the alley in which he slept. And after he has woke, he may go to his usual street corner and hold his cardboard sign, that says "$ 4 FOOD", up towards on-coming traffic. And with the money he makes from the corner, which may not amount to much, he may buy a meal from a fast food restaurant and then may use the rest of his money to sit at the bar and drink until he is drunk enough to go back to the alley. The man with the scraggily hair may, eventually, after months or years more of his routine, leave the streets on which he has spent most his life and stumble into the woods that flank the city. And in the woods, he may lie down wearing all of this clothes, although it may be warm out. And beneath a tree, he may take his last breath and it is unclear if anybody will find him. And it is unclear whether if somebody finds him, what they, the finder, will do. But that is yet to pass, and as the young man walks back to his apartment in the sun and as the bartender is stealing the money left by the young man, the man with the scraggily hair is finishing his beer and looking up at the clock hung on the wall and wondering if the time is in AM or PM as the seconds innocently tic by.

(UN)CLEAN

You wake up with a headache [one]. Since this (the headache) is a regular occurrence (or at least something that happens at a minimum of twice per week) you reach for the bottle beside your bed [two] and take a prescribed amount [three] (or at least the amount that you have self-prescribed) dry [three (a)(b)], after you sit up and push your wrinkled sheets off of your sleep stiff body.

And from your bedroom, you walk to the bathroom and get in the shower [four]. And from the shower (through the window in the grey tile wall beside the shower) you can see the sky [five] as well as the grass of your backyard [six].

Soon the shower is over [seven] and still dripping (wrapped in a towel that is frayed on the edges) you look in the mirror, and in that mirror you look and feel the same [eight] as before, but maybe now a bit cleaner.

And from the shower, you walk to the kitchen (still in the towel that is frayed at the edges) and you put on the kettle to boil [nine].

one Upon waking with this headache, you begin to ponder (rather anxiously) how and why you have this headache and why today (of all days) you have to have a headache (as if any day is a good day to have a headache) and upon waking with this headache (which is slowly worsening from a mere throb to a pounding nearly blinding migraine) you come up with three reasons why you may have this headache; the first reason being that you had three or four (you can't quite remember how many but you know it was no less than three and no more than four) beers (and not three or four of those light, three percent alcohol, piss tasting beers; you drank three or four real, eight percent stouts that [each stout] is the consistency of syrup and has as many calories as a loaf of bread) and therefore you may be just a bit hungover from said three or four beers; the second reason is that you didn't drink any water last night and have not drank any water in recent memory and on top of the beers you are possibly and probably and (now that you think about it) almost certainly, extremely dehydrated; and the third reason being that you need coffee (although you still hold true to the idea that you choose to drink coffee every morning because you 'enjoy it' even though you know deep down that it is not at all a choice to drink coffee, you need it) and since you have spent the minutes after waking up, in the white Saturday morning light trying to figure out why on earth your head is pounding like a goddamn thunderstorm, you have not yet drank coffee and therefore have not yet been able to fulfill that urge and (fine, you admit to yourself) addiction to the coffee or more, the caffeine that is in the coffee. And as you think more and more about why you have a headache, and the possible reasons you have said headache, you realize that the reasons (previously listed) are not mutually exclusive and in fact could be and are most likely working off of each other to make said headache even worse than it would be were only one of the possible reasons (instead of all three) the cause.

two You bought this bottle about a month and a half ago on a day much like today (or at least on a day which started out in the same painful way as today). However, the day on which you purchased said bottle of pills, (pills that are little and red and supposedly made to numb your headache as well as any or all other bodily aches and pains [of which you have a few, specifically in the area of your lower back, an area which was injured years ago but has never healed]) you also had a terrible headache (much like, but perhaps a bit less extreme, as the headache which you have now) but unlike today you did not have a handy little bottle of pills beside your bed that day (and the little in reference to the bottle references that size of the bottle in respect to its size in relation to the rest of the items in your bedroom, not in terms of the actual size of the pill bottle because said bottle was in fact the biggest size that could be legally purchased at the store at which you purchased it) and were forced to go outside with a terrible headache (free of whatever aid the pills provide) to go buy said pills to help with said headache.

three Said prescribed amount of pills (or more, self-prescribed amount of pills) has been slowly increasing since said pill bottle was purchased (see two) i.e. your tolerance has grown to said chemical combination since the pill bottle purchase, and although the bottle indicates and suggests two pills every six hours and no more than six pills in less than twenty four hours, you started with three pills and have worked your way up to five pills every six hours (or at least five pills each morning, you usually forget to take the pills after the first dose in the morning).

three (a) You take these pills dry even though beside your bed (in front of the bottle of pills) there is a cup of water (which is three quarters empty [or one quarter full] depending on your mood) and you could have taken the pills with said water, but you kind of forgot it was there and have grown used to taking the pills dry because most of the time you forget to fill the cup with water before bed (and the bit of water in the cup has been in said cup for who knows how long [certainly not you] and if water can go bad then this water certainly has long ago done so).

three (b) On the other side of the bottle of pills than the cup with the bit of water in it, there is a ceramic, egg shell white mug with no handle and in said egg shell white mug with no handle is soil and from said soil grows an inch-tall sprout of a plant you were told is some sort of succulent. You purchased said supposed succulent because you wanted to have something alive other than yourself to care for but didn't want something that needed a lot of care (or water) because you sometimes have a hard time surviving on your own without anything or anybody else to care for, so you opted for a plant but wanted something that was like super low maintenance and said as much to the man at the plant store and said plant store man told you about and showed you to the succulent section and in said succulent section you picked out the plant which is now beside your bed in the egg shell white mug with no handle. This succulent has now survived three months under your care and has shed a layer of its skin (or whatever outer-membrane plants have) a couple of times, but it seems to be doing ok (or at least looking not much different than it looked when you bought it). Also ever since you bought this succulent you have had this omnipresent but not overwhelming fear that this plant is dead but that you don't know what a dead plant such as this looks like when it is dead and therefore you have been watering and caring for something that is in fact not alive, but because you can't tell if it is in fact dead or alive you have decided that you might as well continue to water it and care for it (when you remember to do so) on the off chance that it is still in fact alive and or until you can for sure determine that it is really dead and therefore in no more need of your care or water. As you finish swallowing the pills you look down towards your supposed succulent, and cannot remember when the last time you watered it (the succulent) was and decide to use the little bit of water in the cup on the other side of the pill bottle to water the succulent.

four Once in the shower (or more once in the basin of the bathtub, naked and shivering in the squint-inducing and unforgiving morning light, atop frigid and immaculately white porcelain) you turn on the water and said water first comes out from the faucet of the tub and the water from said faucet is ice cold for only a couple of seconds (but seems like much, much longer) and said cold water climbs up the white of the tub until it pools around your feet making, you sort of lean from side to side on your feet in order to try and get out of said cold water until the water in the faucet finally warms up (which it, as always, eventually does). And when it does, when the water warms to a temperature that is not horrid, you switch the place from which the water pours from the bathtub faucet to the showerhead using a thin metal tab which is mounted atop the bathtub faucet and with the act of pulling the tab (after a half second of delay) warm water falls, like a liquid deep breath, onto a body that is as much yours as is it a gear in the grind of something big that you don't quite understand or love.

five In that sky, in that infinite thing above, besides a blue that is as endless as it is deep, there is one cloud and said cloud is straight and narrow and is cutting across the sky like a scar from a knee surgery on the kneecap of someone learning to walk again.

six In that grass, lies a bunny, asleep, and as it sleeps its light grey and white fur slightly rustles with a breeze that you imagine as warm (but are not sure actually is, and based on the weather report for yesterday, is most certainly cold and has a nip that indicates tonight there will be snow or rain or something wet and cold from the sky).

[seven] and with it ends the womb like golden heat of the water and the sense of disconnection, freedom and release that accompanies a much-needed shower in a morning (like so many others) when being awake is as hard (or harder) than most anything else.

[eight] Yes, you feel the same and there are still sirens out there beyond the walls of your rented house, and there is still air pollution and crime and women who wear their hair in ponytails and necklaces made of silver with turquoise pennants. There are still Sundays at diners with friends and poor quality coffee, there are still romantic walks in the rain. There is still everything that there once was, and your headache is still there, although the pills which you took are beginning to kick in and said headache is beginning to fade like the fingers of a nightmare you just awoke from sweaty and alone in the night.

[nine] because even if coffee (or lack thereof) is not the only cause of your headache, it certainly will be the start to a cure.

UNDERTOW

There is a sandy parking lot. There is also a sign that is white and on it there is a man drowning; this sign says not to swim but I plan to ignore this sign. No laminated metal with some crude drawing of a dying thing can hold me.

I park my car, and I can hear little bits of something wet dripping on the engine and evaporating with little pings into the white and striated sky as I get out and close the door behind me. My feet are bare and there are shards of gravel in the parking lot which poke into the bottoms of my feet and make my face scrunch up with pain. If the parking lot was entirely gravel or entirely sand I would be able to walk across it to the path which leads down to the beach and the waves and that wild ocean where I am not supposed to swim, but it's not and walking to the path is a slow sort of torture, not painful enough to do anything about but annoying nonetheless. A particularly sharp and pointy piece of rock stabs into the sole of my left foot right below my pinky toe and I think it is bleeding but I don't check because whether or not it is bleeding nothing can be done; I have no bandages or antiseptic to stop the bleeding nor the time to apply those things I don't have even if I did have them. I decide the grey sand of the parking lot will be my medicine and I grind my injured foot into it as I walk towards the path to the beach.

I can hear the waves before I see them, and smell the salt on the wind. Today is colder than most in this place: I was alone when I stopped my car and assume I will continue to be so on the beach.

Every year there is a tourist who dies at this beach because of the under-tow; some weak child or half-dead elder or some cocky young man showing off for his friends who tires himself out swimming against the ever pulling current and ends up sinking below the surface never to emerge. But I am smarter and stronger than them and I am well practiced in these callous tides; I have lived near this deadly place almost all my life and I have long felt the pull of the waters at my ankles: I know how to survive here or at least I should.

I am bare-chested and wearing a light blue bathing suit which reaches down to just above my knees. Airborne and breeze sped grains and grit like tiny bees sting my exposed skin and I squint my eyes as I step onto the soft sand at the far side of the beach and head towards that swelling liquid infinity.

It is bright today even with the bad weather and the refection of the cold sun on the white ground shines my eyes half blind as I stumble on.

There is not a soul on this beach besides my own and sometimes I doubt if mine is even there anymore. The wind and the chill in the air is too much for the tourists and the locals shun this area like the plague this time of year.

My ears are filled with nothing but the roar of the crashing waves and that the trickling of the sand sliding sideways across itself.

I am here today on this frigid day in December, standing almost naked alone in this vacant and wind-flattened sand because I am addicted; I now live to be engulfed in the froth and tumble of the surf. I have long looked for god and I think I may have found it in that moment my foot touches the edge of the water; that microsecond of bliss as I dive beneath the first, pulsating wave, letting the swirling white eat me whole, letting all sound and feeling wane to that of rushing salt and sea; allowing my body to be thrashed and trampled by that holy and ever loving force. I am now forever dry with a brackish finish to my skin. My beard is coarse like the rope attached to an anchor sunk in the deep.

The bumps and stood up hairs across my sun darkened flesh are both from the cold and the thrill of what is to come. I am but feet away from my lover the sea and that sacred moment when I am allowed to enter her hallowed profundity.

And if I am to be pulled away by those glacial fingers of dark blue; if my breath is slowly taken away and replaced by seawater and brine, so be it. I welcome that sweet breathlessness and floating, forever bliss in that ever-churning swell.

VACANT

When my father screamed, and stomped around the house in that slow and terrifying way that always seemed to mean trouble and the eventual casting of blame on me, (although whatever had angered my father was most often not my fault), I would escape through the back door of the house. The back door was a screen door on which the hydraulic sliding mechanism which makes doors slowly close had long since broken and thus when this back door was opened and closed it slammed shut against the off white painted door frame, a sound which both alerted my father to my position and angered him even more because he considered my banging of the door against the house a disrespect to the house itself and to him as the owner and supposed caretaker of the house (although I was the one who actually did most of the chores and basic upkeep of the house in the afternoons after school and on the weekends as my father watched from the kitchen or from a chair with a beer in his hand barking orders like the nasty old dog he was). So, as I left the house through the back door I would carefully close said door so that nearly no sound was made by my exit.

And through that back door I would run across the grass of the back yard (grass which I had most likely just mowed, or would have to soon), my laces flopping in my too big shoes and white socks worn so much that they were then a faded and fragile looking grey. I would hop over the chain link fence which separated the back yard of my house from the back yard of the neighbor's house. From the neighbor's back yard, I would diverge onto a public (albeit somewhat secret) footpath that ran parallel to their property and along the tall wooden fence of the nicest house in the neighborhood (which was diagonal to my house and next to the house behind mine) and I would take said somewhat secret footpath to the quiet, suburban street that ran in front of the house behind mine.

From there everything was available, although I could hear my father screaming for me I was free from his grasp and his long piercing looks; free from that stomping which would more or less haunt me for the rest of my life, I could go where I wanted; wherever that was.

The first time I got away I didn't know what to do; where to go; how to breathe with a heart beating at a normal pace, so I just bumbled along the winding streets looking into the windows of the houses of the nice families which surrounded my sordid home, wondering what it would be like to have a father that would play catch with me or a mother that would really do anything at all. My father always said that my mother was gone before I had even been wiped off and wrapped in a blanket. He said that it was as if he looked at me for a second and she has somehow snuck out of the room never to be seen by either of us again. Growing up I always liked to pretend that her and I were somehow so spiritually connected that she and I couldn't exist in the same space and that is why she had never come back or tried to make contact, that she loved me so much that she couldn't bear to see me, (although of course that wasn't the case) That first day, I walked until I was sure my feet were bleeding from the blisters and from the rubbing and sliding of my feet in the too big shoes. When it was dark and my feet seemed to be on fire in a wet and sweaty sort of way I took my shoes and socks off and headed home, trying to walk mainly on the grass of the lawns of the houses I had been walking past all day (which was nice on my feet but also a bit riskier than the sidewalk as most lawns were not as well kempt as mine was and therefore I had to look out for piles of dog waste and for prickly, thorns, both of which I walked through multiple times on my way back home). When I finally did get back to my house, and snuck quietly through that screen door (carefully shutting it as to not let it bang and clack) I expected to get it from my father but I could hear him snoring in the living room; the gunfire and grunts from some action movie garbled out from the speakers of the TV. He was passed out for the night and I was safe until morning at least. I slept deeply that night and dreamt I was an avalanche sliding silently down a mountainside easily uprooting hundred-year-old trees and wiping away everything in my frigid wake.

After that first day, something had been lifted; a weight; a chain; a sense of stuckness was gone, I was free to roam; free to explore, all it took was me sneaking out that screen door and hopping the fence. I quickly became bored of simply wandering the streets of my neighborhood. My neighborhood wasn't rich but it wasn't as poor as others, however my house was a mere fifteen-minute walk to one of the poorest places in the country. This place was a neighborhood mashed between a sprawling graveyard and a highway always loud and clogged with the sound of upshifting trucks and smog from the cars and the crematorium that was located on the edge of the graveyard (the crematorium was used for the bodies of people from families that couldn't afford to purchase a plot of land for a grave or for a burial but still needed to dispose of the body of the deceased and seemed to always be spouting white grey smoke from its many chimneys). I started to walk down to this neighborhood dressed in dirty faded jeans and a dark grey hoodie which I would pull down over my forehead to hide my face.

I started exploring the empty houses block by block; I'm not sure what I was looking for then, maybe some soft and calm place of my own, away from the stomping and the tension and the chores and those angry eyes which could somehow pierce through walls. Yeah, I think I was trying to find someplace for me to be, simply and safely. I entered each empty house in a different way whether through a broken window or a bashed in side door or an unlocked basement window or simply by walking up to the front door and opening it. It seemed that these hollow shells of once maybe warm and cared for things had no need to be shut off from the rest of the world; there was no need to close and lock anything, everything of value had been taken out either by the people who had been evicted from these houses or by the police or by the groups of men in trench coats who waited outside like little crabs beside the carcass of a whale on the ocean floor, waiting for the bigger and meaner things to move on so they could move in and pick at the remains.

I could tell which houses were vacant by the red signs nailed to the front doors and sometimes by the yellow police tape that was lazily wrapped (and easily ducked under) around the front porches. Sometimes, surrounding the houses that were deemed more dangerous than others or which had been set to be demolished, there were plywood fences scrapped together and put up around the property line, but these fences seemed more to be for liability reasons then for actually keeping people out. In fact, the houses with the fences were the ones at which I had the closest calls with the various bums or addicts that were my peers in the trade of exploring (or in their case more living in) these broken-down spaces, so I stayed to the ones without fences, the houses that even the homeless and strung out stayed away from. I looked for the most dilapidated dwellings. The piles of vines and broken glass and rotten wood were my domain; I searched for those places that were more nature than not; the places had been taken back by the stems and the soil.

I found my haven; my Eden of cracked bricks, dead grass and dripping soft wood. It was sat at the end of one of the longest, emptiest streets in that forsaken place where all the nothing and nobodies lingered. Pushed up against a concrete wall on the other side of which was the ever bustling and filthy, loud highway, was my harbor; a half collapsed two story house with a lawn so overgrown that it completely hid the walkway up to what used to be the front porch (but was by then a gaping hole filled with debris and half of the roof that used to cover said front porch which had long since collapsed from age and wear). It was said by the bums and by the kids at school that a crazy woman had lived in this place; that it was cursed and that it was doomed to fall onto itself any day now; I figured a day alone in a house that may actually collapse was better than any time spent in my room watching the door and listening to my father stomp around the house waiting to be screamed at or punished for something that I most likely had nothing to do with. At least in the rubble of that timeworn thing I had my choice of danger and the swift and sweet death of being quickly crushed, instead of being worn away and beaten down again and again.

I took to sitting in my newfound palace every afternoon and on the weekends, sneaking away whenever I could. I stole a lawn chair from my father's garage and set it up in the soggy living room of that beautifully wretched thing beside a wall of ivy and a ceiling that bulged like a boil filled with rancid water and asbestos dust. There beside walls thick with wet blue-grey mold and a floor that squeaked and leaked as I stepped upon it, with a flashlight held tight between my lips I would do my schoolwork and eat what little food I could take from the kitchen without being seen by my father.

This place was my new comfort; my new room of contentment away from that house that never really felt even close to a home. This broken-down shack on the edge of a neighborhood so dangerous that the police wouldn't ever even come near, pushed up against the back of the highway and next to a graveyard filled with the rotting and worm filled bodies of those rich enough to live far away but who's bodies somehow ended up in the soggy and dark brown ground here, was my new home and within its walls the screams and open handed hits and piercing eyes of my father and the rest of the city simply faded away and I was left with the sound of dripping pipes and the cars passing across the wet asphalt above.

That place of rotted wood was my salvation and I went there as much as I could. One day I went there and found it gone. Somebody with a mass of compact steel and a crane had knocked it down. I looked at the rubble of a thing I had loved and held so dear. I stared at the dusty corpse of my haven. Then I began a slow walk back to a house that never felt anything like a home.

WATER

The water in the pot is about to boil but is not yet boiling. Instead it is at that point at which water sort of smokes right before it starts bubbling and creating steam in the way that water does when it is really, really boiling hot. The water is in a pot but not in a kettle because the kettle is broken and leaking (or at least leaks when filled with water, which it currently is not). The pot is a stainless steel that has lost its sheen from use, but still holds its form well. The broken kettle, which is in the cupboard beside the oven, is a light, muted periwinkle blue and was one of her favorite possessions before it broke, although even when broken she supposes that it still is something she is quite fond of.

Beside and below the stove there is a white tile floor that is cold to the touch and grainy with bits of ground up food and on that white tile floor she sits holding a white mug with a large handle. The cup is empty except for a tea bag (peppermint) and a dollop of honey that is collected on the very bottom of the cup and will need to be stirred into the rest of the cup once the water (from the now almost boiling pot) is hot.

She is alone there on the kitchen floor, cold from not only the tile; she is chilled by something wicked and bitter. She often looks at the door as if she is expecting someone and to be honest she is, but her expectations are not logical. She looks to the door wishing for someone who left long ago, to come through that very door holding a bouquet of yellow flowers (she doesn't care what kind) or take-out Chinese food in styrofoam or just a worn leather suitcase that he will leave at the front door as he walks in a please-forgive-me-stupor to where she sits with her unmade tea.

Outside the wind howls like it knows a secret too dark to keep and the snow is falling side-ways; now is a perfect time for someone long gone to come home.

But he won't, at least he most likely won't and this dream she has of him busting through the door is more something to pass the time than a real wish. This isn't his home anymore, maybe it never was, he left so long ago that in the time since he has been gone she has bought the (now broken) kettle and used said kettle for long enough that it broke from overuse (which she would consider a long time).

She is not sure where he where he went or if he will ever come back and if he does come back, through that door (the front door, which she can see from her spot on the floor and which [said door] is moving in a way that resembles the movements of a bird's shallow and fragile breath) she doesn't know what she would say if he walked in the door, she doesn't know what she would do.

But now the water is boiling, for real now and since it is not in any kettle, but just a lidless stainless steel pot, instead of a whistle to tell her the water is ready for tea (which she may have not been able to hear over the melancholic hum of the wind) there is a just a bubbling and that bubbling is the only sound and moving thing in the house.

All else is still; waiting maybe for something, anything, someone, anyone to come, although perhaps nothing, nobody ever will.

TO WE

His mattress used to be on the floor and he liked it that way, but it's not anymore, it's up on a bed frame which was expensive and more or less unnecessary. For years, he loved coming home from work or from wherever and flopping down on his mattress on the floor. There was something so simple and comforting about having the bed on the floor, but it's up now on that bed frame that she wanted and that he obliged in getting.

And really it isn't so bad to have a bedframe he concedes, but he still liked his mattress on the floor and often wishes for those simpler times. But things are bigger now, what was once an I has now become a we and an us and that we is soon to be an official and legal we; a permanent us, and in part that we, that us, means for him that there will never again be a mattress on a floor. It is bedframes and more than one fork and one knife in the drawer and sweaters hung up in the closet and drives to the countryside and dinners that are had more for the taste then for filling one up.

He is now more than just a man, alone, and today is that day on which he will declare to all of those who show up to see it, that he does in fact wish his life to be forever changed. And he thinks he does, he thinks he is ready for something more, and in reality, this something more is something that he does in fact really want to do and has wished and hoped for, for years prior to this day. There is, however, a lack of stillness in him this morning that he did not think would come during this day. There is a lack of calm and something within that is frenzied and honestly that frenzy, that internal thrashing on an important day like today, terrifies him.

There are things he wishes he did differently, there are places he wishes he saw, things he wishes he said, people he wishes that he would've or could've done something with other than what he did with them at the time. Maybe if he had in fact done those things, if he had not done what he did, maybe he would not be doing what he is actually doing now. Maybe if he had made other choices, he would have felt differently than he does now. Maybe if he had made other choices, met other people, seen truer things, maybe he wouldn't feel this frenzy that he feels now. But he does feel it (the frenzy) and he didn't do the things he wishes he had done and he is there in that bed in the frame in a room in which he once had his mattress on the floor, in a room in which what is now the us, the we, was once just an I and that I could've (and maybe should've) made different choices.

It's not that he regrets what he has become (or what he, later today, will become) because he really doesn't. It's not that he is unhappy in being part of a we, of an us, of being forever connected to someone else. It's not that he doesn't love leaning over in the night and feeling that warmth beside him, or having a hand to hold; an ear; a neck; a mouth. Yes, he does enjoy those things. He loves what he has become and loves who has helped him to become who he is today. He loves that she, that she who is the other part to his whole (and other bubbly love stuff like that) he really does. But one feeling doesn't take away another, blocking one river doesn't erase the sea. There is a swelling in him, a tidal un-nerving that quakes him and that has been quaking him for some time now, but that quaking is worse this morning. That quaking is worse today, the worst it has ever been. And because of his fear and unease with what will proceed today. He is more present than he has ever been. He is thinking one slow and thick seeming thought at a time and those thoughts are all consuming.

He is lying in bed and is wearing black boxer briefs (but everything below his torso is under a down comforter so nobody could see his black boxer briefs anyway [if there was anybody else in the room, which there is not]) and above the comforter and his underwear he is shirtless and is wearing a necklace that was given to him by the other half of what is now or will officially his we, his us, his soon to be forever, and right now that necklace feels heavy and sharp in a way that rusty metal feels sharp; the necklace feels sort of dangerously and sickeningly there on his neck like a noose, a collar, a choke chain.

It's not that he isn't happy or satisfied, because in reality he is happier and more satisfied than he has ever been: it seems to him that he is as happy and as content as he possibly can be or maybe ever will be. Maybe there is something inside of him that is broken; tainted; spinning in place.

This is all he ever wanted, this we, this us. But it's not what he thought it would be. It's not just mornings sitting in bed watching the snow fall through the window, it's not just tearing the wall paper off of the walls of the living room and then repainting the whole thing with a color between blue and white that they made together, it's not just a late breakfast out at some sidewalk café, it's not running through the rain, it's not laying on a blanket in a tall grassy field alone, together in the sun. But sometimes it is and those days are something special, those things are exactly what he always dreamed they would be, but in those visions of what could be those sepia things were a constant, not just occasional moments in the grey. And that's what started this internal spinning, that grey that has always been there, that he thought would go away when the he, the I finally and suddenly became a we; an us; a more than me. But it didn't. Life went on. There were still splinters and broken cups and sore throats and cold mornings on the way to work. There were still tragedies on the news and clouds on days when it should have been sunny (or at least when he wanted it to be). Life wasn't any worse as a we, as an us, as a together forever, but it wasn't really any better, and he always thought that it would make everything better. He always thought that the other, the her, the she, the one (or a one, he wasn't sure if he believes [or believed] in a singular one for him) would make it all ok, that somehow that person would seep into those places where he was lacking and fill them up, fill him up.

The bed is a queen size and is moderate in terms of give. He prefers a bit more give than the bed and his soon to be legally forever beloved prefers a bed that is much more stiff and so they decided to compromise and get a bed that was in between their preferences and while compromise is what supposedly makes a relationship work, a we stay a we, the compromise in the bed resulted in both of the bed's occupants sleeping in a bed that was not comfortable or restful for either of them. And if he really thinks about it, he really can't remember a single time that he has slept well in the bed that they share. The last time he slept well and fully and deeply enough for him to have to sort of come to for like a half an hour after waking up was way back when he had his mattress on the floor, before the new mattress that nobody likes, before the bedframe, before the we.

His other part, his missing piece, his dearly almost betrothed is in the shower in the bathroom which is connected to the bedroom that they share, (the bed in which he still lies). He can hear the shower running and he can hear the dropping of the droplets of the water and the differences in the sounds of the droplets that have dropped off of the body of his her and the droplets that have missed the body and have gone directly down onto the floor of the shower. The door of the bathroom is closed and between the carpet of the bedroom and the bottom of the now closed (but most often open) bathroom door there is about an inch of space and from that inch of space there is a viscous looking yellow light pouring out and making a perfectly straight line of light on the carpet outside and in front of the door. The light that is pouring out from underneath the door is very different in color and consistency than the light which is lighting the room in which he still lies in the bed (on the bedframe). Along with the droplets of water from the shower, he can hear that his her is humming and the humming is soft and gentle (like her) and is light but melancholic in the way that so many great but deeply sad songs are. Although the humming is faint and seems like it is coming from farther than just a couple of feet and a closed door away, it still gives him a chill.

He gets up from his bed, the greying carpet feels scratchy but not entirely unpleasant on his bare and still unraveling from sleep, feet. Well he isn't entirely up, he is sitting on the bed now, instead of laying down, and the down comforter is off of him and he is slightly colder than he was when he was half under the down comforter, but he knows that today is a big day and that he will most certainly go through with what he has promised to do. But part of him wants to go back under the cover of the down comforter, but this time all the way under, and hide under there until he is absolutely sure of everything, or until everything just simply fades into white away.

Denying his urge to hide, he stands on the carpet and tries to decide between going to the porch for a cigarette or joining his almost wife in the shower.

Zoo

Her hand was cold and hard that day, my grandmother's. But when I knew her it was warm, and her hair looked different than it usually did, down there in that hardwood and fake looking make up; in those clothes that I know she never would have chosen as her final outfit; she was much too fashionable and colorful for that.

We used to go to the zoo her and I. Starting on Thursdays when I was in third grade and it was still warm out just after the school year had begun she would pick me up as the final bell rung. I was always excited those days and I would bring some extra food in my lunch box for the ride from my elementary school to the zoo (although I knew she would always bring me some candy or an apple). We would ride in her big cushy car that always smelled sweet with a musky perfume (perfume she sprayed to cover the smell of cigarettes, and even though she was never able to fully cover the smell of the cigarettes I never said anything and I always told her that her car smelled good). And at first I remember asking my mom why I had to go with her (my grandmother) to the zoo every week and why I couldn't just come home and watch TV or go over to my friend's house and my mother said to me that I was lucky to have a grandmother that wanted to spent time with me at all and that I should cherish any moments I could have with her. I did as I was told; I didn't have another choice and I was barely nine years old so I went to the zoo with my grandmother every week for years.

I didn't even like the zoo; all those caged and once wild things pacing and looking beat down. Although my young mind with its limited vocabulary and simple, childish understanding of the world couldn't put words to it, there was a feeling of rot at the zoo; a portrait of the great lie of man's dominion of nature; a mirror image of living in a cage. I was a wild girl and sitting in a class room all day was torture. My grandmother must have been wild too, I saw the flame (or what was left of it) in her eyes when she would lean over and give me a big sloppy kiss as I plopped down into the leather, passenger seat beside her in her old silver, musky car. I knew she knew the fire within me and while we were at the zoo she would let me run uninhibited and sometimes she would run with me in her flowery dress, all her loose and wrinkled skin flopping and her tangled beehive of silver blonde hair bobbing on her head. I quickly began to look forward to Thursdays and I learned to cherish every minute at the zoo with my grandmother.

We would growl at the lions, howl at the wolves and make faces at the monkeys. We got to feed the giraffes and one time we were able to feed a fish to a seal. One day we even went into the insect room (a place we both avoided like the plague) and held a tarantula. I held it together as I felt that hairy wicked beast crawl across my arm and shoulder; I tried to be brave for my grandmother, I tried to show her I could be strong like she was. When the man who was in charge of the insects put the spider on her hand she flinched like she was being shocked by an electrical current and ran out of the room squealing; I followed her with tears streaming out of my eyes, both of us gagging on giggles and getting as far away from all those bugs as possible.

As we walked from cage to cage and tried to memorize the Latin names of the animals (if I correctly identified ten Latin names right she would buy me ice cream, but I usually didn't and she bought me ice cream anyways) we held hands and that is when I learned of her warm hands and the way her rings (of which she had many) felt when clenched tightly against my un-ringed and soft, unspoiled hand. She would get ice cream for herself too; I always liked chocolate and usually dripped some of it on my shirt and on my face (she would get the drips off of my face with a handkerchief from her purse that she wet with her own spit, and which I would vehemently object to but which objections she would ignore as she snickered and wiped the chocolate from around my mouth). She would always get mint chocolate chip ice cream that was a teal in color which I always said looked like boogers to which she would reply by putting some on her nose and trying to get me to lick it off as we both cracked wide smiles and walked on.

And that's how I want to remember her, laughing with that ice cream on her nose with her hair a mess and her fingers filled with rings; not dressed in this tight and lifeless black, laying cold in a room designed to be as bleak as possible, filled with tissues and people whimpering into their hands. I chose to remember her running in the sun with me; facing the lions together and baring our teeth for the world to see. I choose to remember our squeals and giggles and smiles in the warm light of a summer that seems so far away but which I will try to never forget in her honor.

Acknowledgements

"Annotated Love Letter" was selected as the winner in the "Love" Category of Tulip Tree Press' 2017 Stories That Need to be Told Contest and published in the subsequent collection of winners from said contest.

"Barber" was published in *Apple In the Dark*'s Spring 2021 Issue

"Breakfast" Received an Honorable Mention in *Glimmer Train Magazine*'s May/June 2017 Short Story Contest.

"Dawn" was published in *Clover: A Literary Rag* Volume 13

"Highway" was published in *Clover: A Literary Rag* Volume 14

"House" was published *Lotus Eater Magazine* Issue 7

"Milk" was adapted into a one act play by the MFA in Theater at Naropa University, during the 2019 Symposium.

I would like to especially thank:

My mother and father. Without you I wouldn't be here, in every sense of what that means.

My sister, for letting me read her my entire first novel on a road trip through Texas and who is always available on the other end of the phone to hear more.

My grandmother who always tells me "Keep Writing" at the end of every email, whether or not she liked what she just read.

The rest of my family: Julie, Chris, and all the others for listening, for rolling your eyes, for laughing, for crying, and for most importantly reading.

My friends and co-conspirators: Jaiden, Spencer, Bradford, Sam, Sasha, Kika, and many more.

My mentors: Jeffery Duvall, Eric Darton, Christopher David Rosales, the late Dobbie Reese Norris, Andrew Schelling, Sean Murphy, Rachel Weaver, Michelle Naka Pierce, J'Lyn Chapman and Dan Beachy-Quick: for the guiding lights and words you have all provided.

Gene, thank you for believing in this book and in me.

Dave and Hank, of course, for without you both I would be lost. I have pictures of you both on my desk.

CPSIA information can be obtained
at www.ICGtesting.com
Printed in the USA
JSHW041407240222
23227JS00005B/12